V. Mahanenko

CONDEMNED

Lord Valevsky: Last of the Line

Books are the lives we don't have time to live,

Vasily Mahanenko

A Progression Fantasy Series
Book 2

Magic Dome Books

Condemned Book 2: A Progression Fantasy Series
(Lord Valevsky: Last of the Line)
Copyright © V. Mahanenko 2023
Cover Art © Lunar 2023
Cover Design V. Manyukhin
English translation copyright © Taylor Elise Margvelashvili 2023
Published by Magic Dome Books, 2023
All Rights Reserved
ISBN: 978-80-7693-092-6

This book is entirely a work of fiction.
Any correlation with real people or events
is coincidental.

All Books
by Vasily Mahanenko:

The Way of the Shaman LitRPG Series

Dark Paladin LitRPG Series

Galactogon LitRPG Series

Invasion LitRPG Series

World of the Changed LitRPG Series

The Alchemist LitRPG Series

The Bear Clan LitRPG Series

Starting Point LitRPG Series

The Bard from Barliona LitRPG series
(with Eugenia Dmitrieva)

Condemned
(Lord Valevsky: Last of The Line)
a Progression Fantasy series

Table of Contents:

Chapter 1

"I SUPPOSE YOU SHOULD give them names," said my mentor.

Once long ago, presumably in a past life, he had been human, but those days were gone forever. Now the Evil Engineer was one of the four dark beasts officially acknowledged as "purified" by the Church of the Light. A convert who had managed to wrest himself free from the control of the dark god Skron. Nonetheless, much of the Evil Engineer's former essence remained. Primarily his aura that manifested as a dark fog, eternally gloomy demeanor, lousy mood and indelible desire to dominate everything and everyone. I could also add sadistic inclinations to the list, of course, but these I think he was born with.

"Why? They're just weapons," I replied, rising from the ground. I wanted to really tear into someone, but managed to contain my emotions.

Everyone who'd come running from all over the arena in anticipation of a free healing was significantly superior to me in strength. The Magical Academy of the Zarak Empire was attended by the chosen ones — children from the highest rungs of society, whose parents spared no expense for their precious progeny. Enhancements had boosted their physical stats immensely, turning the young men and women into real monsters. What could I say when my partner, Karina Fardi, could easily bench press a hundred and twenty kilograms? A twenty-year-old girl with a figure like a concubine from a romance novel!

"Healing's over!" the Evil Engineer called out loudly without removing his heavy gaze from me. "Just weapons? You called your katars 'just weapons?' Get up, peasant! This obstacle course won't run itself! Fardi, enough wallowing around! In plank position! One handed, dipstick! Other behind your back. Max, Skron mark me, if you fall off again you'll be down there with your partner! You have to pass the pendulums! Move it, dead weight!"

This was how my training sessions passed, serenaded by my mentor's encouraging and occasionally motivating diatribes. But I should probably say a few words about myself to explain how I became destined to such a complete shitshow of a life.

I'm a doomed soldier by the alias Max, once from the glorious Valevsky Barony. "Once," past tense, because officially, the barony no longer exists. The Duke of Odoevsky framed my family — there's not a doubt in my mind — and then had them all executed. No trial, no investigation, although on paper, I was told, everything had been above board. Even the emperor approved of this demonstrative flogging of some insignificant family, just so the whole empire understood: only a chosen few have rights in this world. I was lucky, if you can say that — instead of the gallows, I was delegated to a particular caste of "doomed soldiers." The qualitative composition of this community was highly specific: murderers, rapists, embezzlers of public funds, those who the highest ranks simply found objectionable — but even here, among the dregs of society, people were further divided into two groups. Those who owned magic stones and everyone else. I fell into the first category and was assigned six months of study at the academy, so that I may at least survive my first encounter with a dark beast. For even among death row inmates, mages had their value. Once I arrived at the academy, I was appointed to a sadist named the Evil Engineer, who for some reason, stubbornly insisted that his bullying was training, as well as a partner who by chance turned out to be the daughter of the very same Duke of Odoevsky. I think that brief summary should catch you up to speed. Although there's one more thing. Those katars...

The weapons had been gifted to me by a doomed soldier who went by the name Countess.

It had once belonged to one of her warriors, but the rifts that spawned dark beasts were merciless. Savage, as the warrior had been known, was gone, but now I had these rather interesting swords. Or, more precisely, long knives. As soon as we got back to the academy however, the monitor assigned to me by the Fortress (the highest governing body/building of the Church of the Light) confiscated my weapons and I never saw them again. Fast forward a day, back at the academy, two shaggy looking schmucks paid me a visit, measured me up and down, so that another *three* days later, Father Nor, the Fortress' official representative at the academy, could, in a very solemn manner (that is, in the presence of the chancellor and head of security), present me with the handiwork of the local artisans. Automated steel katars tailored to my body. The very same spring action mechanics, in fact, but executed with much more skill and grace. The length of the retractable blade had been increased to twenty-five centimeters, and it had also gained the ability to transform. From now on, I could summon forth either a thin spike capable of boring a hole in even the thickest set of armor, or a wide double-edged blade designed to shred flesh. But the strangest and most unusual thing was that I was allowed to carry this weapon freely within the academy! For from now on it was an integral part of the doomed soldier named Max. And, it's worth noting, the fit was significantly better than the previous pair.

"We're done with our warm ups for today!"

said the Evil Engineer when I once again fell off the obstacle course. "Max is at the training grounds this afternoon, Fardi is free for today. Doomer, make sure your partner makes it to breakfast."

"I want to go to the training grounds too!" croaked Fardi, holding herself horizontal with the last of her strength. It's hard enough to hold a plank, let alone one-handed, and with two ten-kilogram plates on your back, it's practically impossible. Impossible for an ordinary person, because Karina had been holding it for several minutes and counting.

"Do you need help, Fortress Sister?" I stopped a few paces from Fardi. A week had passed since our return from the rift, during which we, without saying a word, had developed a new style of communication. Deliberately amicable, with the clear knowledge that in six months, we would turn back into enemies. Someday I would kill Karina. Or she me. There was no other option, no matter what you read in romance novels. Just as the Valevsky family ceased to exist, so the Fardi family would cease to exist. No other choice was given.

"If it's not too much trouble, Doomer Brother," Karina replied just as courteously, allowing me to do something that, in polite society, would be grounds for a duel. I stood the girl on her feet and began patting the sticky sawdust, shavings, and lord knows what else from her jumpsuit. Karina's bottom, on which she had fallen repeatedly, was particularly affected. However, Fardi calmly endured this treatment. It was much more important for her to leave the arena clean than not to be touched by a doomer. An entity that, officially, does not exist.

"Will you make it there yourself, or shall I escort you, Fortress Sister?"

"I would like to give up your company, Doomer Brother, but I have no such occasion." Karina all but collapsed on me. She no longer had the strength to move of her own volition. On top of that, no one had lifted the rule set down in our first training session stating that we were forbidden from taking recovery elixirs until we made it to our own beds. The two servants of the Light assigned to Fardi and I as monitors watched closely to ensure compliance.

What other notable things happened this week? There were perhaps two events worth singling out. For starters, I received a clear daily schedule. Up at five thirty. Half an hour for personal hygiene and transportation to the arena. Two-hour warm up, after which I either dragged Karina back, or she me. We switched roles frequently. Shower. Breakfast. From ten to two in the afternoon was a series of classes, some of which I took with the first year groups. And the looks I got from the first years on day one! There was so much fear in their eyes, it was as if a krona had appeared before them. Worse — a doomer with a weapon! Save yourselves while you can! But I'm waxing poetic. At two o'clock I had a hearty lunch, after which the heat really came down — my main training with the Evil Engineer. From four o'clock until I could no longer breathe. Then another half hour. Dinner technically started at nine, but in all seven days, I still had never managed to crawl there on time. After a shower, I fell into bed and got something I had never even hoped for: personal time. Two hours of personal time! True, I had to spend it solely on reading textbooks, but my doomer neighbors used theirs to the fullest, playing some kind of game with dice made from chunks of bread. At exactly 11 p.m., the changing of the guards took place, books were taken away and lights were turned off. The clerics were careful to ensure that doomers got their rest before the next day. They basically only followed me — the other guys were just my companions in suffering.

That was the first notable item. The second was the daily one-hour meetings with Father Nor and one of the red robes. And the meeting times were constantly changing. Sometimes I was pulled out of exercises, from training, deprived of lunch — nothing seemed to faze the servants of the Light. They seated me at the table, sat down opposite and started asking me the same thing for the hundredth time. Everyone was interested in this piece of the map. The churchmen's excitement when I told them what I had received from the Master was beyond words. I've never seen so many members of the Fortress security services in one place. It seemed as if they'd fill the whole academy. What didn't they do to me in those first few days — studied, tested, took some sort of analyses...even took a peek in areas that should never see the sun. And to top it all off, they warned me right off the bat that any disobedience would lead them to beat me to death and snatch the piece of the map from my corpse. Apparently, the only thing stopping the clerics from taking this measure was the fear that they wouldn't be able to obtain anything from a dark creature. I had to draw the map fragment, which was located in a special tab on my status bar, three times, each time explaining that it would be impossible to fill in the missing pieces. Because I only had one of five fragments. I did not inform the representatives of the Fortress about the fact that somewhere inside me was also one of the twelve shards of the *Amplify* stone. This was my ticket to freedom and I had no intention of giving it to anyone. There was a significant gap in my education in the subjects of both geography and heraldry, so I had no clue which part of our world was being depicted in the drawing. Although it became clear from the churchmen's reactions that they understood perfectly well what region it was referencing. But, of course, no one was going to inform me. Not 'til I'm older.

I set off along the familiar route. First, I dragged Karina back to my place, where I collapsed on the bed, held up the full vial of recovery elixir for our monitors to see, gulped it down, then got up and dragged my partner to her bed. The right to enter the academy dorms had been personally granted to me by Zurgan Shor. In Karina's room, I had to once again demonstrate the vial was full, then poured the entirety of the contents into Fardi's mouth and enjoyed a few minutes of peace. It was a rare moment away from the watchful eyes of our overseers. Both clerics had left the girl's room and shut the door tightly behind them.

"Fuck, when will I die already?" Karina whispered as the wave of warmth passed through her body.

"Just say the word and I can arrange that for you in an instant," I offered, sitting down near the bed. Despite the elixir's effects, my body still ached. "As long as you let the churchmen know that you're acting of your own free will. Without coercion."

"Don't get your hopes up. I already wrote my father to tell him you're still alive and seeking revenge. I'm sure you won't last a week in the Fortress. The Duke of Odoevsky has great power, a broad circle of connections and very long arms."

"I don't give a damn about your daddy's long arms." I clenched my fist just right, causing the katars to spring out. With a characteristic click, a long spike appeared, but immediately vanished again. Don't get provoked. Not in the presence of a Fardi. "I'll be so close to him that his long arms will only get in the way."

"I'll kill you first," Karina assured me, her eyes never leaving my weapon. "And I'll take those katars for myself. You know, our mentor was right — masterpieces like that really do deserve their own names. May I suggest 'Weak' and 'Helpless?'"

Your natural states of being."

"As long as they're not 'Smug Bitch' or 'Soulless Harpy.' You back to normal yet? Can you make it to breakfast yourself or do I have to drag you there too?"

"Just what I need! They already look at me like a leper because I train with you. Go fail your lessons. I'll see you tomorrow. I hope I'm lucky and you die at the training grounds."

"You make sure you don't accidentally get yourself killed before then. I want to finish you off myself."

Karina and I had been exchanging such pleasantries all week. For some reason, the clerics were not afraid to leave us on our own. Leaving the room, I found myself in a thick stream of people — students in a hurry to have breakfast so they would be on time to their favorite classes. It was the fourth years, and some groups of third years, who had been stuck in the arena since morning. The first and second years contrived to sleep in as long as possible. Although, judging by some of their puffy faces, they hadn't gotten to sleep that night. But the arrival of an "elite" tore us all away from the unexpected freedom.

"Princess!" A muffled whisper moved through the rows, causing everyone to press against the wall. Including me. The youngest daughter of the emperor lived in a hostel among us mere mortals. Of course, she enjoyed the liberties dictated by her status: personal bodyguards, who had nearly beaten me up once; her own separate floor, where, without invitation, no student, or even teacher of the academy would dare set foot; a personal chef and even a team of lackeys that was always ready to bear her well-fed majesty off to unknown distances. Miralda Lertan strode regally down the corridor, basking in the attention, when — and this made me rather unhappy — her gaze lingered on me. A terrible look. Anticipation. Stopping nearby, Miralda turned to one of the girls accompanying her:

"It's only when you lose someone that you begin to realize how much they meant to you. Count Khamalsky, although he was not a traditionally handsome man, and his jokes sooner evoked boredom than a smile, he did everything whole-heartedly, never asking stupid questions. Those who are willing to die for their princess, for a fleeting chance to become one of her favorites, are too few and far between to leave their death unrequited. If you thought your churchmen could protect you, swine, then you were deeply mistaken. Count Khamalsky will be avenged!"

The sudden blow to the back of the head was so strong I thought it must have decapitated me, but instead, it only gave rise to a large sheaf of sparks. Along with the weapon, I had earned the right to keep the rest of my mana and, as a result, almost never switched off my protection. This greatly accelerated my progress through the arena, allowing me to block some of the extremely fast grappling dummies that I had been physically unable to dodge at my current stage of development. This infuriated the mentor, but he realized that he needed to get used to this new reality, since I had turned out to be so weak.

A heart-rending cry was heard and the students rushed out of the corridor in a panic, stampeding toward the doors. Miralda was tucked away behind the enormous shields carried by her two faithful bodyguards, but continued to survey the situation. Armed, I'm sure, with more protection amulets than could be found in the rift below our feet. I noticed all this in passing as I jumped back, pressing my back against the wall so that I'd have time to react to a new attack. Judging by the fact that my mana bar had dropped by half, the blow had been from a very close distance, and would have been fatal. But there was no one near me. Just three poor fellows lying face down on the floor, staining the floor with a huge pool of red. Even Magister Smalog couldn't help them now. It's difficult to heal a person who's missing half his head.

I felt the movement rather than saw it — the space next to me suddenly gained density, transforming into a member of the Noctural Brotherhood. An all-black suit, with only a slit for the eyes to suggest that it was a human attacking, and not the darkness itself. Another close-range blow, this time to the stomach, and I couldn't dodge or react, so I did something Father Nor and Magister Shor would certainly not give me a pat on the head for.

I activated *Dark Spike* at the same time as the

sword slammed into my defenses, and then threw both hands forward, releasing the katars. My stomach cramped in wild pain — my shield burst and the assassin's blade entered my body. The student uniform did little to protect me. However, I succeeded as well — the explosion behind my opponent was unexpected enough to throw him forward. Right onto the steel spikes of my katars. If the killer had any amulets, they succumbed to the academy's gifts. A cloud of stone fragments covered us and I fell to the floor, thoroughly wounded. Zero mana, nothing to heal me, stomach burning as if on fire, threatening to engulf me whole, and my face had taken a good beating too...One thing made me glad: the katars had worked their magic. The freak that had attacked me was gone, once and for all.

"Finish him off!" the princess squealed as soon as the darkness had dissipated. "Kill the dark beast! Immediately!"

One of her guards set his shield aside and even took a step in my direction before a voice full of venom was heard:

"Does the princess wish to encroach on Fortress property?"

The voice belonged to Karina. Knowing full well that I risked losing consciousness from the slightest movement, I tilted my head. Fardi was standing at the doorway I had just recently stepped through. Wet, covered in soap suds, hastily wrapped in a towel that hid nothing from my eyes. But this didn't bother my partner. She stared at the princess and held her hand out in front of her. The girl was preparing to attack.

"You wouldn't dare!" Notes of panic rose in Miralda's voice. The little spectacle she had rehearsed was starting to go off the rails. According to her plan, her chubby little legs should be kicking me in the side at that very moment.

"Watch me. Take another step and I'll attack! Fardi's word of honor! Fortress' honor! This doomer belongs to the church, and it's not for you to take him!"

Something in Karina's voice said she wasn't bluffing. The girl really would attack the princess or her body guards if they got any closer to me.

"He's done for anyway," the princess said with vitriol. "Magister Smalog is not at the academy! He won't survive with a wound like that. Let's go, I've seen all I wanted to."

A dark haze began to swim before my eyes. The blow to my stomach had proved too serious a wound. I could no longer collect myself enough to stare after the princess. Any movement now would be my last. So all I could do was look up at Fardi, rejoicing that the last thing I saw in this life was not the bared muzzle of a beast biting into my throat, but a beautiful naked female form. Even if it belonged to someone that I would have gladly finished off at the first opportunity.

"Drink! Drink, you bastard!" Karina leaned over me and tried to pry open my mouth. I made an incredible effort and parted my lips and the life-giving moisture of the recovery potion flowed inside.

"Shit, the wound's too deep. Hold on!" Karina disappeared into the room, only to return immediately with a few more vials. "Drink and turn on your aura! Turn it on, dark beast! And don't you dare shut it off early!"

Another stream of liquid went down my gullet and my mana bar jumped sharply up. The *Healing Aura* pictogram was right there on my status bar, as close as it could be, but it took an incredible amount of effort to get to. Nevertheless, I succeeded, and for eighty seconds my condition improved. The wound, miraculously, was still not healed, but I at least had a hope for salvation. The dark haze cleared from my vision.

"More!" I croaked as soon as the aura ran out. Karina sat next to me the whole time, motionless. The girl understood that any movement was akin to death for me now.

"Not so fast, doomer. You owe me your life, got it? Confirm you understand. Nod, mumble, crap yourself, I don't care, but I need you to know, dark beast, that you're in my debt! Or you can die in my arms and I'll be all in tears, telling the tale of the bad, bad princess who struck down the hero of the rift. You. Owe. Me. Your. Life! And I don't give a damn that you're a doomer!"

"Yes," I croaked without even pausing to think. Without mana, I was dead. Without healing elixirs I was dead. Without outside help — dead. And it didn't matter who I owed now. It wasn't to

Skron, so it was a way out.

"Drink!" The contents of yet another mana flask vanished down my throat, and Fardi poured another recovery potion on top. My partner was furious. Her movements were ragged, twitchy. She didn't look like herself at all, and I couldn't believe that it was due to the stress she was under. There's no such thing as stress for a person who managed to maintain consciousness during their first foray into the rift. Something incomprehensible was happening to her, but she continued to pour potion after potion into me, trying to pull me back to this world.

When the red robes arrived, I didn't look up. At some point, the corridor filled with people and there was a rumble of voices, but I couldn't make anything out. My condition was so dire that I had to skip every other breath. Soon the heaviness in my chest lifted — they removed the bodies of the killers. The fire in my stomach, which had subsided, flared up again, but I managed to remain conscious. My mana was steadily approaching zero, and I needed a new dose of elixir.

I certainly wasn't about to give up. Because today, I made a new enemy...

(Turb, capital of the Zarak Empire, present)

"Magister Elor, I have good news. We have found a way to fulfill your order." The servant bowed, waiting for a reaction.

"Explain," demanded Magister Elor. Preparations for the Wave had drained all the strength from the highest hierarch of the dark god Skron. The slightest error in the huge, six-meter tall pictogram would force them to start over from scratch. The summoning magic Skron had bestowed upon his nearest servants did not require magic stones, amplifiers, or other attributes familiar to mages. Just knowledge, accuracy and a strict sequence of actions and words. Master Elor's best time to finish a pictogram was two and a half months. But that goal seemed unrealistic now — they'd had to start over from scratch three times already.

"Students are constantly ordering food from local eateries. The guards turn the other cheek — they're used to the familiar faces that deliver meals. No one checks their bags. A week ago, one of our brothers got a job at a café and just made his first delivery to the academy today. He was checked — a new face. But after three or four weeks, once he becomes familiar, we can stick a well-packaged body into his bag and pass it along to our man within the academy. The deliveries are constant. If necessary, we can deliver ten bodies in a couple of days to initiate the Wave. All your inside man will need to do is perform the ritual correctly.

"This is good news," Magister Elor nodded and looked up at the pictogram. The dark one preferred the version where the Wave came up through the rift, and not through the pictogram.

The feedback was entirely different, and they wouldn't need to draw anything in the rift.

"Four weeks?" The master looked back at his servant, who nodded confidently. "Okay, you have your chance. Prove that the capital's coven can keep its word, and Skron will exalt you. I haven't had pupils for quite some time…"

(Odoevsk, Office of the Duke of Odoevsky, present)

"Your radiance, we have the initial results!" Tari tried to save face and even stopped at the door to wait for permission to enter, but then the duke's assistant couldn't help himself, bursting in without consent and launching fervently into his story:

"The chrone was brought to your laboratory under the greatest secrecy. The courier who delivered the parcel certainly won't be telling anyone. We set everything up, conducted tests, and got this. It works, sir! The equipment you received works! The magical academy is no longer the exclusive producer of magical elixirs!"

With trembling hands, Tari handed his master a small vial, awaiting his response with bated breath. Baleymore Fardi, Duke of Odoevsky, took the vial and drank the contents in one gulp. He had no doubts about the servant — people were people, but this one would not poison him. Not now, when the goal was so close at hand.

The familiar heaviness washed over his head. The duke closed his eyes, surrendering to the will of his senses, and presented his magic stones. One of them needed just one more elixir to boost it up a level. A bright light flashed in his head, causing him to breathe heavily. His auxiliary stone had been boosted one level. A whole level, practically for free!

"How many elixirs can we make?"

"Level boosters — up to fifty units a week. It just depends on the amount of chrone we can get, but our doomers are bringing it in regularly. There's also a lot of nux, but we're holding that, as you ordered."

"We need more. Work round the clock, don't sleep, I don't care how you get it done, but the apparatus cannot stop, not even for a second. The sooner we produce a thousand elixirs, the sooner we get the next apparatus. Move!"

Tari left, and the duke leaned back in his chair, a mysterious grin running across his face. They were six months ahead of schedule. The master would be pleased with these results.

Chapter 2

"YOU ARE FREE. Class starts in five minutes." Father Nor shut his notebook, demonstrating that the hearing was over.

"Class?" I asked, still palpitating my stomach. The nasty scar would remain with me until I could get to a healer. "Hasn't the chancellor left on important business?"

"He has a substitute. I believe this will be a good lesson for you. We really need to reconsider your training regime in light of recent discoveries. I have already conveyed my thoughts on the matter to the High Priest and he has taken a pause for reflection. Go, dark one. Don't tempt me to start listing your sins for what happened today…"

This phrase was enough to send me flying out of the office as fast as my legs would take me. I'd been patched up quite quickly — among the clerics was a healer. Not as strong as Magister Smalog, but it was enough to save me from my terrible stomach wound. From what I saw, some of my innards had ended up on the outside, so it couldn't be repaired in the usual way. The treatment had caused the healer cleric to turn stark white and lose consciousness, completely drained of power, and I was left with this hideous scar across my stomach. The red robes took statements from me and Karina, Magister Zurgan Shor interviewed dozens of ordinary students in order to reconstruct a picture of what happened, and pretty quickly, everyone understood exactly what had gone down in the dorms. The princess, using her privileged position, had snuck a member of the forbidden nocturnal brotherhood into the academy. Any other student would be sitting in shackles in front of Zurgan Shor right now, fervently confessing to how they organized the hit and where they found the assassin's contact, but not Miralda Lertan. Only the emperor had the right to interrogate the princess. The chancellor did do something, however. Something that made the hairs stand up on the back of a lot of necks — he placed Miralda Lertan in a punishment cell. No house arrest, no sending her back to daddy for re-education, no scolding. They had locked her in a cold, solitary confinement cell in the basement of the academy! There was no ceremony whatsoever when dealing with the princess' bodyguards. Both young lads were dragged off to some unknown location by Zurgan Shor's soldiers. Soon a brigade of builders appeared and began to patch up the damage in the corridor as if nothing had happened. Security guards were scurrying around everywhere, both in the academy and at the Fortress. Overall, the machine moved smoothly as the whole world worked together to fix one person's screw-up.

Soon the chancellor left for the palace, demanding that no one release the offender from her cell prior to his return, even if all the armies of this world fell upon the academy at once. The student body was aboil for some time, digesting what had happened, but the teeth-chattering chime of the clock tower sent everyone off to their respective classrooms. War was war, but classes continued on schedule. They sent me off to my studies as well. All I could do was smirk. I'd grown accustomed to the churchmen's soullessness long ago. Am I alive? Can I lift a finger? Can I think and move? Excellent — then off to class! Dark beasts won't study themselves! But when I entered the classroom, I had the creeping feeling that we wouldn't be studying dark beasts today. The entire hall had been cleared of furniture.

"Good morning, students. Today I will be leading this class. The chancellor had an urgent matter to attend to and had to temporarily leave the academy grounds. Line up in two semicircles. Boys on the right, girls on the left. Doomed soldier, you're coming with me."

The flabbergasted first-years complied. Judging by their faces, everyone knew the charming young woman who couldn't be a day over thirty, but didn't understand why she was the one who had shown up to teach a class on dark beasts. The strikingly pretty — one might even say unbelievably beautiful woman was short in stature and her thick, brown hair was pulled back into a tight ponytail. Her standard-issue academy jumpsuit hugged her body so tightly that my mouth went dry. A nice round butt, a perky, voluminous chest, waspish waist, delicate arms — the jumpsuit hid nothing. And she carried herself with such confidence, such ease, it was as if she was draped in the most magnificent gown. I was face to face with the feminine ideal. Just the way she pointed her finger to indicate where to stand was enough to make me twitch. Each movement seemed so measured, incredibly smooth and enchanting.

"I haven't crossed paths with the first years yet, so let me introduce myself. My name is Tarra Lloyd, and I teach dance at the academy. Under normal circumstances, we wouldn't meet until next semester, but, in my view, the sooner the better. Alright, students, line up by height and we'll pair you off. I know that there are fewer girls than boys, so I'm afraid some of you ladies will have to suffer through two partners. Or not suffer, it all depends on your partner's experience level. Ah, it worked out magnificently — ten girls and twenty boys. Perfect! So this is how we'll divide up..."

How grateful I was to Gustav and the twins! Words couldn't even convey my gratitude! First he

had taught me combat meditation, and second —
how not to get shy in front of gorgeous women.
Looking around at my group as they blushed,
shied away and sweated at the merest touch from
Magister Lloyd, I simply put up my mirror that
allowed me to control my emotions in the rift.
Whether it worked or not, it's hard to say — one
glance at how the woman moved and my insides
were all aflutter. Nonetheless, I managed to
maintain my composure where most of my
provisional peers did not. Some joked, laughed
loudly, pretty much everyone turned beet red, even
the girls, but the professor seemed as if she didn't
notice, continuing to arrange the students like
chess pieces around the hall. Hoping to somehow
distract myself from overindulging in the
delectable figure of Tarra Lloyd (I couldn't even
bring myself to call her Magister in my head), I
tried to calculate how many students were in the
school. Four courses overall with two groups in
each. I had no idea how many students were in
each group, but if I was to assume that they were
around the same size as this one, there were sixty
in each course, or two hundred and forty in the
entire academy. A miniscule attendance,
considering the size of the Zarak number, as well
as the number of different families.

"Gentlemen, please enter," Magister Lloyd
said as she strode over to the door to let the
musicians in. The troupe set up chairs, dragged in
their instruments, and soon struck up a familiar
melody.

"Young men standing to the right of their ladies, invite them to dance. Those on the left go stand by the wall. We'll switch in ten minutes. Ladies, it's all in your hands. Bask in it. Doomer, you're working with me."

"May I, Madam?" She didn't have to ask me twice. Turning to the magister, I inclined my head slightly and held out my hand, initiating the "duel." So many strangenesses had occurred since the moment I first became a doomer that I wasn't even taken aback by the fact that instead of studying dark beasts, we were learning to dance.

Since they were teaching it, it must mean we needed to know it. I didn't love dancing, but I knew how. A young baron's education was chock full of a variety of subjects, including such things as dance.

Tarra Lloyd gallantly accepted my invitation with a curtsy, after which she pressed herself tightly against me and my mirror nearly cracked. My heart, in any case, began to beat furiously, threatening to jump clear out of my chest. Her perfume was the exact same one that Serlena Przhedetskaya, the love of my former life, used to wear. The memory flooded my mind and I surrendered to it completely. Two years ago, I had met Serlena for the first time and she had accepted my offer to dance. We only met that once, but the girl had worked her way so deeply into my heart that even the twins couldn't shake her image from my mind. And now, two years later, in another life, I was dancing once more. In my arms was the enchanting Professor Tarra Lloyd, miles ahead of any other women out there. In my arms was Serlena Przhedetskaya, smiling and perspiring. A fleeting moment of joy remaining from my past life.

The music ended and I stopped, letting go of the magister. Serlena graced me with one last smile and her image evaporated. That part of my past was gone forever.

"That was…unexpected," Tarra said, and I grinned. Now, having parted with Serlena, I saw only a beautiful woman standing before me. Maybe even a perfect woman, but a flesh-and-blood woman nonetheless. Not some distant, unattainable angel.

"Change partners!" Tarra ordered and the first-years regrouped. The music started up again and ten pairs started spinning around the room. She spent some time assessing the smoothness and quality of each pair's movements, after which she turned back to me.

"She was someone special to you?"

I nodded, perturbed by the question. Could the magister have, in some unfathomable way, felt everything that I had just experienced?

"You're the first doomer I've ever had in my class, so I'm not exactly sure how to behave around you. But since you're here, it means you have the right to be here, and you'll do the work like any other student. The way you expressed your emotions, allowing them to dissolve into movements, your breath, the surroundings … It's amazing. This is what I want to achieve from each of my students. You definitely need practice. Your movements are ragged and wrong, but your emotions, passion...perhaps this is due to your status. A doomer who could die at any moment. A doomer who sucks everything from life while he has the opportunity. I don't know. One thing I can say for sure is that it will be an interesting experience for both of us. Now in position. It's time to sort out your mistakes..."

These four hours were the happiest I'd spent in the academy. Tarra, with amazing patience for a teacher, explained both to me and the entire class what our mistakes had been, after which we started practicing. Next dance. Serlena didn't visit me anymore, but I didn't need her — I was able to immerse myself in my emotions without outside help. The tempo Tarra set turned out to be impossible for many. The first students began to fall off after the first two hours, collapsing against the wall with a groan. For me, it was a labor of love. The thousands of repetitions of the same movements, millions of steps forward, side, back, the endless turns of the head — compared to what the Evil Engineer bullied me with every day, Tarra was a blessing. The last thirty minutes of the lesson turned into a one-on-one session. Only the two of us remained on our feet. When the bell rang, I was surprised to notice that I was soaked through to the skin, while my teacher hadn't even broken a sweat. I had no doubt that she was another consumer of enhancement elixirs.

"It was a pleasure working with you."

Magister Loyd smiled, taking two steps back. How did she move like that? No master of martial arts could achieve such fluidity! "Attention class! Thank you all for this lesson, I'll see you next semester. Remember, dance is one of the mandatory exams you must pass, so don't expect any concessions from my end. The elite of the Zarak Empire study at our academy! And you must prove your worth, not just on the Wall, but also at the ball, constantly being the center of attention. Because this is the true vocation of the elites — to always be at the forefront and to lead those behind them. Thank you, sirs, for your assistance."

The last she addressed to the musicians. They all began to bow to one another and shake hands. I slowly edged toward the exit — at this celebration of life, I was simply a squeaky wheel. The first years shared their impressions of the lesson, the guys made unambiguous remarks about the teacher's appearance, and someone even attempted to utter the word "doomer," but was immediately stifled by his friends. Apparently, the whole academy already knew what had happened that morning.

They were waiting for me at the exit. Four red-robed clerics immediately stuffed me in a box and escorted me in this manner to the dining room. There, I was received by Zurgan Shor's people, who brought me to the table and then surrounded it from all sides. They didn't even permit me to stand in line — my food was brought by pallid chefs who had personally tasted each dish. Wow, really? So they were planning to poison me now?

"Until the contract holder cancels the order, the Nocturnal Guild will not back down. It always completes the task it sets out to do." The fat old man sat down across from me. "And judging by the customer's disposition, she won't be canceling anytime soon. She's relying on her status. Of course, I'm not particularly pleased to have these guys on the territory I've been entrusted to protect, but I must admit — in just one morning, you've already paid off all the resources invested in you."

"The *Cloak* stone you pulled off the body?" I hazarded a guess.

"And not just that. There were a few other interesting abilities, and if the princess hadn't demanded a demonstrative death, with blood, you certainly wouldn't have made it out alive. Extremely rare, if not entirely unique stones, is what I'm trying to say. I even began to wonder: is your fate truly just a series of accidents, or has Skron placed a curse on you and you're now doomed to suffer for the rest of your days? Which are clearly few in number, but no doubt exceedingly intense."

"Am I expected to respond to that, or was it a rhetorical question?" I pushed my empty plate away. Even the awful old fat man's company didn't spoil my appetite.

"You are permitted to carry mana and recovery elixirs on your person." Magister Shor placed six vials on the table, one by one. Three of each type. "Your partner may not always be nearby."

"But you didn't come here just to delight me with the news that you're loosening my collar." I held Magister Shor's gaze. He habitually chewed his lips and agreed:

"Until the esteemed chancellor returns, you will need to travel around the academy in my presence. Finished eating? Then let's go, I'll hand you over to Father Nor's care."

I even began to wonder — why Zurgan Shor in particular? There were two options: either he hoped that his presence would neutralize any of the particularly violent ones, since there certainly would be hot heads who decided I was the reason their beloved princess had been imprisoned. Or he had some sort of ability that allowed him to identify assassins lurking in the shadows. And, being near to me, Magister Shor would be able to sniff out these killers and end their lives with one fell swoop. Maybe more than one, but you get the picture. Both options were plausible and had the right to exist, both separately and in tandem.

"Thank you for escorting him, Magister." At the training grounds, I was met with a new brigade. "I'll be keeping him until late this evening, so no need to rush back. Dark one, follow me. You have work to do."

The cleric had managed to pique my interest, especially considering that we were so close to the first level of the training grounds. The dark beasts here didn't scare me, even when out of their cages, so they clearly hadn't dragged me here for training. For help?...What sort of assistance could a doomer have to offer? Just our one and only purpose: killing a dark beast. There really wasn't anything else we were good for.

The first cave on the beginner level turned out to be full. There weren't that many people, just six total, but I noticed the peculiarities right away: none of them were wearing an academy uniform. And the age of the group suggested that I had been brought to a parent gathering for graduates. And one more thing...I turned sharply in the direction of Father Nor, pointing to the cage with the dark one. It had always held a common beast before, but now there was an elite krona sitting inside. One I hadn't encountered, a beast from the fourth level of the rift.

"The Fortress has carefully studied your development path and decided to reiterate it. Those you see before you are weapon masters. Sword masters, spear masters. Each of them spent more than a decade on the Wall, fighting side-by-side with doomed soldiers. Three had a chance to resist the Wave. They understand combat meditation firsthand."

"But something's wrong," I guessed. "I can even predict exactly what it is, right off the bat: they can't block the dark beast's influence. No, I misspoke — they can't activate their mirror. Why? The answer is clear, but I don't understand what I'm doing here? You already know why."

"Because they've spent ten years on the Wall,"

Father Nor nodded. "The habit of putting up an inner wall to block off their emotions is too deeply embedded in their being to break it so easily. Your task is to explain to them what to do and how. Any methods are permitted, up to and including physical. Right here and now, you have full authority as their commander. We need mirrors, Dark Max. We need answers."

"Have you considered the fact that the mirror might be an ability only bestowed by dark stones?"

"We consider every factor that might produce results. There are six people here. Three of them have received their abilities through the standard means, while three received stones through fire. Exactly the same as you did. You won't know who is who until the end."

"Cool...I can't refuse, as I understand it?" I glanced up at the cleric, who shook his head. "So they've enlisted me as a mentor too..."

"We all have unusual duties we must perform," Father Nor replied coolly. "I, for example, in lieu of burning this dark one at the stake in a final bid to save his soul, stand next to him and persuade him to work for the good of the Light. Such is life, no matter how we may all wish it were otherwise."

"Alright guys, break's over, everyone eyes on me!" I shouted to get everyone's attention. Having a discussion with Father Nor was, of course, endlessly exciting, but for some reason it always boiled down to the same thing: follow orders or it's the stake for you. After waiting for all six to stop their stupid murmuring, I took a couple of steps forward, sat down and pointed to the seats in front of me.

"Take a seat and we'll begin. The sooner we figure out how to solve this problem, the sooner we can go to dinner."

"Who's he?" asked some bastard with a scar slashed across his face, turning to Father Nor.

"He's the one who's going to help you with your problem. For the moment, he is your commander."

"This pipsqueak?" another chortled. The masters of the Wall were subordinate to the emperor, not to the High Priest, so there was no question of any subordination. The men knew their own worth and were trying to figure out why in Skron's name I had been foisted on them.

"And with kid's toys instead of weapons." My katars didn't escape another mercenary's attention. "Are those toothpicks?"

"In other words, you don't intend to listen to me or do what I tell you to, is that right?" I chuckled. If he thought he'd have the last word on that, he was sorely mistaken. The churchman had given me a direct task and was awaiting its completion. The fact that nature had deprived me of any natural charms or charisma was my own problem. That just meant I'd have to carry out my orders a different way. And I think I knew what it was. One where I had no possible chance of winning. Then they'd be forced to use it.

"Father Nor, we clearly need a small

demonstration. You said these men were all real masters of the Wall? Will you give them weapons? They won't listen until they test for themselves. I wouldn't either."

Father Nor had clearly been counting on something like this — after a few moments, their weapons had all been dragged from the second cave. Three swordsmen, three spearmen. Not bad. Judging by the different lengths and girths of the weapons, they weren't standard poles from our armory. They were obviously personal weapons to which the masters have become accustomed in the ten years of their patrol.

"You should step aside and cover yourself," I said to the churchman as I strode to the center of the cave. The weapons masters, without even saying a word, formed a circle around me, surrounding me from all sides. Judging by their malicious smirks, they didn't consider me a threat at all. In fact, I completely agreed with them — one man with a sword, even the toughest one, couldn't do anything against three spear masters covered by three sword masters. The idea I had decided to roll with was the peak of idiocy, but this was precisely why there was a chance to succeed. A small chance at victory, but a chance nonetheless.

"Before we begin, does everyone have protection amulets?"

No one bothered to answer me, but I wasn't counting on it. At least I warned them that they might be needed. The rest was up to them. If someone accidentally got hurt...I'd had too tough a morning to worry about such trifles now.

"Alright, gentlemen, let's start on the count of three. Your task is to survive. At least thirty seconds. Ready? One! Two! Three!"

Gustav always taught me to never underestimate your opponent. Even if you think he's weak, act as if you're fighting against the deadliest enemy in the world. But this was not my problem — I knew I had no chance against any one of them individually, let alone all six. Whatever anyone might say, they were masters, and Gustav, who had taught me, was never a master. But I had one hope for victory: the elite beast from level four of the rift. Along with my charm, of course — where would I be without it?

I went into my mirror state in a matter of moments. I had my improved golden shield raised, a full mana bar, *Dark Spike* loaded and ready to tear into the enemy, katars in combat mode, and as soon as I shouted "Three!" all spears moved toward me and I went dark. But I wasn't just any beast — one equal in strength to the creature hiding in the cage. I became an elite krona from the fourth level of the rift.

I knew perfectly well what the consequences of this action would be. Losing consciousness was the easiest way out. However, astoundingly, I managed to stay on my feet, and even see some things through the hazy fog that clouded my vision. It was difficult. Extremely. But the pressure was nowhere close to what I had experienced near the Warden's cave. Concentrating, I saw my opponents and could not help but grin. These were the Wall masters who had been fighting dark beasts for the past ten years? Were they doing it by written correspondence?

Five of the men fell straight back on their asses and confidently paddled with all four limbs, trying to get as far away from me as possible. Judging by the look of terror in his eyes he clearly had no intention of attacking. One stayed on his feet, but tottered like a willowy tree during a hurricane. If not for the spear, I'm sure this one would have collapsed to the floor too. My ears began to buzz — I was approaching my limit. That thing in the cage was far too strong, so I had to hurry. Biting my lip, I took a few steps forward, slashing a katar across my opponent's skin to signify a fatal blow. One down. I slashed the cheek of another. Two. I turned around and, with monumental efforts, slashed two more. Then another, and I was left with only one. The same staggering spearman who wouldn't fall.

Before I blacked out completely, I gave up. This wasn't one of my training sessions. I just had to prove to the masters that I was worthy of teaching them. Five out of six should be good enough to get their attention. My mirror flew off into the distance and I fell to my knees with a loud sigh. Alright, enough heroism for today. Now for the lengthy discussions about how...What was that strange muttering?

The sixth master who I hadn't managed to strike down was behaving rather strangely. Not only was he still staggering, even after the dark aura had dissipated, but he was also muttering inarticulately. It caused a wave of rage to well up inside of me and I wanted nothing more than to shut his mouth and stop the mumbling. I had never heard the language of the dark ones, but some sixth sense told me that's what it was. The words the master was mumbling had meaning. Finally, he raised his hands high, as if ending his speech, and I heard the monstrously calm voice of Father Nor:

"Max, don't let him finish that spell. That's not a human. It's a convert…"

Chapter 3

I ALWAYS THOUGHT the stories about converts were just fairytales spread by the church, solely so that the people would have a common enemy to fear more than they did the fanatics at the Fortress. If you don't do your training, the converts will come and snatch you. If you don't eat your porridge, the converts will get you. If you're a bad boy…I think the general message is clear: fear the dark ones and do as you're told. Otherwise bad things will happen.

But standing face-to-face with such a creature, I knew that the stories about the converts couldn't convey even half the horror of the real thing. Father Nor ordered me to stop the spell? No questions asked — over the past week, I'd grown accustomed to carrying out the cleric's orders with no hesitation. But approaching the creature proved an impossible task. The man, hands still uplifted in holy ecstasy, was surrounded by a magical force field, and my katars weren't long enough to pierce through. *Dark Spike* was always a good response to this — not so much to do damage, but to simply change the enemy's position. The explosion was tremendous. It wasn't enough to puncture the shield, which was expected, but the dark one was thrown aside. He could barely stand on his feet, so he collapsed like a felled tree, not even thinking to put his hands out to soften the blow. His mumbling continued from the ground and only then did I realize that I was on my own. The masters who supposedly fought such enemies in their line of work were laying on the floor, unmoving. Only two of them made any effort to rise, while the other three were statues. Just like the other churchmen — everyone was wallowing on the floor except for Father Nor. But even he looked grim — his face was covered in large drops of sweat.

"Break the spell," the cleric's voice sounded calmly again, for which he paid the price. Blood was streaming from Father Nor's nose. Grabbing a spear from the ground, I leapt toward the dark one and brought the weapon down with all my might. There was the crack of breaking wood and the shaft of the spear was torn from my hands. The steel tip of the spear passed through the shield without issue, but as soon as the wood hit, it got stuck. The impact was strong enough to break the spear, but not enough to propel the spear tip forward on its deadly path. It reached the dark one, but rather than piercing the body, it fell inertly on his face and rolled onto the rocks. The dark one gave no sign of ceasing his serenade.

Break the spell...

Don't hesitate. Don't die. Just stop it...

How could I stop something I couldn't reach? I started to look around, hoping for some clue. They never taught me how to fight converts! Push-ups, running, jumping — sure, but fighting against beasts under such powerful protection — No! I needed help! But no help was coming. Father Nor had already begun to stagger. The cleric's eyes closed, sweat streaming down his face. It was evident that he was relying solely on his morals and strong will. I glanced around again. The katars were useless, even if I took them off and tried to throw them at the dark one. The other swords too — although their blades were made of steel, the guard and handle were other materials. They'd suffer the same fate as the spear. The spears, respectively, were also a no-go. *Dark Spike* rolls back every five seconds, it just recharged...but it's useless!

And then I did the only thing I could think of. I went dark again!

Since the convert had revealed himself upon meeting a fourth-level elite, that meant there was something about this beast he wasn't fond of. It seemed to help — the muttering stopped. Although I may have just been deafened. The pressure from the beast in the cage was insane. The convert lowered his arms and rose to his feet in one jerking motion like a marionette. With a twitchy gait, he moved toward the cage, obviously with ill intentions, so I was forced to use *Dark Spike* for the third time, knocking the dark one aside. I tried not to think about the fact that some of the damage was taken by the Wall masters still lying on the ground.

Once again, the convert's defenses proved their worth, completely blocking the blow. His head jerked strangely and two dark eyes turned to face me. His gaze was exceedingly unsettling — there was not a drop of humanity left. The convert turned around and threw his leg forward exactly like a puppet on a string. Living beings don't walk like that. The other leg followed. The creature was clearly trying to approach me. I took a step back, wracking my brain for a way to survive. My mirror prevented the convert from casting the spell, but it turned him aggressive. If I put the mirror down, then...the convert's hands flew back up to the sky and the cave was once again filled with that excruciating murmur.

But this time, I knew what to do: as I retreated, I stumbled over the body of a cleric. He lay motionless on the floor, one sleeve rolled up to reveal a miniature crossbow. Same as the one I got shot with once upon a time. It didn't take a lot of time to figure out how it worked — it was a simple mechanical device, not magic. I deployed the steel arms of the crossbow and fed a steel bolt into the groove, then twisted the poor guy's arm to aim at the dark creature's head and pulled the trigger.

The muttering stopped, the man fell to the floor, a steel bolt through his brain. A chorus of moans rang out. The masters and churchmen had regained control of their bodies. I flooded the cave with *Healing Aura* in an attempt to somehow help the wounded, and at that moment, I nearly went deaf. The beast with a bolt through its brain was squealing and twitching as if alive! For some reason, my aura still had an effect on the lifeless body.

"He must be quartered," I heard Father Nor say. "Skron controls him, even in death."

Cutting the body to pieces proved rather simple, as it no longer had a shield. Picking up a sword from the floor, I played butcher, dividing the dark one into small pieces. I knew then I'd never forget the sight of his severed head opening its mouth to scream, and those hands grasping at anything they could reach long after they had been separated from the body. Skron not only controlled the body, he controlled every piece of it!

The door to the training grounds opened and two red-robed churchmen ran into the cave. One collapsed instantly to the floor, joining the ranks of the weak, while the other managed to stay standing.

"We need a bonfire. Only fire can destroy a dark one. Max, drag everyone outside. Skron's influence will not be felt there."

Grabbing the swordmaster nearest to me by the legs, I dragged him toward the exit. The red-robed monk had already escaped the training ground and was giving out orders, demanding dry logs be brought to the site. I pulled Father Nor out on my second trip. Carefully, as he was of great value to the academy.

"The others." Father Nor's tone was almost emotional. "Get them out. There are servants of the Light in the second cave as well. Don't leave them alone with the dark one. Don't turn off your healing aura...Don't stop. Burn the beast!"

Even on the verge of consciousness, Father Nor continued to think of the battle against the dark beast. I had to make twenty trips before only the wiggling remains of the convert were left on the training grounds. By the time I finished my part of the work, Father Nor had been thoroughly patched up by the healers. The cleric began to pace between the pale weapons masters and servants of the Light I had pulled out of the training ground, leaning over each and peering into their faces for a long time. The red robes took the last of my loads from me and immediately tied his arms and legs, sitting him down with the others. Everyone who had fallen under the convert's influence and lost consciousness were bound.

"Max, the body of the dark beast must be burned," Father Nor pointed to a huge bundle of firewood that had been dragged here from all over the academy. "It will burn quickly. When the master was still a human, he was given the dark stone *Siphon Life*. Don't go near the fire after you finish burning the corpse. You don't need this stone. Go! The training ground needs a thorough cleansing."

Siphon Life? The stone's properties were unfamiliar to me, but the name alone turned my stomach. I didn't want to siphon anyone's life. Now, if it had been a *Destroy Fardi* stone, I would have taken it, even against Father Nor's wishes, but unfortunately, no such stone had yet been discovered at the academy. The creature's body really did burn beautifully. It smoked mercilessly, of course, but it burned. Half an hour later, when I left the training grounds, all of those whom I had pulled out were gone. I was greeted by the imperturbable Father Nor, who had changed from his soiled mantle to a new, snow-white vestment.

"What will happen to them?" I nodded to the place where they had lain.

"The fire," the cleric replied calmly, as a matter of course. "Anyone who cannot keep control of their own minds in the presence of a convert must burn. Such is the price of weakness."

"Isn't that a little harsh?" I asked, astonished.

"Their minds have been touched by darkness. I gazed into all their eyes and saw Skron there. He has already enslaved them. He has made them his servants, even if they themselves do not realize. Sooner or later, a dark one will come to them with an offer of power and we will have more converts. We are both morally and legally required to stop this."

"Two of the masters were moving," I recalled. "They weren't under the influence."

"Those with dark stones," Father Nor nodded.

"I saw them fight. They will be granted life, but only after careful scrutiny."

"And I suppose it's hopeless to ask what happened here?"

"Why? No one prohibited you from asking. The only limitations are on the responses. But we're always willing to hear your concerns."

"You checked all the masters before sending them to the academy, correct?" I asked, and without waiting for a response, continued the thought: "There's no way they can get in without being vetted. The Wall isn't a place where sloppiness is permitted. This is purely my opinion, not based on any facts. So, they were vetted, but nothing dangerous was found. Which means either the master wasn't yet a convert at the time of the screening, or was so strong that he managed to fool your test. If the former is true, what was the impetus for going over to Skron's side? That I put up my mirror? Or that the mirror turned me into an elite from level four of the rift? The master saw the terrible beast in me, got scared and sold his soul in exchange for salvation. Does that really seem feasible? As my mentor would say, it's like pulling an owl out of a globe, trying to tie one fact to the other. The master would not have had time to sell himself to Skron so quickly. Again, purely my opinion. Plus, his shield is a meter in diameter. Where did it come from? It was obviously made to guard against swordsmen and spearmen. So most likely it's the latter, that there was a problem with the vetting process. And so a new, unpleasant question arises: If they made that mistake, perhaps they made a mistake in my case as well?"

"You definitely need an education," sighed Father Nor. "You spin complete nonsense with a look on your face as if a revelation has dawned on you from above. Yes, there was a problem with the testing. But not because it's ineffective, but rather because the convert who appeared in the academy came from the highest ranks of Skron's army. I don't recall ever seeing a convert as strong as he was. He nearly broke me. Plus the spell — Skron may be able to control a body, but he couldn't make it speak. That spell the convert was mumbling, he had to learn it first. The Darkness tried to throw one of his agents at us, and if he had succeeded, he would have been a very dangerous agent with access to too many influential people and too much information. We are fortunate that you used the mirror. Fortunate that the dark one blundered and was not prepared to encounter a dark beast from level four of the rift. Skron was forced to take control of his puppet. And we're fortunate that the influence of a convert's aura doesn't affect dark ones. So much good fortune, and once again, it's circling around the doomed soldier named Max. You should be asking another question. What if it all happened to serve a singular goal: to show us your value and start trusting you? What if Skron is so impressed with your results that he decided to sacrifice one of his most valuable converts to protect you? What do you say to that, Doomer Max?"

"That you have too active an imagination. You stopped calling me Dark One. Why?"

But his response was cut short by the strange clerics coming out of the training grounds. I had never seen such dark robes in my life. They held long steel tongs, at the end of which magic stones hissed in the direct sunlight.

"*Siphon Life* and *Cloak Essence*," one of them uttered, answering Father Nor's unspoken question. "The second stone's ability can only be surmised from its name. The description is hidden, I've never seen one like it before. Eight stones, irretrievably lost."

"How did you manage to extract *Siphon Life* if the stone was obtained through fire?" I frowned, but the black robes were in no hurry to answer me. It was clear that to them, I didn't exist. Father Nor stared at the tongs for a long time before speaking:

"Thank you for your help, brothers. You can return to the Fortress. I will be most grateful if you leave me a copy of your report from studying *Cloak Essence*. I want to understand how the dark one was able to cheat our security system and what we must do to close this gap."

The dark robes left and a brigade of white robes removed the cage and prepared the first cave for cleansing, while I stood near Father Nor and waited for some sort of response. Or for him to send me off somewhere far away. Which was also a response, by the way. And very revealing. Father Nor was silent for a long time, but then said:

"Two weeks ago, a doomer with a very

interesting stone showed up at the Fortress. At the present moment, we have yet to witness another golden dome such as yours. Unless that's what the convert had today, or something comparable. We had no right to risk losing the stone because of some accident. Having discovered how the stone was forged, our researchers started conducting tests. I don't know how many doomers died during that time. All I know is that the presentation before the High Priest consisted of initiation, murder and further extraction of the stone from the body of the dark one. Now we are nearly certain that if, after your death, your body falls into the hands of our researchers, they will be able to pull the elite stones from your body. In your case, *Golden Dome of Protection* and *Steel Resistance.*"

"So *Cloak Essence* is also elite? And did you implant *Siphon Life* in advance, knowing that the masters wouldn't live?"

"All participants in the experiment signed a contract. They knew what they were risking. They could have become an order of magnitude stronger, but they broke down, unable to defeat the influence of the convert. As for what happened…You won't make a mentor. Arranging a fight with six weapon masters at once, without even the slightest idea how they handle their weapons, is the height of unprofessionalism."

"Funny, I thought it was rather well thought out," I contested. "It's true I didn't know their strength, but they didn't know what to expect either. Did any of them really think they would just be waving their iron sticks around the cave? When I saw the dark beast you dragged in...Why, by the way?"

"For training purposes. One of our specialists has developed a curriculum for your training, including improving your concentration and ability to maintain your mirror state."

"In other words, by your own admission, you acted as you always did and managed to make a ton of mistakes? Stop looking at me like that and threatening to burn me at the stake. There was a mistake in your methodology from the very beginning, and I'm surprised that no one noticed it. Tell me, why did you praise my partner during our first training?"

Because she was able to pass through ten caves," Father Nor frowned, trying to figure out what I was getting at, and then quickly grimaced rather quickly. "Mirror! You mimic the darkness, not the influence it has on others!"

"For Fardi, the number of caves was irrelevant. She had gotten a dose of the common beast in the first cave, and the others only served to toughen her skin. That's why I managed to shake the convert, because I reflected the full power of the creature you caged. Not the tiny amount that managed to seep through the steel."

"Are you trying to tell me that you're already capable of holding back fourth-level dark elites?" Father Nor clearly didn't believe me.

"With difficulty, it's a real strain, but I can do it. Just don't forget — the beasts we don't encounter until the fourth level here are running around on the second, and even first levels of other rifts. Give me six hours and I'll barely even notice this beast. Am I being sent to another rift, Father Nor?"

"It's being discussed. No one has ever pulled a map fragment from a Rift Master before. Especially not incorporeal copies. Who knows what will occur if you obtain the full map? Anything could happen. Positive or negative. Before we take risks, we must consider carefully. We must not allow our careless actions to open a new door for the dark ones."

Another important feature I'd noticed in the churchman was the fanatic need to double-check everyone and everything. They dare not take a single step without knowing what this step might lead to. Take, for example, the *Analyze* stone that Magister Nor so badly wanted to see on the academy grounds. A rare stone, most likely elite. But before handing it over to some unknown dark one, they needed to guarantee that the stone would be returned to its rightful home. And how could this be accomplished? Why not just snuff out the lives of a few dozen doomers to test that the valuable materials can be extracted? And to make a presentation of it in front of the High Priest...Heartless fanatics.

"Well, since you yourself stated that six hours is sufficient time to adapt to the elite dark beast, that's what you'll have. You can't return to the academy yet, as the nocturnal guild's contract has not yet been canceled. I wouldn't want to lose you just because of one individual's stupidity. Go on, today the training grounds are your only task. If you see anyone other than myself or one of my companions, feel free to destroy them."

By companions, Father Nor was referring to the four constantly changing overseers who monitored my every step. I must confess, the idea of simply sitting in silence appealed to me, but the fact that I'd be experiencing pain the whole time was less so. On the other hand, what did I know of pain? Just over yonder there were men burning for the mere fact that they were unable to resist the influence.

In reality, it only took me three hours. The fourth I spent amusing myself, walking up to the entrance of the cage and reaching my hands into the darkness, trying to grasp it. When they came for me, I was sitting right next to the krona, separated only by steel bars. Dark brothers for eternity. When I was taken back to the doomer den, I could only sigh sadly. I guess tonight would be another night without supper.

(Chancellor's office, Magical Academy, that evening)

"Great light, why are some people so complicated?" Kimal Sarento leaned back wearily in his chair.

"Not everyone is happy to answer rhetorical

questions." Father Nor waited patiently as the chancellor deigned to notify the supreme council of the academy about his trip to see the emperor.

"No one is asking you to, Father Nor. No one's asking. I apologize for my overt sentimentality. When I first appeared before the emperor, he wouldn't even hear me and demanded his daughter be released immediately. I was given a day to comply with his orders or the empire would recognize the academy as a threat to the state. That deadline, incidentally, just expired."

"Was the High Priest present at the meeting?" Father Nor asked. Receiving a nod, the cleric relaxed. "That means the threat was nothing more than hot air. The emperor would never go against the church. Even for the sake of his daughter."

"Yes, I must acknowledge Father Urg's enormous contributions in resolving the conflict," the chancellor said. "If not for him, our sovereign may have said too much. Miralda Lertan will be released in two days and will receive a transcript and diploma with whatever grades she earns on the final exam. No favors."

"So just a blank sheet?" Zurgan Shor chortled.

"If that's what the Light wills," Father Nor shrugged his shoulders. "We are all equal before the Light. What about the doomer?"

"So he's just a doomer now? Not a dark one?" The chancellor was surprised.

"Today, on the training grounds, he detected and destroyed a convert from Skron's highest ranks," Father Nor reported calmly, causing the other two to start. "Now I am certain that until he meets with the incarnation of Skron himself, he will be able to block out his own dark essence."

"You didn't say it was a supreme convert!" Zurgan Shor chewed his lips unpleasantly.

"As soon as I leave for half a day, something happens," Kimal Sarento grumbled in displeasure. "Tell me, what did your protégé do this time?"

"I will be sure to regale you, along with my own suggestions on how we should utilize this new knowledge, but first, we must deal with the assassin's guild. Has the princess canceled the contract?"

"It was canceled by the emperor, as a legal representative of Miralda Lertan," said the chancellor.

"For now, there is nothing threatening Max, so tell me, how did a supreme convert end up in my academy and how many students and professors did it cost me?"

(Private quarters of the chancellor of the Magical Academy, that night)

"What say you?"

"This will cost you dearly, young one. As for binding him to me, I will, of course, do so, but his soul has been given to another. Until that feeling passes, we won't be able to turn him into a loyal dog. How much time this will take, Skron alone knows. You made a mistake in calling him a backwoods boy — he knows a woman's body and what to do with it. Languid sighs and promises won't work here. You have to give yourself completely. We've got six months. You'll be fine. As always. I need a good lap dog, and only you can arrange it for me. Now come here. When you've got Max on top of you, I want you to remember what a real man can do..."

Chapter 4

THE NEXT MORNING began with another surprise. Apparently the Fortress was also home to blue robes. Whites were the common churchmen. Red was security. Black — research. Gold was the High Priest. What were the blue robes responsible for? I received my answer almost immediately — seeing that I'd awoken, the well-fed man held out a sheet of paper:

"Read and confirm receipt."

Intrigued, I read a few lines and my eyebrows raised, despite myself.

"What is this?"

"Your share of the winnings for the campaign through the rift. Thanks to the actions of one short-sighted woman, you have become an official doomer until you leave the academy. It completely destroyed our entire bookkeeping system. We had to figure out a way to include you on the doomer register while assigning you the status 'unable to send on tasks.' I hate setting up caveats where they're not not needed. That's why it took so long to calculate everything."

"Am I out of the loop again?" I read the list over. "Where did this all come from? It certainly wasn't in the rift..."

"What would you have done with nux? Or unrefined amulets? Or magic stones? Young man, don't feed me nonsense, my head's already jam-packed with it. According to ancient tradition, doomed soldiers who clean out rifts receive ten percent of the loot obtained therein. Each participant's share is determined by the commander, but in your case, we had to calculate it ourselves."

"Ninety-two recovery potions, seventy-two vials of mana, thirty-two gold, seventy-two silver coins," I read each item aloud. This was a significant sum of gold — in our barony, one could live quite comfortably on such a salary for several months before running out. How could I complain when my mentor Gustav's wages totaled just fifteen gold a month?

"I know full well what's written there," the blue-frocked cleric said, pursing his lips in displeasure. "I wrote it myself. Young man, are you going to sign or not?"

"I'll sign, of course, but I have one question — why do I need all this? Doesn't the Fortress provide doomed soldiers with everything they need?"

"It does. But don't confuse necessity with

demand. The more effectively our doomed soldiers fight, the more rifts they close, the more opportunity they have to purchase or commission better armor or weapons. To customize. Adapt. To order things that may not be allowed under standard circumstances. They can even save up for enhancement elixirs. You will receive a list of items and prices at the Fortress. Do you need a pen?"

"I have nowhere to put this all now. Is it possible to leave it at the Fortress for safekeeping?"

"Young man, we are a church, not some manner of bank. My task was to correctly calculate and deliver your due, and not to concern myself with where to store it. There's a branch of the Imperial Bank at the academy. You can leave your savings there. Although they are unlikely to work with doomers. You can put the coins in your nightstand and forget all about them when you come to the Fortress. You can give them to those in need. The Fortress doesn't care how you spend your earnings. Doomers are free to dispose of their wages at their discretion. However, so that you will sign this piece of paper as soon as possible, I will give you a piece of free advice: try to find yourself a good smith who can customize your equipment specifically for combat in the rifts. I am sure that the academy will do no worse a job at this than the Fortress. Would you like to verify the contents yourself, or will you take the word of a servant of the Light?"

"A certain short-sighted woman who awarded me the right to accept this prize taught me not to trust anyone. Especially unknown clerics in strange robes. Yes, I would like to check."

The man pursed his lips in displeasure, but said nothing, pouring the gold onto my bed. My roommates' eyes lit up. They had never seen so much gold in one place in all their lives. Both men jumped out of bed and watched as I put the coins back into the purse one by one. Everything was exactly as listed — the gold, silver, and two boxes of elixirs were placed next to the bed. I really didn't have the slightest idea what to do with all this, but since they were giving it out, I wasn't about to refuse. After signing the paper, I sent the churchman on his way and looked out the window. There were only ten minutes left before my "warm up."

"Look after the elixirs. Don't lose a single one," I ordered, tossing two gold pieces into the air. One for each doomer.

"We won't," the tall one assured me. The fat one nodded quickly, testing the coin with his teeth. Soon a satisfied smirk stretched across his face.

"Know where I can spend this?" I nodded toward the coins.

"On food, of course," the tall one twirled the coin and stuck it in his pocket. "We've already figured it all out. They have a menu here, you can order food even from the most expensive restaurant in the capital. All that's important is that you can pay. I've always dreamed of trying the imperial cake. They're sending us to the Fortress in two months anyway, why bother saving up? I'm definitely ordering a cake."

"Maybe we should order you something too?" Fatty put away his coin. "Just tell us and we'll arrange it for you right away. You're the one they're always fucking with, they mostly leave me and my brother alone."

"I have everything I need." I pulled on my jumpsuit, threw the gold into my backpack, took a couple of vials just in case and ran to the arena. The Evil Engineer would eat me alive if I was even a minute late.

But it seemed there was no avoiding punishment today. When I sprinted over to the meeting point, the Evil Engineer was in a darker mood than usual. My mentor threw me a glance and muttered something under his breath, then nodded to one of the new teachers, indicating that I was all his. He wasted no time and beckoned me over to him. The same way we would call a stableboy when we needed to go somewhere. If this new guy thought I would run toward him with open arms, he was sorely mistaken. As ordered by Father Nor, I had only one mentor in the arena. Anyone else can gesture all they like. Defiantly turning away, I started doing squats. Even though the Evil Engineer had refused to start our warmup, I certainly wasn't going to let my muscles get cold.

"What are you standing around for?" I asked Karina, who was frozen nearby.

"Magister Hwang called you." Judging by her tone of voice, the professor's identity was only a mystery to me.

"And? Anyone who likes can summon me, but that doesn't mean I'm going to rush over there and ignore the orders of my mentor. Even if the cat got his tongue this morning." These last words I addressed directly to the Evil Engineer.

"But it's Magister Hwan!" Fardi whispered.

"And because of you, Miralda Lertan will soon be sent to the rift," I got angry. "For some reason, you don't have any emotions about the princess, but here comes Master Hwang! If my mentor says that warmup today is canceled, postponed or rescheduled, and other teachers have the right to manage my time, then by all means. I'll spring to attention at Magister Hwan's beck and call. He whistles, pats his leg, even scratches his ass and I'll come running. But as long as my mentor is silent, I'll stay on schedule. Warm up. Which is what I advise you do too."

"Magister Hwan...is head..." Karina began, but stopped short, staring over my shoulder. Judging by the way the Evil Engineer's face twisted, Hwan was standing right behind me. I wanted to turn around. I really did. It felt as if I'd give everything I had in this life to just turn around and look at Magister Hwan. My hands started to shake and an unpleasant bitterness filled my mouth. My eyes became heavy as if I hadn't slept for three days. The only thing I felt now was the obsessive need to turn around so all this would end, but I stood and faced the Evil Engineer. The dark one crossed his arms over his chest and stared at me, somehow magically managing to avoid direct eye contact. However, I did notice something. The indifference, or neglect in the mentor's face had been replaced by interest.

The desire to turn around became so strong that I made one last attempt to avoid it — I pulled my mirror over myself, hiding all my emotions behind an impenetrable wall. It didn't help. It was clear that I was being influenced by some ability, but it had nothing to do with darkness. So, I didn't have a single chance to block it. My head began to spin, I staggered, and the idea occurred to simply fall face down and ignore everything else, but I did not allow myself such weakness. Stand! Die, but stay standing! And never turn around!

"I, naturally, don't give a damn what you do. What's one pupil more or less to me? But if you continue like this, you'll have to explain yourself to Father Nor. Why one of his favorites suddenly lost his mind."

The Evil Engineer's voice sounded as if it was coming from the bottom of a barrel. The pressure vanished abruptly, as did the urge to turn around. Control returned to my body, and I wanted to fall to my knees and sigh with relief, but the inherent sense of danger didn't permit this. All I allowed myself was to lean over to my backpack and pull out one of the recovery elixirs. Judging by the trembling of my hands and my wobbly legs, the healing aura wouldn't be enough now. The contents of the vial passed through my body in a warm wave, and as soon as I regained the ability to speak without a tremble in my voice, I clarified with the Evil Engineer:

"Mentor, should I keep doing squats or should I head to the obstacle course?"

I'd never seen a dark one laugh. It not only sounded, but looked ghastly! The darkness he was exuding condensed, nearly becoming solid.

"Today you will be studying with a new teacher. On special discharge for pains in the ass like you. Magister Hwang, he's all yours. He has breakfast in two hours, try not to kill him by then. Fardi, you're off today — I give you the right to come up with your own punishment. Or did you think your training today would consist of standing and gaping at Magister Hwang? Ten laps in full gear around the arena! While you run, think about your punishment. Move!"

Karina took off with such speed that I was caught in her dust cloud. The Evil Engineer stepped aside, showing that he no longer had anything to do with me, and I finally did what I had so desired a few moments ago. I turned around to face my new teacher.

Magister Hwan had all the typical features of a resident of the Shurgan Empire — his complexion, slanting eyes, the particular way he tied up his hair. His arms crossed in a peculiar manner, hidden in his sleeves, he looked down on me with the full authority of his age and stature. The long, snow-white hair and beard told me that this was a man clearly quite advanced in years. Although time seemed to have passed him by — hair color aside, not one wrinkle had touched the man's face.

I stood and looked at Master Hwang, not sure how to behave. As to who he was, I still had no idea. But, judging by Karina's reaction, this was a fairly well-known figure, the mere appearance of whom in our arena was deemed nearly impossible. Deciding that it was only proper to greet the magister, I bowed my head.

"Welcome, Magister Hwan. I'm eager to experience the wisdom you came here to impart."

"I take it you have no idea who I am and what I'm doing here?"

"Forgive me, teacher. The fame of your exploits was not passed along by word of mouth in the barony where I was raised. I don't know what Magister Hwang is famous for and why his appearance in the magical academy arena has caused such a stir. I've never seen the fourth years push themselves so hard during a morning workout. Even the most notorious slackers are training."

My comment was on point — today the arena was literally teeming. Never before had there been so many people here. It seemed as if the entire third- and fourth-year classes had run to the arena this morning to warm up. Everyone was hard at work, even the teachers — they were driving their students harder than the Evil Engineer did.

"I own a small school in Turb, only select students may attend. Only select professors have the right to cross the threshold of my institution, and only a few are allowed to demonstrate their skills."

"Is that supposed to motivate me to do something?" I still didn't know why he had been called here. "I know my limits, Magister. Even in my most flattering dreams, I never considered myself the cream of the crop. Your school certainly gives its students incredible power, but this is far from my level. You can see for yourself that anyone present here is capable of defeating me with the little toe of his left foot. Why are you here?"

"I'm here upon request," Magister Hwan replied reluctantly. "We all owe someone something, and there comes a time when you must repay your debts. I was asked to take a look at you, evaluate your potential, and give my assessment."

"Just in case, I want to remind the respected magister, in case he has not been informed, that I am a doomed soldier. Faithful slave of the Fortress. The purpose of my existence is to destroy the darkness in all its manifestations. Both in the form of creatures, and in the form of converts. In five months I will be sent to the Fortress, and with a fifty percent chance I'll die during my first trip into the rift. Alright, maybe my second. It's not clear why you're evaluating my potential. Why invite such a busy man as yourself here when they already know the answer? No one cares what potential I have."

"You said a key phrase, Doomer Max." Magister Hwang finally pulled a hand out from his sleeve and stroked his long beard. "Destroy the darkness in all its manifestations. The school I run, in addition to offering direct instruction on wielding weapons, also specializes in hunting out and destroying converts. Creatures that hide among ordinary people and strike when no one expects it. Five laps around the arena. You have one minute a lap. If you're not standing in front of me in five minutes, this conversation is over. Time starts now."

I still had no idea why I had to break a sweat for this guy, but since the Evil Engineer "gave" me to Magister Hwan, I had to obey. A minute a lap — that was Fardi's average time, but I really had to strain to keep the right pace. It was harder to run without her familiar back in front of me.

"Four minutes and twenty seconds. I can't say I'm thrilled, but now at least I know what I'm working with." The Magister stroked his beard, dissatisfied. Fighting converts is not the same as fighting dark beasts. A different approach is required. All these hurdles, kettlebells, obstacle courses — they are just toys. The real weapon is here, in your heart. I was informed that you were given katars. Why can't I see them?"

"Bringing weapons to training is forbidden. Mentor's orders."

"What are they training you to do here? Move furniture?" Magister Hwan surveyed the area with displeasure. Not one of the students had a weapon. "Running, jumping, pull-ups...Silly and pointless exercises that only build up your muscle mass so you're juicer when you're fed to the dark ones. No, that won't suit us. Follow me! We're going to my school. If I'm going to teach you anything, it'll be in an environment where you can actually learn something!"

"I'm afraid that Sir Magister does not fully understand the breadth of my situation. I'm not just a student at the academy. I'm a doomer. I'm prohibited from leaving campus under threat of death. Do you see those servants of the Light? They have an order from the High Priest to strike me down at the first hint that I might be trying to escape. I am unable to go with you to your school, however much you might wish to take me."

"*I* might wish?!" The old man looked as if he might have a stroke.

"You. You've already drawn your own conclusions. I'm sure they're not too different from my own — I'm mediocre with a side of incompetence. No one would argue otherwise. Someone like me has no place in your school. But ask yourself, why are you here? Likely because our esteemed chancellor — because Father Nor would definitely have warned me — invited you at such an early hour to witness a simple warm-up of some mediocre student? And a doomer at that. To jokingly call in a debt you allegedly owe him? Or is there some real reason why you're here?"

"Well, you certainly know how to wield your sharp tongue. Let's see if your weapon skills are worthy of your big mouth. We'll do without the katars for now. Give him a rapier."

One of the magister's pupils unrolled a long bundle to reveal a weapon. They brought me a standard rapier of the variety that was always on the hip of the highest aristocracy. A useless toy against the sword that Gustav had taught me to wield. Magister Hwang grimaced as soon as I took the sword and gave it a few test swings.

"Great Light, what backwater village did you come from? Have you never held a rapier in your hands?"

"I was prepared for the Wall," I replied coolly. Hiding the truth now would be the height of idiocy. "With a longsword and a spear. Not a rapier. You can't fight dark beasts with this thing."

"This is precisely the sword to use against converts. When these creatures finally reveal their true natures, there won't be a sword or spear in sight. But everyone carries a rapier!"

"Everyone whose status permits. Don't forget, Magister — I'm a doomer. Any place where rapier holders gather simply won't let me in."

"Test him." Magister Hwan nodded to one of his pupils. "Try not to kill him."

"I beg your pardon, Magister, but am I allowed to use all the means of defense at my disposal? Or should I limit myself to the sword?"

"Give him all you've got. But don't run away. If I see your back, I will forever forget the name Max. Let's go!"

The golden dome flickered on, and in that

instant, I was attacked. Magister Hwan's pupil moved with incredible speed. Almost as fast as Rabblerouser. But while a doomer's movements always had a clear purpose — to topple and destroy the opponent, there was something flowery about his motions. Ostentatious. As if the student had already decided he knew the outcome of the battle and was simply demonstrating his extraordinary agility for his master. So I didn't beat around the bush. I took a step forward, provoking him to strike, the golden dome enthusiastically flung his weapon aside and it scratched the leg of an oblivious student along the way. As he tried to scrabble for his weapon, I finished the movement and, with a blow of the hilt, sent the poor fellow off to dreamland to gallivant with the hot babes. What else would a young man of our age dream of?

"This one's broken. Got another?"

"So you have protection against steel?" I had to give the magister credit, he caught up quickly. There was no confusion or shock on his face. Bending down, he raised his sword and with a beautiful gesture saluted me in an invitation to duel. "Perhaps this will be interesting. Shall we commence the duel?"

And commence we did...Although could the beating I got from that old man really be called a duel? Rabblerouser was a snail on a casual stroll compared to him. It felt as if he was surrounding me on all sides at once, and the only thing that saved me from my ultimate demise was the golden dome.

He magnificently blocked all reflection damage as if it barely registered to him. The sparks flying indicated that the dome was doing everything it could, really giving its all, but to no avail — a real sword master laughs in the face of weapon rebound. And most unpleasant of all, when I pulled out an elixir to restore my mana, Hwan somehow managed to knock it from my grasp.

I don't know how, but the open vial flew from my hands, spilling its contents onto the ground. No mana meant one thing: within a few moments, the tip of his blade was hovering a millimeter from my throat.

"The best fencers of the empire come to me to hone their skills, and I'm accustomed to dividing my students into different categories based on skill. Advanced. Elementary. Beginner. Today I witnessed a new category. Yours. Abominable. You don't feel the sword, don't hear its song. You hold it as if it were a shovel and not the weapon of the elite."

"And yet, it was he who destroyed the supreme convert that infiltrated our academy," the chancellor's velvety voice rang out. Kimal Sarento had come to personally oversee my training. "And not only destroyed, but was able to detect him. The clerics are already driving themselves mad trying to figure out how to use the new ability that has opened up to them. We have no choice, Magister Hwan. Max must learn to use the rapier, and there's no one in this world more qualified for that task than you."

"A supreme convert?" The old man frowned, starting to see me in a new light. "His aura alone would sweep Max off his feet like a hurricane would a house of cards!"

"Nevertheless, this is fact. Thirty people were unable to resist the influence and were sent to the pyre back at the Fortress, but not Max. He finished the beast off and managed to keep his mind intact. Incidentally, didn't he also effectively resist your influence? And, as I understand it, you didn't plan to hold back."

"I won't deal with him personally, Kimal," the old man responded after a long pause. "The public won't understand. I turn away the best and brightest, but agree to take this boy on and teach him from scratch...How often would he attend class?"

"Four hours a day, seven days a week," replied the chancellor, causing me to stare at him in astonishment. Four hours how? Where was he going to cram them in? "Beginning at five-thirty in the morning, and by nine thirty you may release him. Five months, Magister, only five months, after which the academy will officially recognize your debt as paid. But this will happen only in one case: if Max can learn how to use a sword at least at a beginner level. Advanced is a pipe dream."

"Then my final question: why? He's a doomed soldier."

"That's your answer, Magister. Because he's

a doomed soldier. What the churchmen have in mind is far too dangerous for any normal person. Max must be able to fend for himself, not just with magic, but also with weapons. Because it's officially open season for converts."

Chapter 5

"DRINK," THE EVIL ENGINEER handed me some ghastly swill that stank for a kilometer in all directions.

"What is that?" I looked doubtfully at the dark liquid.

"Just pretend it's coffee. Drink!" he barked.

Considering how he was balling his fist, I anticipated a blow to the head for insubordination, so I had to risk drinking the sludge, trying not to taste it. To my surprise, it left a pleasant aftertaste on my tongue.

"Tonight we're going to the rift," the Evil Engineer said when I'd set the empty cup down on the table. "That's so you don't nod off. It'll wake you up better than coffee, but there are side effects. Tomorrow morning you'll feel like shit."

"I have training." I listened as my stomach desperately tried to digest the monstrous mixture

I'd swallowed.

"That's not my problem. If the chancellor decided to teach you to wave a toothpick around for fun, that's his business. Who am I to interfere? Although I don't understand why Father Nor allowed for such frank madness to occur."

"And by 'madness' you mean training with other mentors or training to use a rapier? Or both? Or something else entirely?"

The Evil Engineer balled his fists, clearly intending to teach me a lesson in holding my tongue, but he restrained himself, and even laughed.

"They warned me, of course, that my pupil was from a different world, but to not see such obvious things...Now I understand why the servants of the Light fawn after you. They love holy fools."

"Ha, ha, ha. What a clever and poignant joke from a dark beast such as yourself," I replied without a hint of humor. "To be able to see the obvious, one must have at least some information. They shove me from one place to another, never deigning to explain the reasons for their behavior. And any time I ask a question, I get a fist in response. What, are you gonna pick on someone who's defenseless, take out your anger on me for the fact that they're giving me new mentors?"

"You're a little boy," scoffed the Evil Engineer. "And you think like a little boy. With that approach, you simply won't live to adulthood. They plan to use you as convert bait. And where do these beasts like to gather? At balls and dinner parties. Events with large gatherings of influential people, where it's easiest to gain their trust, where you can make good connections. But for people like you, doomer, these places are not just a battlefield, they're level ten of the rift, where one wrong step may send you to your grave. Any single guest at one of those parties has the full right to kill you on the spot, no trial or investigation, and even the High Priest's protection won't save you. You will be on the razor's edge, but hunting out converts, and at the same time, in order to at least try and avoid this fate, you'll be blessing a new trainer with your talent. It would be one thing if they were teaching you something relevant, but no — rapier skills! The most useless of all possible types of weapon."

I remained silent, digesting what I'd heard.

"In the rift, you're on the same level as the beasts. They're dangerous, deadly, but you know what to expect. They won't poison your goblet of wine or stick a knife in your back, no one will use you as fodder to demonstrate their magic skills while trying to impress some small potato. Even if the beasts are dangerous, they're honest. They don't hide behind the norms of decency, don't cover their asses with made up laws. But, naturally, it's so much more important to learn to wave a toothpick around so that you can follow the chancellor around like a little lap dog and jump for your bone."

"Like I have a choice," I muttered. "Didn't you

teach me that any disobedience means death?”

“To the Fortress. Not the chancellor. You don’t understand what he’s doing, don’t know why, but accept any decision he makes as law. As for the Fortress…Sometimes it’s easier to die than to lose the last remnants of your honor. Doomers are slaves to the Fortress. This is fact. You just met the Countess and her crew. Did you see them prostrating themselves before every churchman? Did they bob about back and forth like a piece of shit in a toilet bowl? Or did they maintain their dignity and distance, fully aware of their own strength and significance? As long as you act like slime, you’ll continue to be slime. But once you turn yourself to granite…Alright, let’s go. I’ve already wasted too much time on useless conversation.”

“You said we’re going to the rift. Didn’t they close it?” I didn’t take kindly to the Evil Engineer’s rebuke, but I had to admit there was a grain of truth in it. It was a point that warranted careful consideration.

“We’ll cloak ourselves, we aren’t touching any beasts. If you’re going to keep jumping through hoops like a circus animal, we’ll need to enhance your abilities.”

“Going off of that speech you gave a minute ago, I should now stand steadfast and demand you explain everything before we go anywhere,” I said, refusing to follow. “Or is it that I can’t be slime around anyone but you? Why don’t you have any idea what a normal mentor-pupil relationship is supposed to look like?”

“You talk too much.” An open-handed slap flew my direction, but at the last moment I dodged and his hand passed over my head. Straightening up, I saw the back of the mentor's head and, more on reflex than anything else, gave it a good whack.

“Oops,” I muttered as the Evil Engineer froze and began to slowly turn in my direction. The dark one's expression held nothing good, so I began to back away, babbling complete nonsense: “It wasn't me. And if it was, it wasn't on purpose.”

“I'll kill you!” he growled. “I'll kill you, bastard!”

“I didn't mean it!” I shouted, fleeing my enraged mentor as fast as my legs would take me. The surrounding trees came to my aid and I dodged between them like a rabbit — this somehow leveled the Evil Engineer's speed advantage.

“Stand and die!” cried the shadow behind me, getting closer and closer every second. I came to the realization that running was not an option — he would catch up with me and kill me. Or maim me in a way I'd remember for the rest of my life. Which, judging by his angry roar, would be short and sweet. What compelled me to duck, allowing his hand to pass over my head again, I can't say — evidently, it was on reflex. The Evil Engineer flew past me and turned to attack again, but no such luck! By that point, I was already climbing a short, thin tree with the dexterity of a monkey.

“Get down here!” the Evil Engineer

demanded, stopping below the tree. "And die with honor!"

"I'm good up here," I replied, testing the neighboring trees just in case he decided to come after me. I'd have to jump.

"Alright, I'm calm. Climb down. If I beat you it won't be too hard," he responded after some time. The rage was gone from his voice, so I had to obey. The pranks that my brother and I used to play on our tormentors taught us an important lesson: know when to stop.

"Never do that again," the Evil Engineer warned. "Lay your hands on me again and you'll lose them. I'll rip them off myself."

"Does that work both ways, or only one?" I said, refusing to be in debt to him. "Or can I also warn you about placing your hands on me?"

"You can warn all you like. But who's going to listen to you? Once you can beat Fardi one-on-one, you'll be deserving of some respect. But for now you're weak and useless."

"That being said, we're heading to the rift. Together. It's unlikely you'd take a weak and helpless little boy with you. You'd take Fardi. The exalted hero, free from fear or reproach. Do you know that Father Nor wants to swear her in as a Sweeper?"

"Someday that tongue of yours will get you in trouble," the Evil Engineer sighed, but stopped and pulled a small metal box out of his pocket. "Starting from the fourth level of the rift, creatures known as ousels start showing up. Don't frown —

they're not mentioned in the textbooks. At least the ones you were given. Ousels are small creatures, slightly smaller than your fist. But among doomers, they're known simply as the little death. Surviving a battle with them is only possible with the support of three or four powerful mages. These are small, nimble and extremely dangerous dark beasts. When we return, I will ask Father Nor to give you a complete description of the creatures of the rift. Our task is to find the ousel habitats and catch one elite."

I took the cube he held out to me and examined it with interest. It looked solid, with walls a couple centimeters thick, although I noticed two small holes. For breathing? Perhaps. What was this box for? Recalling the beginning of the conversation, I realized that there wasn't a line the churchmen wouldn't cross.

"Get the picture? I see that you do. Now think about how you're going to use this thing. You'll have to face a crowd of aristocrats alone, put up your mirror and hope that there's a convert among them and that he manages to break through the protective amulets of the rest. So that the clerics will throw everyone on the bonfire as servants of Skron. Because otherwise, as soon as you let your mirror down, the high-borns regain consciousness and crap themselves from fear. Then your life won't be worth a thing to them. An abomination that can only be cleansed with blood. But instead of trying to figure out how to live longer, you, like an idiot, are all excited about learning to use a rapier...Alright, we're here."

"What is this?" The entrance to the rift was in the basement of the academy, but we were approaching the back lawn, where a small, nondescript building was waiting.

"The mine. My main task for the past seven years. I've made it to level eight, but stopped for now. I'm waiting for them to bring the steel sheets to line the walls and make a place for a door. Don't tell me that you were narrow-minded enough to think we were going to pass through all the levels of the rift?"

I'd learned to determine which questions were rhetorical and didn't require a reply. And I didn't want to reply — anything I said, my mentor would just use as fuel for fresh mockery. The Evil Engineer leaned over the heavy steel trapdoor and lifted it with an audible creak of his joints. I gulped — the slab was thicker than the length of my katars. A narrow passage to the lower floor opened up. Descending the vertical ladder, I greeted one of the clerics on duty at his level. He paid no attention to me, immersed in meditation. Soon the Evil Engineer also descended, tightly closing the upper hatch behind him.

"Main rule of the mines: only one door open at a time," he said. "It's a rule written in blood. Two years ago, a beast from level six broke into the fourth through the mine. I don't feel sorry for the idiots who allowed it to happen, but I do for the nearly two dozen students and teachers who suffered for it. So now there's only one right way:

open, climb through, close, and only then can you open the next door. This is the exit to level one. We're going deeper."

There were meditating churchmen on all levels of the mine. After descending to the fourth level, I opened myself up to the sensations I was feeling. I had never been so far beneath the ground before. Everything was calm — the steel walls completely blocked out the dark influence.

"We move quietly, don't attract too much attention, no chatting. The beasts don't like it. We find the ousels, stick one in the box, and head back. Should take about ten minutes total. Father, we're going in."

The cleric opened his eyes and a shiver went down my spine. Blind! Although the servant of the Light moved quite confidently for a blind man, as if he saw everything perfectly clearly. The lock clicked and the massive steel plate slid to one side. I wheezed from the pain that rolled over me — despite the fact that I had just been practically cuddling with that elite in the training grounds, the pressure on level four proved much stronger and sharper.

"Come on," ordered the Evil Engineer, fading into the shadows. Gulping, I took a few stiff steps and heard a click behind me. The door slid into place and the cleric blocked off the passage.

"It's heavy," I admitted, leaning against the wall. A krona passing nearby started at the sound of a human voice and did a quick lap around the cave. Not finding anything suspicious, it went about its business. The Evil Engineer remained silent, allowing me to recover. I couldn't see my mentor, but I had no doubt that he was right on my heels, deftly avoiding any encounters with dark beasts. Gathering myself, I slowly advanced, continuing to cling to the walls — any attempt to move away nearly caused me to topple. As soon as I entered the next cave, however, I completely forgot about holding on to the wall. The enormous cave was a living sea of dark beasts. Kronos, lurges, a few schtryks, rapses hanging from the ceiling — countless monsters. I even turned to try and catch my mentor's gaze. I wanted to see the answer in his eyes. Was this a normal amount of beasts? It was impossible to walk without stepping on something!

But the Evil Engineer was nowhere to be found. The ability he was using hid him not only from the beasts, but from me. Seeing a passage on the opposite side of the cave, I sighed and inched forward, periodically stepping on the paws of monsters. At some point, I realized that my path took me as far as possible from the schtryks. I didn't want to be anywhere near those horrible spiders. And it wasn't just me — judging by the small motes of clear space surrounding them, even the dark beasts themselves were terrified of the schtryks.

In the next cave, we found the same thing: it was packed so full of beasts that they were barely able to move. Next cave. And the next. Everywhere, the story was the same. My hands were itching to kill something. I even touched one of the larger elite kronas, reasoning that the other beasts wouldn't even notice the loss, but then stopped in my tracks at the entrance to the next cave. It was empty. There was no overpopulation problem here, which was extremely intriguing. Why were the beasts suddenly shying away from this free space?

I got my answer a couple meters in. The crushing pressure coming from the cave was so heavy that I didn't have the strength to move on. Whatever was lurking in this cave had an influence on par with a Warden. If not greater.

"Clear the cave..." the Evil Engineer's whisper came from right behind me. He didn't have to tell me twice. I lowered my arms toward the nearest creatures and activated the katars. The dark beasts twitched, but immediately fell silent. Their legs buckled, but the enormous density of the beasts prevented them from falling over. I moved away from the dangerous passageway and surveyed the area. I had my work cut out for me...

The schtryks turned out to be extremely difficult to kill. After I finished off the kronas and lurges, I approached the first spider. How grateful was I to Rabblerouser for telling me how to deal with these monsters: a blow to the nerve center gave me thirty seconds to find both hearts. Twice the blade hit bone and ricocheted, nearly twisting my arm out of its joint. I had to start from scratch — strike the nerve center again and then stab into each heart. Although I suffered with the first one, I got rid of the rest of the schtryks much faster. I didn't touch the rapses — only those I saw along the way. Looking around, I sighed heavily. There were at least seven elites here that I could pull some nice trophies from. But, Skron damn them all, we weren't here for trophies.

Making sure the only remaining rapses were on the other side of the cave, I threw a couple of bodies aside, clearing a space for myself, and then looked up at the freshly re-substantiated Evil Engineer.

"Is that normal for level four?" I nodded toward the cave, which had become a temporary graveyard for hundreds of creatures. Within a few hours, the monsters from the neighboring caves would devour their fellows and become that much stronger.

"This one's far from a level twelve," I said, stating the obvious. "So what's sitting in that cave?"

"Some sort of exclusive beast."

"A red beast on level four?" I said, astonished.

"Can you shut up for even a minute?" my mentor snarled angrily. "An exclusive on level four...that means the fifth level beasts are already under the range. That's impossible..."

"If you're going to talk out loud, at least let me in on the details, it'll be easier for everyone," I suggested, ignoring his previous remark. "What's a range and when is it encountered? By the way, let's move closer to the passage. The more I feel that creature's influence, the faster I'll get used to it."

The Evil Engineer shot me a murderous look, but silently got up and helped clear a place near the passage. I staggered and blood came out of my nose, but I wasn't about to retreat. Sitting on the stone floor, I closed my eyes and controlled my breath.

"A range is a place with a strong concentration of dark beasts. Elites, exclusives — the best of the best, any one of them capable of tearing apart half the academy. These ranges are located every four levels, excluding the first. So if there's a range on the fifth, that means it's on the ninth and thirteenth…That's not possible! The rift can't reach down to level fourteen already!"

"If I may, what threat does this present?" I asked through clenched teeth. My head was already so heavy my eyes felt ready to pop out of their sockets.

"At the fifteenth level, the Master can create a dark new species. It's called a metamorph. An exclusive beast of extreme power, capable of destroying the entire capital on its own. I'm not sure even our chancellor would win in a one-on-one battle. In our entire history, we've only seen two metamorphs. The last one was around fifteen hundred years ago. The result was the Harley Desert, once the trading center of the Caliman Empire. We have no right to let this exclusive live. The beast must be destroyed. How long will it take you to train your mirror up?"

"Six hours, no less." I remembered Father Tyut's assessment.

"Six it is. Time is no object when an exclusive beast is at hand. Sit here and train. I'll patrol the floor. We need to take out some of the elites and find you an ousel. Even if we destroy the Rift Master itself, Father Nor still wouldn't be pleased if we don't carry out his order."

Every fifteen minutes I moved closer to the passageway, cursing the dark beasts with all my might. My head had finally lost touch with reality, my eyes had popped out of the socket three times, but begrudgingly went back in, my body was twisted like rope, and even my dinner — such a rare guest in my stomach — was trying to jump back out my throat to get away from the exclusive beast. The only thing that kept it in was the mulish obstinance of a psychologically unsound man. I suffered, even though I didn't fully understand why I was suffering. Why would I need beasts from the rift if I was being sent out to hunt converts? What was I doing at all? Why was I here?

It took four and a half hours for me to reach the cave. The Evil Engineer returned and put the closed box in my bag. Apparently, the influence of one dark beast was not enough for me and he needed to add more. I made one last effort and moved into the room, assessing our prospects.

"What is this?" I said, dumbfounded, staring at a spherical furry flying thing that clearly exceeded my head in size. Several smaller spheres — about the size of a fist — were flying nearby. The large ball had a red dark aura, while the smaller ones had a golden dark aura. An exclusive monster in the company of the four elite. A raw deal for me, considering that I had no idea how to destroy these creatures.

"Ousels. Almost no weak points. No heart, no internal organs, no one knows how they fly or feed themselves. Upon contact, they release a caustic toxin that kills a person within a day. It's killed by thermal processing — burning or freezing — or in our case, by mincing. Turning one ball into a set of smaller ones. Keep in mind that they have incredible regeneration. And with that ends the brief digression on how to fight ousels. You need a plan, apprentice. How will we destroy all of them? Simply leaving them alone and going on our merry way is not an option. Red beasts have no place in this world."

"For starters, we need to get a little closer," I got up with difficulty and took a few hesitant steps toward the flying spheres. They noticed me and reacted — one of the golden ones flew in my direction. The Evil Engineer immediately became invisible, and I stood there like a deer in the headlights. I really wanted to put up my protection, but now was not the time. It might provoke the enemy. The sphere circled around me and returned to its master.

I took a step and another elite hovered over to me, as if to signal I should not move any further. On my third step, the whole quartet began to circle around me, fur bristling. There was something glistening at the tip of each hair — evidently the toxin that the Evil Engineer had warned me about.

Raising my arms so that the blades of my katars pointed toward the spheres, I waited for the right moment to strike. I didn't have the slightest idea how to properly destroy the flyers — I had nothing to create fire or ice. But I had a piercing-slashing weapon of enormous power, which I fully intended to use. My eyes nearly popped out of their sockets as I tried to simultaneously track the position of all four Elite ousels. They circled around me in an irregular pattern, some faster, some slower. Occasionally, their paths would intersect, and that was the moment I was waiting for. And I needed to take out not just two or three, but all of them at once. Two per katar.

I had to wait ten minutes — my shoulders even went numb. But I didn't budge, patiently waiting for my chance. The cycle started over and I moved my fingers to activate the blades. This time I needed a spike, not a flat blade. Two sharp stingers flew out of the grooves, easily threading through the four spheres. At the same time, I activated my dome shield and switched on the healing aura, trying to cause as much harm to the dark beasts as possible.

A blow to the chest almost knocked me over. The speed with which the huge ousel crashed into me was frightening. The ball bristled with hairs, throwing out the most dangerous poison in my direction. My shield performed its function perfectly: some of the drops froze in the air, some flew off to the side, and some ricocheted back. I don't know if it slowed the giant ousel's rapid jumps or what, but the creature was directly in front of me, within striking distance. Without thinking twice, I stabbed the monster and, continuing the motion, crashed into the wall, finally blocking the creatures. I didn't turn off the healing aura for a second, but after half a minute I had to call out to my mentor:

"Mana! I need mana! Pour an elixir in my mouth!"

"Hold them there! Cover your eyes!"

The Evil Engineer appeared at my side, holding an extinguished torch. He struck two stones together to create a spark and carefully fanned the flame. After a couple of moments, the torch began to shine furiously, as if wrapped with a freshly oiled cloth.

"Don't even think about pulling away, even if you get burnt! Resist!"

With these words, the sadist placed the torch under my katars. The ousels burned silently. They fluttered and slid over the weapons, but did it all noiselessly. As for me, I was screaming like my lungs were being ripped out. Tongues of flame licked my fists, causing monstrous pain, but I didn't dare to twitch, continuing to press my fists against the wall. I knew the exact moment when it was all over — through my tear-filled eyes, clear as day, a message burned:

1 of 12 *Amplify* shards obtained. Total: 2 of 12.

"Where are you going?" the Evil Engineer barked as I yanked my arms out and deactivated the katars. My fingers were so stiff they almost wouldn't bend, but I still managed to pull out one of the recovery elixirs and drink it in one gulp. Next came a mana potion to activate the healing aura. The blisters on my fingers began to heal over before my very eyes, unable to withstand the double dose of treatment.

"They're dead," I explained, blowing on my healing hands.

"How did you know?" The mentor narrowed his eyes in disbelief.

"I got a notification. Did you forget I'm dark too? You know, mentor, you should learn to trust me a little more. I could, for instance, suggest that we are killing red beasts not because they present a danger to the world, but because they have a chance of dropping a shard of a very valuable stone. One which can grant a doomer his freedom. Does Father Nor know that you're secretly building an *Amplify* stone? Or have you decided to keep this a secret?"

"You know Max, I'm seriously considering just finishing you off here and telling the churchmen that I couldn't save you. No one knows about the amplification stone. And it should stay that way."

"Did it drop a piece of the map too?" I looked at the Evil Engineer and chuckled. "Of course it did, what else. But you didn't say anything about it either, decided to keep this knowledge to yourself. Why? What happens when you collect all five fragments?"

"I still don't have a full map," he replied after a pause. "Masters control a certain territory and in order to get a fragment, you must clear rifts in this territory. The most I've been able to collect is three out of five."

"How many rifts have you cleared?"

"You want a full count? I'll just tell you: I have eight fragments, two entire *Amplify* stones and three fragments, but I already collected one stone in this rift. Exclusive creatures can usually only be found from the seventh level down, they've never climbed up so high before. Their stones are not formed through the churchmen's skills."

"Just like that stone you connected them to," I nodded knowingly. "Yellow or red ability? I know, stupid question. The churchmen can find elite stones anywhere. So you snatched an exclusive ability somewhere and strengthened it with two exclusive stones. Not bad for a Fortress slave."

"Father Nor knows nothing about the amplification stone," the Evil Engineer stated, for some reason.

"He wouldn't have found out about the map if you had even a drop of trust in me." I refused to be in debt to him. "Why should you tell me about the specifics of dark beings? About the maps, the shards? Maybe something else will surprise me and I'll run off to the churchmen, asking them to explain whatever it is that just popped up before my eyes."

"So you still believe in the impossible — you think there's a way out of this rift for you?" asked the Evil Engineer. "After everything you've said?"

"I not only believe it, I'm now certain that you and I will return here together very soon. Not tomorrow night, of course, but the night after. The sooner I can get used to the seventh level, the sooner we can start hunting exclusive creatures. I need an *Amplify*, mentor. And before I am sent to the Fortress. I don't have the slightest desire to become a faithful slave. And you will help me."

"You have training in an hour," he replied. "Deal with Fardi and you might pique my interest. As long as she is stronger than you, you won't even dream of fighting exclusives. Rest tonight, tomorrow we go to the fifth. We'll see how long you last."

Chapter 6

"THIS IS WHAT I'M SUPPOSED to teach?" The petite girl, my height and only five years my senior, walked over me with such a look of contempt that I felt uneasy. I didn't have time to take a shower, so I had come to practice straight from the rift. Smeared with dark slime from head to toe, angry and tired. A true apprentice of the Evil Engineer.

"Welcome, mentor." I barely managed to tack "mentor" onto the end. I wanted to say "beautiful," or even offer to take her back to my place so that we could talk in a more pleasant environment. Nevertheless, I held back. Life had already taught me that appearances can often be deceiving. Karina Fardi didn't look like she would pack a punch either, but...Skron damn her! When would the image of her benching a hundred and twenty kilos leave my head?

"I beg your pardon for my appearance. I just

came from the rift."

"Is that supposed to make me feel better?" The girl wrinkled her nose in displeasure. "I refuse to work with someone who might give me something nasty! You need to shower before we continue. Make note that class is already underway and you're wasting your own time."

"You know what, gorgeous, I don't really give a shit about your class," I fumed. "You don't want to train me, you don't have to. You can pack up and leave! If you think Magister Hwan sent you here as punishment, I won't try to dissuade you. Think about it. Either you suck it up and we start class, or there won't be any more classes. You can explain to Magister Hwan yourself. I had too hard a night to come here and tiptoe around you."

"You're dead, doomer!" The girl suddenly transformed into a deadly shrew. Drawing her sword, she delivered a lightning-fast jab aimed directly at my heart, but what could her steel do against my golden dome? The rapier was thrown to one side, although not as far as the previous student's had been. I noticed the amulet around her neck and, without thinking twice, activated *Dark Spike*. She hadn't announced the beginning of training and I had been attacked, so by law, I had every right to defend myself. The darkness exploded extravagantly. I was thrown back, even though I'd had time to prepare, so my opponent stood no chance. She was blown five meters away. There she lay, completely stunned by the explosion, even as I approached. Triggering the katars, I touched one blade to her neck, causing a thin stream of blood to trickle out.

"You're dead, mentor. Shall I recite the laws of the Zarak Empire that would permit me to pierce through your pretty little neck without risking my own? I won't, out of respect for Magister Hwan and the chancellor, but remember: the next time you try to kill a doomer, be prepared for the doomer to kill you right back. I suggest we start from scratch. Hi, my name is Max, I'm a doomer who needs to be trained to use a rapier. This was a task given by Magister Hwan, so I cannot refuse. I promise to be a diligent student, to obey and absorb your wisdom with as open of a mind as I am capable of having. Your turn."

I removed the blade from her neck and extended a hand. Naturally, she did not take it. In a single motion, like a true acrobat, she jumped to her feet and examined the remains of the amulet that once hung around her neck.

"This amulet protects against lethal damage. If not for it, I'd be dead right now! Do you know how much these cost?!" Evidently, the full gravity of the situation was only now hitting her.

"Have a nice day!" I nodded and turned around. Apparently, I'd have to go back to training with the Evil Engineer after just half an hour. My fencing lessons clearly weren't working out.

"Ursula de Vrath," she spat at my back, forcing me to stop. "My name is Ursula de Vrath, and you can call me master, mentor or Ursula. Makes no difference to me. What's your skill level with a rapier?"

"Magister Hwan called it 'abominable,'" I replied, turning toward the girl. Alright, I'd give her a chance. But I certainly wasn't going to let my shield down. Ursula grimaced in displeasure. She was obviously not pleased with the news.

"Why do you need rapiers anyway? They're useless in the rifts you just crawled out of."

"I do not have the right to divulge that information," I responded, acknowledging the fact that the girl could put two and two together. "Ask Magister Hwan for details. Where do we start?"

"With the basics," Ursula sighed, resigning herself to the inevitable. "Pick up the rapier. Let's see what you can do."

The answer turned out to be: not much. The rapier was so different from the longsword to which I was accustomed that even the few small movements I made were very unsatisfying. As for Ursula, she barely restrained herself from groaning. She cursed, swearing even more than the sailors in the port, and several times she tried to abandon her thankless task, but every time she came back and started over again, step by step, gesture by gesture, demonstrating the fundamental movements. We started with the very basics: how to hold the sword correctly, how to strike, how to block an opponent's attack, how to move your finger joints. Everything that ordinary aristocrats went through in childhood, I now had to learn at eighteen. But I didn't cry or protest, even when doing seemingly ridiculous exercises at

Ursula's request. Even when the students who came early to warm-up started to mock me.

"Alright, you've learned to hold a sword. Try to get back from the rift a little earlier next time, if you decide to go back. And take a shower. We're done for today." Four hours later, she allowed me to lower my sword and I sighed with relief. My arms were trembling from the tension — wielding the blade required muscles I didn't even know I had. My hand throbbed mercilessly — even the healing aura didn't help. I needed a recovery elixir, but the supply in my bag had run dry and I'd never made it home. Fardi was already limping from her warm-up, like the rest of the students. Only the Evil Engineer paid close attention to how long I held the rapier at arm's length. Having katars in no way made things easier for me. My arm kept wanting to fall, but my mischievous mentor corrected me over and over again.

"And where are you going?" the dark one asked as I followed Ursula.

"To class," I replied.

"Uh huh, back to class," my mentor nodded fervently. "And what class are you going to, exactly, when your teacher is standing right here?"

"I have Dark Beasts and their Habitats now," I frowned. "Chancellor's class."

"Well, if it's the chancellor's class, then yes, I suppose you should go...Just one question, Max: What's the point of studying something that you will never encounter? Most of the dark beasts that the chancellor mentions are on the Wall. They simply aren't found in the rifts. And they certainly won't be invited to any balls. Since when did they start preparing you for the Wall?"

I closed my eyes, trying to stifle my rage. He could get under my skin even worse than Fardi sometimes. Why couldn't he just speak frankly?

"I was with Father Nor this morning. He shares my concerns about the rift, but requires proof. I won't be here for the next few days — I'm leading a total purge of level five. If it indeed is a range, I may find some chabre — a relatively rare alchemical material. They didn't permit you to go with me — apparently, they've got other plans for you. Tonight, Doomer Max, under the escort of the servants of the Light, will visit a certain pointless event on the occasion of the birthday of a certain pointless aristocrat."

"So you deprived me of my breakfast just to inform me of this upcoming event? Or did you have another bomb to drop?"

"A bomb?" The Evil Engineer chuckled. "Maybe it is a bomb. *You* can drop and hold a one-armed plank for one minute, then switch sides. Five sets to start, and then maybe I'll drop something else on you. Move!"

The way he barked at me, I didn't hesitate for a second and fell into a plank. My body trembled from my previous workout, and I knew full well that I wouldn't last another couple of hours with the Evil Engineer. No way. After a few moments, however, I forgot about the pain — My dark mentor sat close to me and began to speak quietly, carefully monitoring my own monitor's movements.

"I should have told you about this when we were down there, but I didn't have the time. Or the desire, honestly. I didn't think they'd put you to work so quickly. The supreme convert you took down was really decked out — the bastard knew he'd have to pass all sorts of inspections, so he defended himself as much as he could before both the clerics and his murderers. I don't know what *Cloak Essence* does, but it will most definitely block any attempts by people like us to squeeze any loot out of him."

"Can you get to the point?" I wheezed, switching arms. "Why are you giving me this history lesson?"

"Today, you'll be using your mirror to detect converts. Normal ones, not supreme. This means there's a high degree of probability that you'll get a drop — one of the twelve *Augment* shards. A stone that improves the quality of other magic stones."

"Improves the quality?" I looked at the dark one in surprise. "I don't understand..."

"Dark one lore." The Evil Engineer shifted to keep my monitor in his line of sight. "It is believed that magic stones have only two variable parameters: the level and number of facets. This is true for common people, but not for dark ones. We have a third parameter: the quality of the stone. You could equate it to an extra cut that improves the parameters and endows the stone with additional abilities. *Augment* shards are only obtained from converts. I don't know of anywhere else. If not for your trip today, I wouldn't even have hinted about it. But who knows what you'll do if a new notification suddenly pops up. I'm sure no one has told you about *Augment* yet, so you don't realize its value. Just take my word for it — it's worth it. Once you collect your stone, you'll understand why it's so hard to describe in words."

"So *Augment* is another exclusive stone? On par with *Amplify?*"

"Correct. There's also *Mentor*, which reduces mana costs, but it only drops from red beasts found on the Wall, so it's of no use to you now. Perhaps you can find other exclusive stones elsewhere, but I know of only these three. No one should ever know that you have fragments or whole stones. Your life depends on it. If anyone, even Father Nor, asks you about these messages or status bar changes, keep quiet. The less they know, the less likely you are to be sent to the pyre. It is easier for churchmen to burn at the stake than to deal with their problems. Enough! Now go take a shower and off to the chancellor's class with you! And just see what happens if you're late!"

I now saw the Evil Engineer through different eyes — the faithful slave of the Fortress had transformed into a plotting schemer. He had his secrets, was extremely reluctant to reveal them, and did everything to keep them for as long a possible. Although I completely agreed with regards to the churchmen. Father Nor was considered quite progressive and something of an innovator, but even he clung to the ingrained order of things with all his might. If he found out about the new stones...They wouldn't touch the Evil Engineer, but they'd scrap me for parts, if only to understand how to obtain these exclusive stones. And was that really something I needed? So I'd keep my mouth shut.

I was almost late for breakfast, but "almost" doesn't count. Hastily cramming food in my mouth, I swallowed it practically without chewing and then flew to class. But my encounters with beautiful women were far from over for the day — instead of dark beasts, Tarra Lloyd awaited me again.

"Good morning, Doomer Max," the woman smiled as I looked around the hall. The rest of the group was missing, although I was certain I'd gotten the room number right. Sensing a trap, I started backing away and nearly knocked over Father Nor, who had sprouted up behind me like a mushroom after a warm rain.

"Today will be your debut appearance," the cleric informed me. "We've chosen your attire. Get dressed, we'll assess if we need to tailor the sleeves to conceal your katars."

One of the servants of the Light brought me my outfit — a rather magnificent and elegant suit. Another brought a dashing pair of boots, a sheath for my rapier, and even a rapier itself. I was never much of a fashion guy myself, so I didn't know how current the trends were, but I couldn't help but note the quality of the fabric. Even the dresses my older brother's wife used to wear were simpler than these garments.

Looking up at Tarra, I realized that she had no intention of turning around. On the contrary, she watched with interest as I undressed. I had to strip down entirely — they even brought me a new pair of underwear. Silky, smooth, pleasant to the touch and ridiculously uncomfortable. They kept getting stuck in places they shouldn't be.

"He needs a barber," said Tarra Loyd, looking at me from all angles. "Such a sparse mustache and sloppy beard will garner unnecessary attention. First laughter, and then annoyance that such a slovenly person was let into this event. To put it nicely, he needs to be whipped into shape. He looks more like a peasant who slipped on his master's outfit. From what I understand, your task is to make him blend in among the other guests?"

I fastened my belt and looked at my reflection — a count, no less! My back straightened automatically, forcing me to recall all my lessons about customs and how to behave properly in a society of peers.

"He'll go to the barber after lunch. Were you informed of your duties?"

"Escort, entry, greetings, three dances," Tarra Loyd confirmed. "Are you attending this class too? No? In that case, please leave us. I was only given four hours to iron out all the wrinkles."

"Escort?" I asked, surprised, once it was just the two of us.

"Don't you know it's bad form to show up to an event alone? Only troublemakers do that. Those who are itching for a fight. They always pay close attention to guests like that, which, as you know, is what we're trying to avoid. That's why they asked me to accompany you today. They can't send a Duke's daughter to the birthday party of a mediocre baron's daughter. They may take it the wrong way."

"Well, you certainly won't be staying out of the limelight." Only now did it register that the professor was not in her tight pair of coveralls, but rather a magnificently elegant dress.

"Why?" Tarra batted her eyes so picturesquely that my pants got tight. She wasn't just gorgeous, she was perfect!

"Because as soon as you arrive, everyone's eyes will be on you. Only eunuchs and castrati could resist your charms."

"Eunuchs and castrati…You really know how to woo a woman, Max," Tarra laughed, making my silk undergarments twitch. I had never heard such an enchanting sound in my life. Damn it! Get it together, Max! Have you never seen a woman before? Why was I suddenly drooling like a schoolboy?

"Thank you for the compliment." She brushed away a tear and cleared her throat, becoming serious. "But you're right, one of my goals is to take all the attention and let you do your thing. Shall we begin? First of all, we need to learn how to move together. You have to stop trembling when

I touch you. It's important."

"Stop?" I put up my mirror, locking up my emotions. My heart continued to beat wildly, but outwardly, I was as calm as Father Nor. "What makes you think that I was trembling at all?"

"Because I can feel your pulse," Tarra whispered in my ear with a voice that made me swallow involuntarily. This woman wasn't just beautiful, she also knew it, and knew how to use it.

"I still haven't learned to control my heartbeat," I grinned apologetically.

"Which is very bad." Tarra took a step back from me. "Control over your emotions must be more than just external. Try to calm down and we'll start again. You have one minute to quiet your rampaging body."

The mirror didn't help. The spell Tarra cast was beyond the capabilities of any normal human. I took several deep breaths and took down the mirror but remained in a state of combat meditation. It wasn't a beautiful woman standing before me — the most beautiful woman I've ever known. Standing before me was a dangerous opponent, capable of seizing my mind with her charms. For some reason, I imagined the Evil Engineer's perpetually dissatisfied face. That was a man who knew how to behave in front of pretty ladies. Why couldn't I, if he could? Was I worse than that dark beast? Since when?

"Shall we try again?" Tarra took a step forward and reached out her hand to touch me. I raised my head and, with a detached gaze, noticed the perfection of her skin. Ordinary human skin wasn't like that. A mole here, a scar there, a flash of hair. But Tarra had none of that — she was flawless in every way. And that's what helped me keep my cool — she wasn't human. So what was the point of trembling with lust?

"Wow, you're starting to get it." The hot breath from Tarra's lips washed over my ear and all my control went out the window. My heart started beating fiercely again and Tarra laughed out loud. "Couldn't keep it up! One minute to rest, then we'll continue! I know you can manage!"

Two hours. It took me two hours to feel comfortable enough being close to Tarra without just staring at her lips the whole time. After that, everything was much easier — dancing, greetings, walking arm in arm — we even worked out how I'd approach the crowd that would undoubtedly gather around my companion, in order to save her from too much attention. For the last hour, I reveled in the fact that I had the perfect woman swaying in my arms, knowing that a cold shower awaited me that evening to somehow quell the passion that had flared up in my chest. From the moment I became a doomed soldier, Tarra was the first woman to simply be there and rejoice in this fact. She didn't keep her distance like the other teachers, she didn't show her contempt for me like my classmates, she didn't turn her nose up in arrogance like Fardi. She was simply perfection, permitting me to be near without demanding anything in return.

"Get changed," ordered one of the clerics who came to retrieve me after four hours. I once again noticed that Tarra made no move to turn around, but now, this didn't faze me. I didn't turn away either, but calmly removed all the clothes I had been given earlier. Tarra looked over my body appraisingly and shot me a coquettish smile. I pulled on my uniform and realized that from now on, all the excitement I had for my partner would be gone.

The next couple of hours were also quite eventful — I was allowed to take a real bath. With oils, fragrances, soaps. The last time I had enjoyed such a pleasure had been in my past life. While I was luxuriating in the warm water, the nail experts came to transform my stumps into decently manicured fingers. Then I got a haircut, shave, ironed clothes...Everything was of such high quality that it gave me a pang in my stomach. None of this extravagance had been available in our barony. My father didn't approve of such things, believing that a man should be adorned with his sweat and scars, not bows and rose water.

As for transportation, the Fortress really pulled out all the stops and got me a real carriage drawn by four horses. Tarra was already aboard, seated with the grace of a real empress. Unwittingly admiring the woman, I missed the moment Father Nor approached.

"Today you have a difficult task ahead of you. The servants of the Light are already in place, including Father Dvar. They are there incognito, with permission from the girl's parents. You will be given a room to conduct the inspections. Do you have the cube with you?"

I held up the steel box.

"What we're doing is a violation of the law, but it's a step the Fortress takes willfully. We are acting in strict cooperation with the secret imperial office. At the event, you will be on your own. None of the guests will know that you're a doomed soldier, but you must plan your actions based on the law. Do not attack first, do not incite violence, no shows of aggression. You will be closely monitored. Each guest at the event must carry an amulet against the influence of converts. If you find the beast, we won't have to burn those who fell into the same circles. Magister Tarra Loyd will explain your duties in more detail. Questions?"

"How many guests will I have to check?"

"Everyone at the event. Invitations were sent out to five hundred families, but not all of them will attend. The Barons of Chescony are not among the circles of influential families, which allows us to conduct an experiment with the least risk of loss to reputation."

"Am I supposed to kill the convert, or do you have your own team on site?"

"You won't be required to kill him. He will be seized and delivered to the Fortress. We have our own ways of obtaining information, even from beasts under Skron's control."

"What do I do with the groups where there are no converts? They'll collapse from fear and start trying to crawl away. Some might even have a stroke. A level-four elite is too serious a beast to take such risks."

"That's why you're starting with the Barons of Chescony. If the experiment proves to be unjustifiable and people suffer, then at least we can quiet them quickly. As for what to do with those who demand satisfaction for the insult inflicted upon them...That's what you've trained for — you must solve the problem yourself. Neither the church nor the empire will interfere. Officially, we won't even be present."

"You speak so calmly about risking the lives of completely innocent people..."

"The war against the darkness requires sacrifices. And the Fortress is prepared to make them. Both in the form of our own servants, and of ordinary civilians living in the Light. If we have found a new way to identify converts, even at the cost of a dozen lives, we will easily agree. The damage that an ordinary convert could deal if he reached the city center and gave himself over to Skron would be much greater."

"Gentlemen, I don't want to interrupt your fascinating conversation, but only the upper classes are allowed to be late for an event. Viscounts, Counts. We have merely an ordinary baron, going to visit another baron."

"One more thing," Father Nor looked into my eyes. "No one will be controlling your actions today. You could take a chance and run away. Perhaps even successfully. But know that the Church of the Light will not rest until it finds you, wherever you may hide. And once we do, your remaining path in this life will be short and straight. To the bonfire. We don't deal with traitors."

"I understand, Father Nor. I have no need to run, and if I accidentally found myself outside of the access zone granted by the church, I'd slowly move toward the academy with my hands up. I don't plan on running. I have other plans, and the academy is the only place where I know how to enact them."

"I sincerely hope so. Today will decide many things for you, Max. Go on, Magister Lloyd is right — you shouldn't dawdle."

The whole way there, I listened to Tarra's bewitching voice explain the plan to me, but when we arrived, my heart betrayed me and skipped a beat. I still couldn't let go of the past, no matter how much I wanted to. It was a blow to the stomach when the herald coughed and announced in a booming voice:

"Baron Maximilian Valevsky and his companion!"

Chapter 7

"VALEVSKY?" I NEARLY SHOUTED at Tarra, but brought it down to a whisper. "Are you serious?"

"I don't understand your surprise. According to the orders of the secret imperial office, we are not permitted to use the name of any existing family lest it negatively affect their reputation. Therefore, they simply put together a random assortment of letters. It is unlikely that anyone present will look into the empire's registry of family lineages to check the records."

"Maximilian Valevsky is my name!"

"Max, you must understand something very important," Tarra turned toward me, ignoring the enthusiastic exclamations. "Maximilian Valevsky is a random name that has no connection to you. The Valevsky family does not exist, and any Maximilian who might have borne this family name — even more so. For the duration of this event, you are an invented person who was given a random name, which will be taken away as soon as the task is completed. The sooner you come to terms with this, the easier it will be for all of us."

"Baron, I'm glad to see you at our celebration!" An elderly couple approached us, forcing us to wrap up our little powwow. In any case, I'd tell Father Nor everything — they should warn me about things like that in advance. The Barons of Chescony had made attempts to appear more youthful, despite the long, gray hair covering their heads and the wrinkles on their faces that didn't lend themselves to cosmetic tightening procedures.

"Baron, Baroness," I inclined my head, greeting the masters of the house. The only people who knew who I was and why I came here. Nevertheless, it was necessary to follow protocol, so I finished the sentence: "Your invitation came as a surprise to me, but I accepted it with much joy."

"Hurry along now, I'll introduce you to my granddaughter, the Belle of today's ball," The Baroness of Chescony took me by the hand and dragged me into the depths of the hall, where a crowd of my peers was clustered. Judging by the constant outbursts of laughter, the party was in full swing. Everyone was already in their own cliques, so it would be impossible to wedge myself in unnoticed. And I didn't want to, to be honest. The girls, without exception, wore magnificently elegant ball gowns, differing only in color and depth of neckline, while the guys showed more diversity in their dress. Some were in an almost exact replica of my own suit, while others wore a strange mixture of leather and armor, deliberately demonstrating the fact that they were one of the emperor's guards. Coming closer, I recognized the academy's insignia on one cuirass — none of the guardsmen here were on active duty. And there were no other representatives of the magical academy. People who studied there should not attend such trifling events.

"Granddaughter, let me introduce you to Baron Maximilian Valevsky, the grandson of one of my old acquaintances" — the baroness brought me over to the "Belle of the ball." No, I had nothing bad to say about Elmira Chescony — she was a girl with two legs, two arms, magnificent breasts, an entirely human face, but when I looked upon her for the first time, she immediately fell to the end of my personal list. Elmira was even lower than the princess, although I would have thought she would remain solidly in last place for the rest of her days.

"Maximilian." She held out her hand for a kiss. Elmira's voice was akin to her looks. It seemed ordinary enough, the same as hundreds of others, but not at all suitable for her appearance. Nevertheless, I had to play my part to the end, gallantly kissing her lace-gloved hand.

"Will you introduce us to your companion?" Elmira asked, only now noticing Tarra's presence beside me. The professor looked like a creature from another world against the background of the other attendees.

"Tarra Lloyd, Baroness. Please extend her your love and hospitality."

"Just Tarra?"One of the future guardsmen wedged himself into the conversation. "No title?" Tarra looked at the young man and shot him such a smile that he involuntarily gulped.

"Just Tarra," I confirmed. "She is my dance teacher."

"Is that all? Of course, *all* the barons drag their dance teachers to balls with them these days," one of the ladies said rather unambiguously, causing the others great amusement.

"If you're wondering if Tarra Lloyd shares a bed with me," I smiled, instantly drawing everyone's attention. A touchy subject had been raised and everyone was dying to hear the answer. "That is none of your business, gentlemen. I ask you to treat my companion with respect and not to insult her with such remarks."

"And yet...?" Actually, the young man so interested in Tarra's status looked an awful lot like the girl who had let the improper phrase slip. "Baron Dahlem, at your service!"

"And yet nothing, Baron. I've no more to say on the matter," I said with as friendly a smile as I could muster."

"The dance, gentlemen, the dance!" The birthday girl threw her hands up, attracting the attention back to her. "Baron Dahlem, I await your invitation!"

"We're not done yet, Baron, my boy," Dahlem said to me, and then bowed to Elmira, inviting her to dance.

"You really know how to make friends," Tarra smiled as we joined the others. I had three mandatory dances ahead of me — you can't argue with longstanding tradition.

"So, Baron I-Don't-Remember-Your-Name, you didn't answer my question," Dahlem immediately appeared next to me during the pause after the first dance. He was accompanied by two friends, future guardsmen like himself. The tone in which Dahlem addressed me obliged me to act, demanding satisfaction. But I had no right to act — several nondescript men at the far wall, who were acting as if they had just happened upon this celebration of life by chance, would not take their eyes off of me. They must be the agents from the secret office Father Nor had warned me would be closely monitoring my behavior. So I had to make sure I drew the boundary lines clearly for them."

"I'm afraid that it's not in my power to satisfy your curiosity today, Baron. Upon accepting my invitation, I promised the hosts that I would not instigate any duels or other such activities. If you still wish to continue our conversation in a more private setting, you'll have to stop running your mouth for a moment and attack me. Although in this case, I wouldn't be breaking my promise, and I could engage in some good fun with you while keeping a clear conscience. All the same, your verbal attacks I must endure with nothing but a bitter smile, ruefully pondering the future of our empire. Indeed, what future awaits us all if His Imperial Majesty's guards have sharper tongues than swords?"

Dahlem bared his teeth.

"You're a dead man, Valevsky! A dead man who dragged his coffin-warming whore here with him. I despise people like you! Attack you? You should be so honored! A dog like you should be thrown to the wolves. Let's go, gentlemen. It stinks like shit in here."

"You *really* know how to make friends." Tarra grabbed my hand, pulling it to her body. "But I dare say you held your composure well. Other young men your age would have taken things outside after the first sentence he uttered. Second dance, Baron! Invite me to dance, quickly, so we can forget the verbal diarrhea the esteemed Baron Dahlem deigned to pour over us."

I heard a disgruntled snort — apparently, several girls had been listening attentively to our every word. The music started up and the huge hall filled with twirling pairs. We didn't lag behind — I rejoiced at every touch, completely shaking Dahlem and his goons out of my head. If I had my way, I would have painstakingly pulled every tooth from his mouth, but I wasn't going to give my life for a moment of moral satisfaction.

But Dahlem clearly did not intend to leave me in peace. Having found himself a whipping boy who couldn't respond, he decided to exercise his wit. As soon as the second dance ended and we stepped to one side, he, accompanied by his faithful comrades, unpleasant sister and friends, appeared before us again. Judging by the smell that wafted over, the baron had already managed to find some alcohol.

"Your lady insulted me, scum! She insulted me and deserves a good spanking! She..."

I even closed my eyes, internally begging the Light for the strength to survive this evening. Father Nor had made a mistake by pairing me up with Fardi. He should have found someone like Dahlem, who I couldn't lay a single finger on. It was an excellent test of patience.

"Does the Baron Dahlem wish to pack his bags at the academy and go straight to the Wall tomorrow?" The words were spoken in a pleasant male bass. I opened my eyes to see my salvation. A man of fifty years, dressed in a formal suit and...that was it! Nothing more could be said about him. An exact copy of Gimlet — everything was so standard that there was nothing whatsoever to catch the eye.

"With whom do I have the honor of speaking? Introduce yourself!" The baron shot the man a look of displeasure.

"Slovan Ousmim, Colonel of His Imperial Majesty's Own Secret Office," he replied, flashing some sort of badge. It had the desired effect — Dahlem straightened up, as did his team. "You've had too much to drink, Baron. You disgrace the honor of that armor you wear. Any more remarks addressed at any of the guests at this esteemed event and there will be a report about your shameful behavior on the chancellor of the academy's desk tomorrow morning. His Imperial Majesty's guards have no right to behave so defiantly. I await your apology to the hosts of this extravagant event. Only then will I consider the possibility of closing my eyes to this flagrant violation of the academy charter. You have ten seconds."

"Don't listen to him, brother! What is a colonel of the secret office doing at such a piddly party as this?" I heard the irritating girl whisper, but the colonel's words had clearly reached Dahlem.

"Elmira Chescony, please accept my apology for my impertinent behavior," said Dahlem, for some reason staring at me. "It won't happen again. Good evening, gentlemen. We'll be leaving!"

"No one will be going anywhere at the moment." Slovan made a gesture with his hand, and two people appeared near each door. One faceless representative of the secret office and one servant of the Light.

"What does that mean?" Dahlem nearly screamed. "You have no grounds to detain us!"

"No one need be detained. Doomer Max, I think it's time we put an end to this little facade. Even a fool could see that nothing good would come of the Fortress' undertaking. It was doomed to fail from the start. You should leave this place. There's no place for you among civil society."

"Doomer?" A wave of astonished murmurs swept through the hall. With one word, Slovan had destroyed the church's entire operation.

"Colonel, I believe we discussed this!" A dead silence hung over the hall as a new voice joined the conversation. Without saying a word, the guests backed toward the walls to get farther away from the red-robed servant of the Light. The fanaticism of the churchmen was no secret to anyone, and those in red robes were especially zealous. But Slovan didn't care at all. He looked at Father Dvar with the same distaste with which he looked upon me.

"The doomer was meant to leave his companion and seclude himself in the room we allocated for him. Instead, he dances among the living, as if it's normal. We discussed many things, Father Dvar, you are right, but not this. Because of your slave's actions, I was forced to intervene and put an end to this operation. Everything was supposed to go smoothly, with no superfluous actions, but you neglected to heed our recommendations. What makes you think that an armed doomed soldier roaming freely among the guests is a great way to improve relations between our departments? And if he had not restrained himself and attacked Dahlem? Who would be to blame in this case? The High Priest? There will be no inspections today. I revoke permission and ask you to leave this event."

"I insist that the inspections are necessary." Father Dvar had lost his patience. Few people in this world could tell a Fortress security service man "no" and live to see another day.

"Father, look around. These are children! Ordinary children, still wet behind the ears. Where do you think you're going to find...what you're looking for?"

"You know very well that darkness doesn't discriminate. If we have the opportunity..."

"But you missed this opportunity by allowing a doomed soldier with a weapon to mingle with normal citizens. Only my respect for your work persuades me to turn a blind eye to your blatant violation of our agreement. You overstepped in every way you possibly could have. Do not abuse my patience, Father Dvar. Walk with the Light. There is nothing else for you here."

"May we talk somewhere with fewer spectators?" Father Dvar clearly wasn't backing down.

"We may. Lieutenant, take the doomed soldier outside," Slovan ordered and another faceless man appeared next to me. Now I knew where Gimlet used to serve. I began to wonder what offense a member of the secret office would have to commit in order to be sentenced to death.

"Madame, if you please," I offered Tarra my hand. She gave me a smile, took me by the elbow, and we left the Chescony family household in complete silence. I didn't even think about what would happen to the elderly couple that had introduced me as one of their old acquaintances. One thing was for sure — Father Nor would eat me alive.

"Your carriage will be arriving momentarily," said one of the clerics who met us on the street. I grinned. The "freedom" Father Nor had spoken of turned out to be a very narrow one, limited only to the confines of the Chescony residence.

"So you're a doomer?" Baron Dahlem's voice sounded like a bolt from the blue.

"So you've only got balls when there's not a secret service member around?"

"Boys, go about your business." Tarra's voice was full of metal. I didn't even know it could sound like that.

"Oh, the dead man's coffin humper said something. Who do you have to be to fuck a corpse? Don't you even dare look in my direction, Father, I'm fully aware of my rights, as well as yours. No one can forbid me from ridding the world of this garbage! You really shouldn't have dragged this cadaver to a ball and introduced it as Baron Valevsky! The whole empire knows what the Duke of Odoevsky did to those derelicts! He burned their hovel to the ground! You'd be hard pressed to find a stupider joke than appearing under the guise of a Valevsky."

I maintained my imperturbable expression, although inside I was boiling — the operation didn't fail because of what occurred inside. It failed as soon as the churchmen assigned me this name! I even had a fleeting moment of gratitude for the drunken asshole — he had given me excellent protection from Father Nor's scorn. Just let him try to shift the blame onto me now.

"You listen here, dead man!" Dahlem clearly didn't appreciate that my thoughtful silence was distracting from his important monologue. The young man drew his sword and pointed it at me. Tarra stepped back behind me, but from the way the woman held herself, it was clear that if this moron decided to attack a professor of the magical academy, he wouldn't like the result.

"Now you die, imposter! No one can ever forbid me, Baron Dahlem, from demanding justice!"

My golden dome flared with bright sparks — Dahlem was on the attack. His sword flew off to the side, forcing him to stumble, but then from the shadows came his team to his aid, the very same future guardsmen who constantly stood behind their commander. Two more swords flew out of their scabbards, forcing me to literally "hold my horses." There were too many witnesses and I needed iron-clad proof that I didn't attack first. For when I was finished with these freaks, even their mother wouldn't recognize them. I wouldn't kill them, they didn't deserve it, but the healer would certainly have a lot of trouble with them.

Sparks flashed and I grinned. Three against one. Fantastic, what gentlemen these guards were! Were honor and principles simply things they read about in books?

"You think you can hide behind your dark magic and just do whatever you want? Try it!" Dahlem was a man with ambitions. How else could he have gotten a crossbow like the ones the clerics wore? That meant he was prepared for anything, even skirmishes like this. A steel bolt flew in my direction, instantly halving my mana bar. There was a cry of pain as the steel ricocheted and hit someone, but I couldn't care about that now. I saw Dahlem's little helpers begin to roll up their sleeves. They had matching sets of crossbows. My shield wouldn't survive another volley, so I did the only thing that occurred to me in the moment. *Dark Spike* wasn't appropriate here — there were too many ordinary people nearby. So I was perfectly within my rights to use the steel cube. Was I going to let my foray into level four be in vain? Without taking my eyes off Dahlem, I grinned and for just a couple of moments became a mirror of the elite beast from level four of the rift.

The result exceeded all my expectations. Dahlem fell to the ground, eyes wide with horror, and began crawling away from me. Any thoughts of attacking had vanished. But the aura affected more than just my harasser. Despite the fact that I only held the mirror up for a couple of seconds, Tarra Lloyd, my monitor, and ten other ordinary onlookers who had gathered to watch the free performance had all fallen under its influence. And while most of them simply fell to the ground with a surge of visceral, animal terror in the face of a horrific dark beast, things were not so simple with one particular member of the student guard.

He remained standing, and as soon as the dark aura disappeared, he raised his hands to the sky and began chanting the dark curse. Skron had lost contact with his faithful slave's mind, so he had taken over his body to wreak havoc. One of Dahlem's goons was a convert!

"Not on my watch," I growled, breaking the spell. The only way this could be done was to turn on the mirror again, causing the entire crowd to suffer. It helped — the muttering stopped. The creature twitched, taking a step to one side. Then another. And another. Skron manipulated his marionette, forcing it out of the aura's range in order to finish the spell. I didn't even want to think about what might come to pass if I let that happen, so just in case, I took a few steps after the dark beast.

He sped up. His movements were twitchy, inanimate, but Skron quickly adapted to the controls. He accelerated even more, so that I had to give it my all to make sure the beast stayed within the mirror's range. The Chescony estate was now far behind us, all those we encountered fell to the ground in horror, but I was glad for one thing — as long as the beast wasn't able to mutter its spell, it wouldn't enslave ordinary people. No one would have to burn.

At some point, I began to seriously consider just snuffing the nimble little beast out. Sure, Father Nor wanted them alive but the speed with which he rushed toward the center of the capital was frightening. The convert ran with too much purpose, as if Skron was leading him toward a particular goal. The creature skirted obstacles, meandered through narrow streets, even tried to get lost in the crowd. But I was not far behind, leaving a path of groaning and trembling citizens in my wake. I realized that I was pushing as hard as I could and couldn't run any faster, even if my life depended on it. However, even the convert had their limits — the human body is imperfect. Nevertheless, we soon turned away from the center and toward the slums.

The house the convert ran toward was visible from afar. It was the only house on the street with a light in the window. There were no streetlights nearby, no random passers-by. A great place to finish off one particularly nimble little student who thought himself a hero. But I didn't pause to try, keeping the convert within a five-meter distance. He sped up and literally crashed into the door, breaking it off its hinges, and disappeared into the depths of the house. I followed, pulling out a vial of mana, just in case. It never reached my lips.

"What…" I heard a voice sound, followed by a soul-wrenching scream. The owner of the house had fallen under my aura. A light loomed ahead and I saw the flicker of the convert's back, causing me to rush forward again. Bursting into a large room, I stopped, catching my breath with difficulty. The convert stopped near the opposite wall. There was nowhere else to run. On the floor, a man in a black hood writhed in fear. Drooling, he squealed and tried to crawl away from me toward the wall. But he was the least of my concerns now. On the floor where he had just been was a huge ring of ornate intertwined threads. Once I was able to focus on it, something clicked in my head and messages flashed in front of my face, knocking me out of my mirror state.

You have learned the symbol "Yat."
1 upgrade available.

The aura evaporated, the screeching stopped, and the room immediately filled with dark murmurs. Skron had once again sensed the freedom of will and wanted to impose his influence wherever he could.

"All right, Father Nor, I hope you'll forgive me for this," I muttered, picking up a piece of the door from the floor. The room was very reminiscent of a dark beast's den. That's why the convert was in such a hurry to get here — he felt good in this place. But, may the Light smite them all, why had the church allowed dark beasts to make a home in Turb, the capital of an enormous empire?

The question was rhetorical, there was no one around who would reply, so I swiftly dealt two precise blows with the plank of wood. One hit the dark hooded figure, who had begun to rise from the floor, and the second hit the muttering beast in the head. It did little good — even from the floor, the convert tried to finish its spell. Mentally scolding Father Nor, I tore off a piece of cloth and stuffed it into the convert's mouth. Unlike the supreme convert that I had encountered previously, this one had no energy dome. He had nothing at all, save for the now useless crossbow hanging from his arm.

The gag helped — the muttering stopped. The convert began to twitch, as if he was about to run away again, but I didn't have the strength for a second round. I had to hold the creature down and bind it with its own clothes. Which, quite frankly, turned out to be a difficult process. Despite his slender physique, the dark beast had immeasurable strength. If I hadn't already learned to fight against these jerky movements, the dark beast may have claimed victory from me. The important thing was binding their hands and feet, and pretty soon I had two twitching cocoons lying in front of me. I also tied up the robed figure, just in case. Even if he wasn't a convert, let the clerics figure out why he was here. I doubt it was just to water the flowers.

I took up a torch and took a tour of the house. The whole thing was empty, abandoned. Returning to the only room where there was any semblance of life, I sat down on the floor and looked at the symbol again. One improvement available...The status bar has already been updated with a new icon that blinked invitingly. Deciding that no harm would come from simply reading the description, I concentrated on the icon and stared at the new window that popped up, bearing a drawing of the symbol and a short paragraph of text:

Yat. *Strengthening symbol. When applied to a*

weapon, damage +50%. When applied to armor: defense +50%. When applied to the body, growth rate of physical parameters +50%. Symbol validity period: 14 days. Requires chabre powder to use.

Chabre...the alchemical material the Evil Engineer went after. I was certain he would know perfectly well what the symbols were, where they came from, what they meant and what they did. I liked what I was reading, but until I understood all the consequences of using it...Great light, I had started thinking like Father Nor! When had he infected me with his distrust of all things new? Had the dark ones granted me new knowledge? Then I should rejoice and try to utilize it as quickly as possible. Weapons and armor were of no import to me, but increasing my physical parameters was too tempting to just pass up. I needed chabre, and there was only one place I could get it.

"Alright, you've had a little rest, now let's go!" Just in case, I drank a vial of recovery elixir and grabbed both cocoons. It was time to plod back to the academy. I hope they stopped to listen before they killed me on the spot...

Chapter 8

(Office of the High Priest, two days later)

"WHAT HAVE WE?" the man robed in gold gazed upon his closest companions. Those endowed with the power and the right to speak their mind.

There were very few, only ten in total, but Father Urg would vouch for each of them. Father Dvar, head of both the internal security service and all covert external operations, took the floor.

"The doomer uncovered one of the capital coven's bases. The convert is useless, just an animal with no mind. But the other dark one who fell into our hands proved a real wellspring of information. He was in charge of the western part of the city, overseeing the activities of new converts. Just a couple of hours ago, we received twenty names. Combat teams are already heading to the location to eliminate this darkness from the world. We also know how many members comprise the capital coven, and confirmed that Magister Elor has come to Turb. Their most recent meeting location has been revealed. The dark ones are careful. Small fry like this one have not been apprised of his plans, but we still found some good information. The darkness is preparing a Wave.

A hum went through the office. This was less than favorable news.

"Why would the darkness want a Wave?" frowned the High Priest. "And in Turb, no less. They know perfectly well the power of the beasts they may summon. They know the city's security systems."

"Could the dark one be lying?" asked a blue robe. The Fortress' financial managers always had a grounded approach, suggesting the most obvious solutions. "Could Magister Elor have deliberately sent us this, as you called him, small fry? To put us on the wrong track. So that we concern ourselves with the Wave while the killing blow is struck elsewhere?"

"We are working to confirm the findings," said Father Dvar.

"Try not to kill the dark one prematurely," the High Priest requested. "His time on the pyre will come. What else can you tell me about the incident?"

"We had to interrogate four hundred and twenty people who succumbed to the darkness," said Father Frass in a gray robe. Few people outside the walls of the Fortress knew gray robes even existed, and if they did, they would never in their lives want to meet the ones who wear them. The Dark Inquisition. Those who decided whether a person deserved to burn. Those who sought out darkness in the minds of others. "We would have obtained our results much faster if our former head of the department had taken part in the interrogation."

"Everyone must walk their own path, Father Frass," came Father Nor's cool response. Few recalled that he had been considered the best Dark Inquisitor for more than twenty years. And those who did were all present at this meeting.

"And so it turns out that a convert under the influence of a dark beast's aura is unable to spread Skron's influence?" said Father Dvar. "How can we use this?"

"We cannot. Despite strictly following the same instructions, we have been unable to recreate the mirror," Father Gron, the owner of the dark robe, responded. The Fortress researchers were granted extensive powers and their experiments absorbed most of the church's resources. Both financial and human.

"Dark Max is unique, at least for the time being. Now we have other projects that take precedence," Father Gron said, finishing his thought.

"And this is our biggest problem," the High Priest sighed. "The secret office demands blood. The citizens who have fallen under the influence of the darkness demand blood. Baron Dahlem demands blood. Everyone wants blood. No one understands the importance of destroying the dark ones, everyone is primarily concerned with their own desires and notions of honor."

"We can put pressure on the Dahlems to quiet their progeny," Father Dvar suggested. "And we can quiet all the others who fell under the mirrored influence the same way. The secret office can be ignored. Since they disrupted our agreed-upon plan, it is pointless to negotiate with them."

"I want to note that it was we who disrupted the operation. Not the servants of the emperor." Father Nor's voice was calm. "It is entirely my fault, and I will admit it. I thought that the doomer would feel more comfortable in the company of his peers if he took on his former name."

"We will not become like the dark ones, giving rise to fear where everything can be solved by peace. We will not defend Max, even though it is thanks to him that, for the first time in twenty years, we got our hands on an active member of the coven. Max broke the law, for which he will be punished. Father Nor, see to it that the doomer receives the punishment he deserves — three days on level five of the rift, I believe, should suffice. Announce our decision to all interested parties. If after his punishment, Max remains alive, all charges will be dropped. If any of those who have staked their claims do not agree with our decision, they are free to go to the fifth level of the rift in order to enact their threats themselves. The doors to the rift are always open. And one more thing,

Father Nor...when Max gets back from the rift, we should return to the issue of his enhancements. I suppose it's time to give him *Analyze*. Does anyone object?"

"We have learned how to extract elite stones, so we're not really risking anything. Unless some beast from the depths of the rift devours the doomer," said the dark robe.

"*Analyze* alone won't be enough," said Father Nor. "Not just that — it will be useless. I expressed my views on the matter at the last meeting."

"So let's do it. In three days, the doomer Max will receive his new stones. The time has come to finally put a limit on the boundless freedoms the respected chancellor Kimal Sarento has enjoyed."

(Magical Academy punishment cell)

The punishment cell...A cold two-by-two meter box with a bed, a hole for a toilet and a tiny window through which the daylight barely broke in. An ideal place to reflect upon your life, your behavior, and to be imbued with respect for the powers that be. The only pleasant aspect was that they fed you well, three times a day. The same ordinary food from our dining room, except without the metal utensils.

The second day of my stay in this endlessly entertaining environment was coming to an end. I wonder if Ursula patiently waited all four hours for me to arrive or left five minutes after the start of class? Or had her classes been canceled altogether — what's the point of teaching me the sword if I'll burn in a couple of days anyway? In order to somehow occupy my brain and drive away the stormy thoughts, I returned to the moment I came back to the academy, once again ignoring the idea of getting lost in the huge city and starting a new life. Maybe even moving to another empire. Was that possible? Yes, it was. Had I considered it while dragging the dark ones to the academy? Boy did I! But one of the few reasons why I didn't was stuck down in the rift for the third day in a row. The Evil Engineer had gone down to level five and no one knew why he'd been down there for so long. And all the nuggets of dark lore I had received over the past week had come from him.

So I was forced to return. A warm welcome was never in store for me — I only managed to get to the academy by morning, when news of my escape had already spread through the whole city. The patrol found me five hundred meters from the park. I was immediately surrounded, taken to the academy under escort and handed over to Father Nor's custody. The cleric met me personally.

Nobody had touched the dark ones, so I had to drag them to the torture chamber where they'd given me enhancements myself. Only then, after the doors were locked, did Father Nor give me five whole minutes to explain the reason why I had fled. It's just that I never got the words out. When I reached the part about the guy in the black robe, the cleric stopped me, called his assistants over, and ordered me to be escorted to the punishment cell. That's it! No swearing, no praise, nothing at all. Complete indifference to my fate, except that they took my katars and the steel box. I really should have made a run for it...

"Step out!" Instead of dinner, one of the churchmen had come to my cell. "Get dressed."

He handed me a jumpsuit. When they'd shoved me in the punishment cell, they hadn't even allowed me to change my clothes. Of course, while I was running after the convert, part of my suit had torn, the sword dangling from my belt had fallen off and was completely lost, but even what was left of the vestments were expensive enough that they shouldn't be left to rot in some jail cell. The servants of the Light didn't care about this, however. They had clearly found the main culprit and were deciding the most efficient way to take care of him.

That being said, the jumpsuit puzzled me. I didn't understand why I'd need it. When they handed me a belt and pouch with various elixirs, it became clear that they wouldn't be burning me right now. Were they planning another training session? It was already so late. The middle of the night!

"Your blades." He pulled out my katars from the bag and even helped me put them on.

"Why?" I couldn't resist asking. "Why such generosity all of the sudden?"

"Because you're being punished," Father Nor's voice came from somewhere off to one side.

He had been lurking in the shadows, so I hadn't noticed him right away. Stepping out into the light and allowing himself to be seen, Father Nor continued: "On order of the High Priest, you will be sent to the fifth level of the rift, where you will spend three days without food and water. During this time, you are free to do whatever you please. Your only task is to survive."

"Isn't the Evil Engineer supposed to be cleansing level five as we speak?" I asked, surprised.

"We haven't seen the dark one in three days. We don't know what he's doing or what's happening to him. We cannot send intelligence to this level. We don't have the resources. If you have the opportunity, find out why your mentor has been in the rift for so long. If no such opportunity arises, don't be a hero. You will go through the fourth level and gradually make your way down. Judging by the information we have, the creatures on level five are an order of magnitude stronger than creatures of the fourth. You must learn to control your mirror."

"This is really a punishment?" I frowned. "It seems more like a training session. And a strange one, at that."

"You have been found guilty of breaking the law. You will be punished. It's not a training session. Don't even mention such stupidity when you speak about how harsh the Fortress can be to someone who brought them two dark beasts."

"Was it even helpful?" I asked, not even

expecting an answer.

"You'll find out after you have served your sentence. They will pick you up in three days in the mine on level five. This is your only way out of the rift. If you decide to exit through level one, you will be brought back. Clear? Good. Escort Max to his punishment."

"Can I bring a bag?" I asked at the door. "If the Evil Engineer is right, then there's chabre to be found on level five. I won't be able to carry much with just my hands."

"You may have a backpack," Father Nor agreed after a pause. "Although the Evil Engineer is panicking for no reason, believing that three ranges have suddenly appeared in the rift, there are other useful materials down there besides chabre. You can leave the nux, but we wouldn't refuse a bag full of chrone. The doors will open to you only after three days. You can't break out before then. Go."

I wanted to ask how I would even know that three days had passed, but didn't want to risk hassling Father Nor again. The guard took me to the mine, descending with me to the fourth level. The servant of Light monitored me carefully to ensure I was following proper door-opening protocol, but made no moves to help. Once we made it down, he spoke with a blind cleric about something and we went even lower, warning him that he'd need to open the door again in three days. But I wasn't paying much attention — as soon as the locked plate clicked open to reveal level five, the blind man released me into the punishment zone. There were no beasts near the mine entrance. Apparently, fourth-level creatures considered this zone to be dangerous. I put up my mirror and boldly went to search for the descent. The caves I had to wade through were still infested with monsters. There seemed to be even more than last time. Unable to resist, I finished off several especially large elite kronas, but did not receive any loot from them. There were no stones to be had — this became clear as soon as they died, and I didn't want to spend the time examining the remains to pick out the valuables. And I didn't have the chance anyway — the monsters standing next to me simply wouldn't understand why I was poking around inside one of them.

So I continued to move from cave to cave, periodically stopping to take out the larger beasts. No matter what anyone said, sooner or later they'd have to be eliminated. Better now, when I had plenty of time. The cave I had cleared earlier, as well as the one where I'd destroyed the red exclusive, was completely brimming with beasts. There was no trace left of the corpses — the dark monsters devoured each other's bodies at lightning speed. I had to spend several hours searching for the descent. By some evil irony, it had been placed in the farthest and most remote cave from the mine. Like all the other rooms on this level, the one containing the passageway to level five was filled with kronas, rapses and other evil spirits, so they all had to be killed. The reason for this was simple. As I approached the opening, the influence from level five began to beat down on me. My defenses threatened to shatter, leaving me all alone with a huge mob of monsters, so I was forced to thin out the crowd. Only after the bodies stopped twitching did I drearily begin the torturous process of acclimatizing. Father Nor wasn't wrong — the beasts on level five really were astoundingly powerful. It took me a long time to even get close to the passage, let alone go down. I trembled terribly. I was even glad I hadn't gotten dinner, otherwise my stomach would have pushed it right back up. Another issue was my lack of partner. In the two-level rift, as well as during our last visit to level four, I had just sat on the ground, and either Gimlet or the Evil Engineer pushed me forward, closer to the source of negative radiation. Now I couldn't enjoy such a privilege and had to edge closer on my own. Which, frankly, turned out to be quite difficult. My body betrayed me, resisting the pressure and making involuntary movements in an attempt to crawl further away from this terrible place. And the closer I got to the opening, the more difficult it became to overcome myself.

I only took my first step down what felt like a full day later. The passage was filled with creatures that had risen from level five, but, oddly enough, their aura was not particularly strong. Common monsters, the same as on the fourth level. Even the magic krona that had broken through with its entourage, and even that couldn't account for a fraction of the horror I felt seeping up from level five. Engaging my katars once again, I cleared a path for myself and started my slow descent. Only one turn of the staircase, but it took me a few hours to pass through. A couple of times, my mirror almost broke, and a few other times I had to turn back, unable to master my reflexes, constantly slaughtering beast after beast that flew at me with monstrous determination. The dark creatures seemed to sense that the cave above had become vacant and rushed to fill it as quickly as possible.

But everything has a beginning and an end. Shit, I was talking like Father Nor again...As soon as I set foot on level five, I had an important realization — being in the company of these beasts made me feel bad, sometimes really awful, but it was entirely tolerable. Apparently I had finally become a card-carrying masochist. Feeling bad made me feel good. Something had to be done about this, and soon — I didn't want to live like this.

Taking a few steps to one side, I nearly growled with rage — aside from the slope leading up to the fourth level, there was another leading down to the sixth! That's why I was having such a rough time! I decided to verify, taking one more step toward the passageway, and it was very nearly my last. My mirror shattered immediately, as if it had never been there! My head became cast-iron, my body cramped, my legs gave way, but by some miracle, I managed to fall backwards instead of forwards. Sparks flew immediately. The creatures in the cave fell on me with a blind thirst for destruction, but I was once again unbelievably lucky. The krona attacking me from above blocked out most of the others, and the majority of them were already dead. It's hard to explain how I was able to restore my mirror. By that point, I was acting on pure reflex. Using the same reflexes, I finished off the creature, which had been completely unfazed by my transformation into a dark one and continued to bash into my shield. The other kronas calmed down, and there were no new attempts to devour me. I had to lie there for several more hours before I had the strength to push the dark one off of me and crawl away from the hole. Level six just wasn't a possibility for me now. In fact, it was still too soon for me to venture out into five — when I crawled toward the passage to the next cave, my body cramped up again. As if the monsters in this cave were just as strong as those on the sixth.

Once again I had to endure it, recklessly downing recovery potions in the process. Now that nearly a day and a half had passed, my body began to remind me that I was a growing boy and needed energy to function. Although honestly, I appreciated Father Nor's wisdom when he forbade me to eat dinner and sent me down here without a single crumb. My bowels hadn't needed emptying yet because there was nothing in there to empty.

Only by the end of the second day did I gain

strength to enter the cave full of beasts on level five. I noticed something was wrong right away — I had never seen such a bright golden glow in my life. When I stood at the edge of the entrance I gulped, horrified by what I saw. There were almost fifty elite creatures here — kronas, lurges, schtryks. Somewhere at the far end, an exclusive creature glowed red. And not a single common, or even magical dark one! What did Father Nor say? That the Evil Engineer was panicking for no reason? What could this be, if not one of the ranges he had warned about? Was it really true that our rift was already fourteen levels deep and that a metamorph would soon appear? If so, I needed to leave the academy as soon as possible. They'd throw the doomers to the beasts first.

I stared at the sea of monsters and a bad premonition arose in my soul. The Evil Engineer had gone to the fifth level in order to clean it. But clearly, the cleansing process was far from finished. And it had been five whole days since he had entered the rift. Did he make it back? It was actually vital that I find out. I couldn't believe that my mentor would allow himself to be devoured. I didn't believe he would disappoint me like that.

But I had to figure out what to do next. Either clean the cave or move on in my search for the Evil Engineer and then cleanse level five together. In the end, selfishness won out — the red krona looked harmless enough. As I understood it, all the horror that had tried to break through my mirror was emanating from this exclusive beast. If I killed it, maybe things would get a little easier. Perhaps I'd even be able to breathe normally instead of the intermittent gasp of air I got now.

But in order to get there, I had to thoroughly cleanse the room. The elites didn't want to let me by and were constantly interfering and getting in my way. They behaved exactly like the ousels on level four. When there were only five creatures left, I had to stop — all five had banded together in one spot and were baring their teeth, growling, preventing me from breaking through to their master. And with the droves of rapses hanging from the ceiling, ready to drop on me from above, my outcome wasn't looking particularly rosy. I could take a risk and test my strength, of course, but the same bad feeling in my gut made me retreat. I would most definitely return to finish them off later, but only after I took a tour around the entire floor and confirmed that the Evil Engineer had already left.

Because I couldn't even imagine the alternative.

The next cave turned out to be just as jam-packed as the previous — one red and a whole mob of gold beasts in their sundry forms. I didn't linger here for long. I just finished off a couple of kronas on my way to the next cave. Where for the first time I could breathe normally — the cave was nearly empty. The few scattered elites devouring the bodies of their fallen brethren didn't count. My dark mentor had passed through, and spent quite a while here. Just in case, after I finished off the cannibals, I ran to the next passage to check. Empty, again, with a rare elite here and there. A satisfied smile began to creep across my face. The last cave had only two passages. The one leading back to where I came and the one that led to this cave. Since this room had been cleared and the Evil Engineer had been nowhere to be found in the last, it meant that I was on the right path. I didn't even consider the idea that he could have been eaten. He regularly frequented levels eight and nine. What were a couple of level five beasts to him? Even if there was a red beast among them.

I went from cave to cave, marveling at the efficiency and strength of the Evil Engineer. There were no creatures anywhere. And the farther along I went, the fewer cannibals I encountered. The final few caves I passed through were completely littered with untouched corpses. More precisely, pieces of corpses. Unlike me, the Evil Engineer tore his opponents apart. When I reached a dead end, I was about to turn back, when I was attracted by some kind of movement. One of the dark beasts shifted. I moved closer to put it out of its misery, but then my eyes fell upon the boot, and a cold chill ran through my body. I rushed forward, throwing the pieces of beast aside. A few moments later and I was staring at the ghastly pale blue body of the Evil Engineer. A body devoid of life. The beasts had done a number on him. Both arms were torn off almost to the shoulders, one leg was missing, as was half his face. Deep, lacerating wounds all over his body completed the terrible picture, but amidst this destruction I saw the convulsive flicker of a shallow breath. Despite everything, his body continued to fight for life. Although it seemed to me that the last drop of life had drained from it long ago.

Chapter 9

"DON'T YOU DARE DIE on me — I'll kill you!" I swore, whipping out a recovery elixir and activating the healing aura. But a problem arose: the Evil Engineer was unable to swallow. The liquid flowed into his mouth, but he immediately vomited it back out. I had to pour it down his throat, literally drop by drop, in tempo with his breath. Flooding his lungs with elixir wasn't ideal, of course, but I couldn't think of anything else right now. The only first aid they teach to doomed soldiers, if at all, consisted of tearing off a piece of paper, spitting on it, and slapping in on a wound. It's easier to recruit new ones than to heal them...

No blood flowed from his stumps. His leg and left arm had been tied with tourniquets. His right had been "patched up" via cauterization. The skin there was dark and threatened to turn gangrenous, so I spent two more vials washing out his wounds. Once again, with no indication that it was helping. I had to feed the last bottle down his throat, just like the first. For a long time, nothing happened and I even began to suspect the worst, but then I saw improvement: his breathing became less intermittent, the deadly blue tinge had left his face. The dark one was still fighting.

"Alright, let's start making our way toward the mine, slowly." I carefully lifted the Evil Engineer into my arms, but almost dropped him when an arm rolled out from under him. He had managed to recapture his limb from the beasts and prevent it from being devoured. I set him back down on the stone floor, stuck the severed arm in my bag, and started digging through the piles. If his arm was here, the rest of him must be around somewhere. Since he'd taken all the trouble to wedge it underneath his body, they must mean something to him. I'd spend a couple more minutes looking. He'd been here for five days already, he could wait a little longer. I uncovered his leg right away, although not in its entirety — it was missing a foot. But I had to sift through a lot before I found the right hand. I even thought the creatures must have eaten it. The last piece of the Evil Engineer I found under a huge pile of monsters a few meters away from the body. After throwing the monster bits aside, I pulled the arm out and was about to put it in my bag when a red glow emanating from the fist caught my attention. I had to break two fingers to pry it from his grasp. Even when separated from the body, the Evil

Engineer's arms were much stronger than mine. Nevertheless, I wasn't giving up, and eventually plucked a small, accurately-hewn hexagon from his fist. With a gulp, I stood frozen, thoughtlessly peering into the stone, as if it held the answers to all my burning questions.

Amplify. No question about it, there were no other red stones in the rift. At least according to the information I had. My mouth became unusually dry once I realized what this was. My ticket to freedom. I had a ticket to freedom! The only thing I had to do was find the cleric to exchange this stone for freedom. Father Nor wasn't a good prospect. Knowing his temperament, he'd simply take the stone and tell me to bring him back more. And that I had ten minutes. No, definitely not Father Nor. Then who? The High Priest? Maybe the chancellor? Surely Kimal Sarento was familiar with the mechanics of turning a doomed soldier back into an ordinary person through these red stones. There was also the Countess, but I didn't have access to her. So what did this mean for me? That I had to wait around and try not to rock the boat, running around with an amplification stone like a beacon, waving it from side to side? No one must know I had it. But then the question arose — where to hide it? I couldn't integrate it into my person. I only knew one way — through fire. This would tie the stone to me permanently...damn it, what was I thinking? My mentor was about to die here! First I'd get us out of here, then figure out what to do with the stone.

Once you make a decision, it always becomes easier to act. Putting all three pieces of the Evil Engineer in my backpack, I hid *Amplify* under my katara mount. It definitely wouldn't budge and the glow wasn't visible. Returning to my mentor, I picked him up again, noticing the small bag that was still attached to his back. From the looks of it, there was something in it. I was forced to sit him up again and remove the additional weight. Peering inside, I frowned. The Evil Engineer had been collecting blue crystals. Exactly the same as those illuminating the rift, except that they were dim. I pulled out a couple and turned them in my hands, wondering what their value was. It was doubtful he'd be collecting useless rocks. So they must have some value. Was this really chabre? The rare material that can only be found on ranges? I could use a couple of them to figure out that symbol business...Alright, I'd deal with this later as well. Bag on my shoulders, Evil Engineer in my arms, I finally escaped that terrible cave.

Finding the mine shaft again took a whole hour. My mentor had absolutely no reaction when I put up my mirror, which immediately raised new questions. Was he immune to the influence of creatures from the very beginning, or did the unconscious body not react to the aura of the dark ones? It was more than just a passing curiosity — this could come in handy in the future. For example, if I knocked someone out, I could drag them to any level of the rift. What a delicious manner of execution: first, they go mad with horror, and then they're devoured by ravenous beasts. Why hadn't I thought of it before?

"Open!" I rapped on the door. My internal clock told me that three days had long since passed, but the blind cleric on the other side of the steel door made no attempts to show he was there. I did not know the secret password, so I had to settle down next to the door, tirelessly pounding on it with my fist. Apparently, the cleric was not only blind, but deaf. The racket I was making must have been heard all over the rift. But the zealot didn't care. He was told only to let me back in after three days, so that's what he would do.

Five thousand knocks! I had to bang on the door five thousand times before it opened! My hand had gone numb. When I heard the click, I jumped to my feet and lifted the Evil Engineer with me. The unpleasant blueness had begun to creep over his face again. Practically shoving the blind man aside as he stood in the doorway with a detached look, I threw my mentor over my shoulders and ascended the ladder. Only at the very top did I stop and wait for the servant of the Light to close the passage to the fifth level. I had enough on my plate without worrying about false accusations that I tried to release the rift beasts on innocent academy residents.

Level four. Three. Two. Everywhere, the same picture — the indifferent expressions of the servants of the Light. Even when I asked for the recovery elixir, I received no response. It was as if they hadn't heard me. I had to crawl up through the levels, guided by my blind faith that I wasn't too late, he wasn't past saving. Although I had no idea how he'd live with one leg. Would he train in a wheelchair? He clearly wouldn't be able to continue digging the mine. With his teeth, maybe...

The last slab slid aside, releasing me into the twilight of the encroaching night.

"Your punishment has been carried out, the charges are dropped. From now on you...what's wrong with him?!"

Father Nor was there to meet me personally. The cleric knew I wouldn't want to linger in the rift any longer than necessary and would leave at the first opportunity.

"Healer! He's barely breathing!" I shifted the Evil Engineer from my shoulders to my arms.

"Follow me!" Father Nor quickly pulled himself together. Turning toward the shadows, he ordered: "Magister Smalog to my office, immediately! Notify the chancellor! Fill a bath with recovery elixirs. Move!"

The shadows shifted — the churchman's assistants rushed to fulfill his orders. But I was no longer paying attention. I moved quickly after Father Nor, who had nearly broken into a run. Once in his office, Father Nor swept everything from his desk onto the floor with no hesitation.

"Lay him down. How long has he been like this?" Astoundingly, a hint of sentiment had crept into the servant of the Light's voice."

"I have no idea. I found him six hours ago. I'd say he'd most likely been lying there for at least a day."

"Why didn't you drag him out right away?"

"Because we sat at the door to the mine for over three hours. Banging, shouting, begging to open it — with no response. They didn't listen. Because Father Nor demanded that his orders be fulfilled to the letter."

"What's going on?" The chancellor swiftly stepped into the room. "Great Light!"

Genuine emotions once again. Like Father Nor, the chancellor seemed sincerely concerned about the Evil Engineer. Soon a small trough appeared, into which the servants began pouring vial after vial of elixir. They placed then lay him down inside, but the deathly blue tinge stubbornly remained.

"Gentlemen, what's this about an urgent call?" Magister Smalog entered the office, saw the trough and stopped short. The skin on the doctor's face became whiter than the cleric's cassock. He stepped back and leaned against the wall, where he remained standing, looking upon the remains of the Evil Engineer with abject horror.

"Magister Smalog, can you do it?" Father Nor understood the healer's reaction all too well.

"This will kill me," Magister Smalog whispered. "Three limbs gone…I can't handle even half of it."

"And if you're not alone?" the chancellor prompted. "The clerics have healers of their own."

"This will require level fifteen *Heal*, minimum." Magister Smalog still couldn't come to his senses. "Two, three healers would be best. If we combine our efforts..."

"The only one with level fifteen in Journal." The chancellor looked at Father Nor. "He won't work for free. Especially if he has to risk his life. Damn it, it's nearly night — the viscount could be anywhere. If I find him and deliver him to you, you must find a way to pay an imperial healer. Magister, can you ensure the dark one does not perish before my return?"

"Keeping him alive — is something I can do," nodded Magister Smalog. "I don't suppose you have the limbs?"

"I do." I threw my backpack on the floor and removed the three lumps of flesh.

"Great light, why is he still in the bath?" the healer nearly cried out. He snatched the pieces from me and began to carefully line them up with their corresponding stumps. His voice even changed — the fear was replaced by a fiery determination. "Yes, Viscount Journal alone will certainly be enough. Since we don't need to rebuild flesh, we can handle it together. The Evil Engineer will live as long as it takes. This I can guarantee. Father Nor, please give the order to transfer the trough to the medical unit."

Four servants of the Light grabbed the trough and had almost carried it out of the office when something incredible happened — the Evil Engineer began to wheeze and choke.

"Bring him back!" Cried Magister Smalog. "Quickly!"

Back in the office, the fit died down and his breathing evened out.

"Max, leave now," Father Nor ordered. I obeyed, but as soon as I moved a few meters away from the Evil Engineer, he started up again. "Come back. Magister, what is it? Why does the dark one get worse when Max moves away?"

"If only I understood." Sweat appeared on the healer's face. "Something binds them together."

"Yes, I surmised that already. That wasn't my question."

"I have no idea!" Magister Smalog flared up. "Perhaps the remains of the aura that the doomer used to heal the dark one. Perhaps the fact that they are both dark and the presence of a servant of the Light affects him negatively. This has never happened before in my practice. If you'd like to excuse me, I can do some research. But I'm not sure the Evil Engineer would survive it. Gentlemen, hoist the trough up again. Max, come along."

There was no third attack — the Evil Engineer calmly endured the transfer to the hospital ward. I was seated in a corner so that I wouldn't interfere and the healers began their strange procedures. They removed the tourniquets, worked over the stumps, and gave him some kind of injections. It was a terribly interesting process, but I wasn't allowed to watch, as Father Nor approached me.

"Tell me what happened."

I had to tear my attention away to retell the story of the last three days. Father Nor wanted to know every detail — how long it took me to adapt to the fifth level, to the cave with the red beast, how I found the Evil Engineer, what I did then, how I healed him, the location of the resources that I was sent so deep to recover.

"Resources?" I interrupted.

"You were on level five for two full days. There should have been some chrone around. Did you collect it?"

"Are you serious? My mentor…"

"We are unable to do anything else to help the dark one now, so we must instead turn to those matters for which we are responsible. So you didn't follow my instructions?"

"No," I replied, furious at the soulless churchman. How could he be talking about some crystals now, with the Evil Engineer in his current condition?

"However, you have two backpacks," said Father Nor. "You were only given one."

"The second isn't mine. Mentor had it when I found him. I don't know what's in it.

"Empty it," Father Nor demanded. Staring blankly at the chabre (if that's what it was) as it spilled onto the floor, the churchman took the backpack and practically tore it to pieces, searching for hidden pockets.

"Are you looking for something in particular?" I asked, surprised.

"How many exclusives did he kill?"

"Around fifteen," I said, estimating the number of caves he'd cleared.

Father Nor nodded and finally left me in peace. By that point, the healers were cutting off the remains of the Evil Engineer's clothing, and the way the cleric closely monitored this process was very revealing. Father Nor was searching for *Amplify,* as if he knew perfectly well how it was obtained. Which raised a series of questions in my mind, both for the cleric himself and my mentor. The Evil Engineer claimed that Father Nor didn't know and shouldn't know anything, but his behavior hinted that one of them was being disingenuous. Weren't they supposed to work together, despite all their assurances to the contrary?

Unbeknownst to myself, I dozed off. The last three days had been hard, and from what I could tell, no one was about to permit me to eat or bathe, so all I could do now was relax and enjoy my fleeting moment of peace. But I somehow missed a whole throng of people entering the ward. If not for the shriek emitted by an unpleasant-looking man, I wouldn't have even thought to open my eyes. But the shrill voice did the impossible — it pulled me from the arms of sleep.

"No, and that's final!" The owner of a chic mustache, somewhat similar to those worn by Gustav, crossed his arms over his chest, trying to demonstrate in every way possible that he wouldn't budge. He wasn't a tall man, and his slender build, along with his extravagant mustache, made him look not unlike a cockroach.

"Kimal, look at him, he's a dead man! The fact that he's breathing is due solely to the enhancements, elixirs, and Skron knows what else he's imbued with. Magically transforming this *thing* into a living being would require all our strength. Sure, you can force Magister Smalog to risk his life. He owes you a debt, so he must carry out any order. But I don't answer to the academy! What will the emperor say if I die now trying to save someone who should have been sent to the stake a long time ago? Father Nor, your ward is dead. Whether you want it or not. Find another dark one. I wash my hands of this."

"We are prepared to pay," Father Nor said, refusing to let up.

"With what? Money? Don't make me laugh — there's not enough money in the whole Fortress. Your protection? I don't need it. I'm under the protection of the emperor and regularly pass checks to test for darkness. Stones, elixirs and other goods the Academy or Fortress has to offer? I can buy them all myself. Not from you, but on the black market. No, gentlemen, you have nothing that could interest me enough to risk my life. I value myself much more than the remnants of a dark beast. My advice is to let him die in peace. Release him to Skron. The darkness is already waiting for him."

The little cockroach was irate. He knew how much they needed him and took full advantage. The chancellor exchanged glances with Father Nor and shook his head — the academy was admitting it was powerless.

The *Amplify* stone began to burn under my wrist plate. Not physically — mentally. Would I ever be able to look in the mirror again if I allowed the Evil Engineer to die now? I'd never had any issues with this before. At one time, I even dreamed of strangling the heartless creature that kept demanding the impossible from me. But now I needed him. He possessed too much knowledge of the kind I severely lacked. Of course, there was no guarantee he'd be in any hurry to blab about the symbols, various stones, and other dark lore, but at least he had the information. There were no other dark humans in the empire. And searching for the remaining three that lived somewhere far beyond the horizon was also not an option. I'd have to make a sacrifice. And really, what was I giving up? Technically, the stone belonged to my mentor, I had just carried it here. I'd receive my own *Amplify* sometime in the near future — I already knew how to obtain the stones, I just had to learn how to destroy red beasts. And once he survived, the Evil Engineer would help. Skron damn it all to hell! I was still so reluctant to part with it.

"I beg your pardon, Viscount Journal, if I can bother you for a moment — would the dark one definitely live? Function normally? Be able to yell like before, use his hands?"

"Who is this unfortunate soul?" The healer responded slowly and looked in my direction with disgust.

"The apprentice who pulled the Evil Engineer out of the rift," the chancellor replied, giving me a suspicious look. Outwardly, I didn't appear as if I could be of any interest to one of the richest men in the empire. The healer snorted and turned around, intending to leave, but then Father Nor's voice sounded. Calm and quiet. The voice I feared most.

"You were asked a question, Viscount Journal. Please reply before you leave our company."

The healer was no fool. He could also hear the dangerous notes in the cleric's tone. Apparently, Father Nor's reputation reached far beyond the walls of the magical academy.

"Yes, he will live," the man replied, grimacing as if he'd just taken a bite out of a lemon. The viscount clearly did not enjoy fielding a question from the lower class. "Run, jump and even talk, if you'd like. Is that it? Satisfied? Or are you now going to make me examine some trinket this...student dredged up from the rift?"

"I am indeed," nodded Father Nor. "Max, did you have something to show us?"

"Here." I removed the katar and pulled out the glowing red stone. "Do you think, Viscount Journal, that the exclusive *Amplify* stone is a valuable enough reward for you to risk your life and save the dark one?"

Such a silence fell over the room that I could even hear the Evil Engineer's quiet breathing.

Smooth, but terribly weak.

"Possibly," whispered the healer. "These stones are the stuff of legend..."

"A legend in the flesh." Father Nor acted as if he had expected this from me. "May I? Yes, this is *Amplify* — that's the characteristic pictograph. Sir Chancellor, I ask you to confirm the authenticity and value of the stone."

"Confirm? This is an exclusive stone, Father Nor! What else needs to be confirmed? But where did he find it?" Kimal Sarento was as impressed as the healer. "Max, we need details!"

"Your question is misplaced," I said, throwing the ball over to the Evil Engineer's court. "When I found him, this stone was in his hand. The one that was cut off. A doomed soldier named the Countess told me a story that those who possess such stones gain their freedom, so I kept it for myself. However, if I have to choose between my freedom and my mentor's life, then it's obvious what must be done. There are plenty of red beasts below us — I'm sure this stone fell out of one of them. I'm going back down to genocide the lot of them. Even if I have to destroy hundreds, I will reach my goal. But only later, once the Evil Engineer is back on his feet."

"So he's also a doomer?!"

Great light, what an annoying voice this cockroach had.

"We need your answer, Viscount." Father Nor brought the conversation back to business. "Are you willing to take the risk for the amplifier?"

"I need a partner, I can't do it alone." Beads of sweat broke out on his forehead. He wouldn't take his eyes off the stone, clearly thinking of how he'd embed it. Even though the stone was considered a fairy tale, the cockroach knew perfectly well what it was capable of.

"Magister Smalog will be your assistant, but the main burden will still fall on you," the chancellor opened the door and invited the magister inside. "What preparations do you need to make?"

"I need recovery elixirs," the healer muttered. "A lot of them...and I also need the stone. Right now. I'll have to insert it in a less than ideal spot and strengthen my *Heal*. I can't do it without it."

"Of course, Viscount. We'll quickly draw up a contract and the stone is yours!" In negotiations, when the other side made demands, Kimal Sarento was always professional. "I suggest you go to my office. Father Nor, may I have the stone? It needs to be prepared for integration. Today, our empire will witness the birth of not just a healer, but a ruler among all healers!"

The procession left the office. Magister Smalog began to fuss over the Evil Engineer's body, preparing it for restoration, and I stared into the eyes of Father Nor, unable to tear my gaze away. He stood only a pace away, giving me a look that made me uncomfortable.

"You acted wisely," said Father Nor at last. "A doomer only has the right to exchange an exclusive stone for his freedom after he has been officially included in the rankings. Despite the fact that you have already gone through one rift and are officially listed as a representative of the Fortress, you are not in the rankings. You can't be given an assignment. Therefore, nothing that you pull from the rift belongs to you. If you had shown me this stone after the viscount left, I would have taken it without further ado. Now about the fact that you lied to me. Didn't finish. Forgot. Choose any excuse you'd like, the essence is the same. What you have done is unacceptable. Apparently, you were given too long a leash. You forgot who you are and what you're doing here. Hand over the katars — the academy does not allow doomed soldiers to carry weapons. Your steel bracelets will be returned to you. Your privileged position is being revoked. No special training, lectures, dances. From now on, you are an ordinary doomer who will pass through our academy in three months. And two weeks have already elapsed.

Chapter 10

(Office of the High Priest, late night)

"WOULD YOU PLEASE EXPLAIN this decision? I thought I made it very clear that Max deserves a reward," the High Priest wearily rested his head on his hand. The highest hierarch of the church permitted himself displays of weakness in front of few people, and Father Nor was one of them.

"Two reasons." The gaunt servant of the Light poured himself a glass of water. It had been an exceedingly difficult day. "First: I really don't like the amount of attention the chancellor is surrounding Max with. Kimal Sarento made his first power move when he sent out his personal weapon, his mistress Tarra Lloyd. It costs her nothing to fool the boy, forcing him to do her bidding, and by proxy, the chancellor's. No matter what anyone might claim to the contrary, our little doomer is still just a brainless boy. While Max was in the punishment cell, Tarra made three attempts to reach him, but each time our brothers in the Light managed to expel her. What could this be, if not a ploy to earn trust and make the doomed soldier a faithful lap dog? I respect this woman as a high-level professional, but when she oversteps into our territory, I become extremely aggressive. It's a great deal easier to fight dark beasts than it is to resist the magic of this woman's charms. I suppose it's worth mentioning offhand to Max that she's actually over sixty years old and not even fit to be his grand-mother — his great-grandmother, maybe. This should at least give him pause, before that satisfied smile breaks across his face from her every touch."

"Do you think the chancellor wants to use Max as a loyal agent within the Fortress?"

"All signs point that way. For instance, making the connection with Magister Hwan and, through him, a beautiful mentor in swordsmanship. I can believe in many things, Father Urg, but not coincidence. Ursula de Vrath is undeniably a professional with a capital 'P,' but she is, first and foremost, a beautiful girl around the same age as Max. I am of the opinion that she was meant to stir up the interest of an eighteen-year-old boy, and that Tarra Loyd, as someone who sees the doomer as more than just empty space, will reap the fruits of their joint labors. I have already stated that Max does not need dance or rapier lessons. The best case scenario would be locking him in the rift and periodically sending down food. Three months and he'd be able to descend to level eight or nine. That's level four or five in a normal rift. However, my suggestions were ignored. Kimal Sarento made it clear that preparing the doomed soldier to enter the Fortress is the academy's responsibility. By surrounding Max with care and beautiful women, the chancellor will make him an addict. Generate a sense of affection. A sense of debt to the Academy. Given the young man's prospects, Kimal Sarento must be stopped at the very start, even if I am wrong and the chancellor's motives are pure."

"Sometimes I get the feeling that you'd suspect even yourself, if the opportunity arose," Father Urg chuckled bitterly. The High Priest had grown to trust his friend.

"I'm only a man and I may be mistaken," Father Nor said, rubbing his eyes. "The incident with the name is proof of this. Everything will become clear within the week. If Tarra jumps into Max's bed, we'll need to pull him out of the academy in three months. I considered using Max as a double agent, leaking false information to the chancellor through him, but it's all too complicated. We need Father Dvar and his resourceful mind, but we must not initiate him into the affairs of the dark. This choice will be fraught with consequences. The second reason is quite simple: I don't like the freedom Max has been enjoying. He stopped fearing me. Soon, he will begin to perceive me as his mentor or friend. This may be acceptable while he is still at the academy, but he may start to get the wrong ideas about his place in the world. I need to keep my distance. The Evil Engineer is enough to handle on his own without allowing another dark one into the close circle. I think it's time to give Max a trusted servant who will make a long-term alliance with him. And don't even look my way — I can't handle two of them. My age won't allow it."

"Where can I find a worthy servant for you?" pondered the High Priest.

"Not just worthy, but someone who will follow along the path with the dark one. Wherever it may lead. As I would with the Evil Engineer. Now I have distanced myself from Max — he must learn to see me as a threat, otherwise, because of his age, he will begin to break the rules one by one. As he would with *Amplify*. He knew what the stone meant, but he thought he was smart enough not just to hold it for safekeeping, but to use it for himself. So no — his sense of brotherhood fled. Now the empire has one more cursed artifact of Skron and something will need to be done about it. I'll have to keep an eye on the viscount too. Where I'll find the time for all this...in short, I believe that only one person should be great and magnanimous — the High Priest. The rest of us need to prepare doomed soldiers for their difficult life in society."

"Are you trying to say that my presence is required at the academy once more?" Father Urg chuckled. "To chide an overzealous fanatic and give Max some of his privileges back? It will reinforce my place as the one making decisions in the doomed soldier's eyes. And, if something happens, he will not go to the chancellor, but will seek a meeting with me. Alright, let's do that. Make a list of what you need to return and warn Kimal that tomorrow, I will visit the academy. It's time for the dark one to receive his rewards."

(Magical Academy, the morning after returning from the rift)

I opened my eyes and stared up at the ceiling. The habit of waking up at half past five had become so ingrained over the past weeks that all hope of sleep evaporated as soon as I woke and my body demanded action. But there would be no action today, except for the three-hour trip to the range. Father Nor was at least consistent in his decision to transform me into an ordinary doomed soldier, deprived of any privileges. My roommates were also shamelessly dozing off — like me, their next activity wasn't scheduled for another three hours. And it was breakfast. Then a four-hour rest and a new activity code-named "lunch." Then another three hours at the training ground, enjoying the company of dark beasts, and one more training session in the form of dinner. That's it! Compared to the nightmare I'd been living in for the past few weeks, it seemed like a cake walk. Unless I considered the fact that two and a half months from now, I'd be thrown out of the academy like a bad dog. And then came the beasts of the rift, strong teeth and a flash of pain, and then eternal darkness. As the Evil Engineer's example had shown, even the most experienced and strongest doomers were never more than guests in the rift.

"Why are you still here?" The chubby roommate asked. I had never learned their names and, if I was being honest, I didn't want to.

"Overslept," I replied, getting out of bed. Alright, that's enough! I couldn't get lazy. As long as I had the opportunity to train, I must! Even the hundredth of a percent I'd gain on my physical parameters would make me stronger and, quite possibly, help me survive. I had a purpose and no one could stand in my way. Even the ever-offended Father Nor!

"What's that?" I asked, nodding in the direction of a sack that had appeared against the far wall. The bag was too large not to be noticed.

"Food," a satisfied grin broke across the fat man's face. "You have no idea what you can order for just one gold! The gruel they serve in the cafeteria doesn't even compare to what you can get from the city bakeries. Do you want a bun? Don't just pass it up, doomed brother! I know you keep your distance, you were an aristocrat in a past life, and the loss is still fresh. We won't impose — if you don't want to talk, don't. But it's also not a good idea to refuse a gift. They got our order wrong. They brought so much that the two of us can't finish it alone. So will you help? It's really a feast for the eyes and stomach. They only brought it last night, still fresh.”

“Alright.” I caved. I've had a sweet tooth since childhood. Gustav constantly grumbled if he caught me with buns. My training sessions were always harder when he did.

“Here!” the tall one opened the bag and, without looking inside, conjured a hearty loaf like a magician. Well packed and protected from air so it wouldn't go stale, soft to the touch. He didn't toss it to me, but delivered it straight to my waiting hands. I nodded gratefully, removed the protective film and nearly choked on my saliva — I hadn't had dinner yesterday. Three days, in fact, without food or water, and here was this delicious morsel.

“You can really put it down, dude!” the fat one drawled enviously, as soon as the huge loaf evaporated in my mouth. It was the most delicious pastry I'd ever had in my life and it went down in a few bites. My roomies weren't wrong — it was an order of magnitude better than our cafeteria food.

“Want more? Don't be shy. Look how much good stuff we have. And the gold was yours anyway. Try another. Go get him one, bro.”

The second roll went down just like the first, but this time I was able to stretch it out and luxuriate in the flavor for several minutes. Digging in my backpack, I pulled out my purse of gold and took out four coins. Two for each.

“I have nowhere to keep them for now, but I see you've managed to fix the place up. That should be rewarded. AND...”

I didn't make it to the end of this sentence before there was a pounding on the door that threatened to break it off its hinges.

"Get up, doomer! Why in Skron's name aren't you at training?"

"What are you doing here?" I opened the door and was face-to-face with Fardi, who was already in her training jumpsuit.

"You plan on training in your underpants?" The girl's voice was full of vitriol. "The dark one woke me up today and ordered me to drag you to training. You have five minutes."

"In case you haven't noticed, I've been given new jewelry," I held up the steel bracelets. It was impossible not to notice them. "And with these tchotchkes, unfortunately, the path to the arena is closed to me."

"What does the arena have to do with it? The dark one is waiting for us at the training grounds. Let's go, faster!"

"Dark one? What dark one?" I heard my fat roommate ask. Karina winced in distaste. She barely had the energy to talk to me, and here was another doomer. A cut-throat murderer from the dregs of society. A perfect conversation partner for the daughter of a duke.

"Bear in mind, doomer, that our mentor gave me strict instructions: if, for some reason, you refuse, I am supposed to twist you into a pretzel and carry you on my back. You already look pretty salty, so it should suit you. And I will carry out this order. I'm not going to get punished because of you. You have four minutes. I'll wait outside."

Fardi was determined, so I had no choice but to obey. Pulling on my jumpsuit, I once again thanked my neighbors for the rolls and ran after the girl. The fact that the Evil Engineer was on his feet already was good news. The fact that he could not come to me on his own was not. Apparently, Father Nor's order left no room for interpretation.

I noticed my mentor from a distance. He was standing next to the training grounds, arms crossed over his chest. His own hands. Whole and healthy. And he stood on two legs. Also intact — the doctors had managed to restore his lost foot.

"You're late." The Evil Engineer's consistently irritated tone was actually comforting. Even if the world turned upside down, the dark one would always be dissatisfied. He paid no attention to me, as if I did not exist at all. "You will be punished for this — no warm up in the arena. For starters, ten laps around the training grounds. Don't feel sorry for yourself, push yourself to the max. If some piddly little runt suddenly starts running behind you, I want you to knock his teeth down his throat after the third lap. What are you waiting for, Fardi, an invitation? March!"

I barely held back a smile. A cleric stood nearby, carefully recording every word the dark one said in his notepad. So formally, I didn't exist for my mentor. Since Father Nor gave the order, it must be obeyed. But this "piddly little runt" remark could mean nothing other than "just you see what happens if you fall behind Fardi — I'll eat you alive." So as soon as Karina rushed off to the races, I was right on her heels. After so many days of training together, I knew very well that my partner still had her limits. They were somewhere in the clouds, but they were clearly defined. Something to strive for, and to one day exceed. As I stuck doggedly to Karina, around the sixth lap, I suddenly realized that this was a comfortable tempo for me. I wasn't at my limit, wasn't tearing my tendons to keep up. This revelation came as such a surprise that I nearly stumbled on a rock. Unlike the pristine arena, the area around the training grounds left much to be desired. We completed another lap and I approached within arm's length of the girl, a task which had seemed impossible just two weeks ago.

I moved to pass her!

Fardi didn't back down. When she noticed I was trying to pass her, she sped up, and for a while we were on equal footing. Now I had to give it my all — but the eight laps behind me and lack of normal food had their effect. But I wasn't about to give up — I was consumed by the excitement of victory. Even if after the tenth lap, I fell and never got up again, for now I'd do everything not only to keep up with Fardi, but to leave her in the dust. All I needed to do was move my legs a little faster.

I don't remember the tenth lap — it became a prolonged struggle to get a full breath of air. My lungs were torn apart, my legs were filled with lead, there was a rumble in my head, and blood might have even trickled from my nose, but I didn't notice any of this, focusing on only one thing: rounding the last bend and seeing my eternally dissatisfied mentor standing there. This was all that mattered, this was my main goal now. Run to the dark one. Crawl. But get there first.

The ground slipped from under my feet as I crossed the finish line. I simply didn't have the strength to stay upright. My chest slammed into the ground and I lay there, convulsively gasping for air. When the buzzing in my ears subsided, I heard the very end of a conversation, and Great Light, I would give anything to have heard the beginning!

"...now he's suffocating! A mistake, a mediocrity who decided to come to warm up this morning!"

"Sir, this is..." Karina still couldn't catch her breath.

"No excuses! Shame on you, Fardi. This is pure disgrace! Take it lying down — one-handed plank. Switch every minute. And don't you dare give up. Or this will be our last training session. Do or die! Move!"

My brain was still barely able to form thoughts, but my body obeyed. My arms began to tremble after just ten seconds due to the catastrophic lack of oxygen. But our mentor's rebuke had affected more than just Karina — I was also inspired. Don't give up, even when it's bad.

"Done!" The Evil Engineer's order cut through the darkness. I collapsed to the ground, falling on my side. Disgust prevented me from falling straight forward. My morning rolls had evacuated my mortal body, unable to withstand the pressure.

"Next exercise. Move, Fardi! Do you want to come in second again?"

Two hours of arrant mockery ended just as deplorably. Karina and I were left lying on the ground, unable to get up. I wasn't the only one who threw up — the golden girl also sullied the soil. And there were no butterflies in it. The Evil Engineer wasn't playing around and kept periodically increasing the load. I hadn't felt so bad since our first training session.

"I have no idea how you'll make it back to your bed, but you can only drink your elixirs there. I'll be waiting for you after lunch. It's time to show you what real training looks like. Now that you're not limited by a weaker partner, you can reach your full potential. You need to work off the effort that has been invested in you, Fardi. Since Father Nor considers you a potential Sweeper, you should at least look like one from a distance."

He turned and set off toward the main building, any interest he had in us gone. But there was no rest for me — Fardi's caustic voice rang in my ear.

"You're a freak, doomer! I hate you, you filthy creature! I would give anything to go back a month. I would beg my father to destroy you! Crush you like a cockroach! I hate you!"

"You're repeating yourself." I tried to get up but my arms gave way. They wouldn't lift me off the ground. Gathering my strength, I growled and rolled onto my back with a jerk. Then onto my stomach. And back again. Somewhere to the side of me was my backpack. It contained a recovery vial. No one had forbidden *me* from drinking recovery elixirs, so within a few minutes, my strength would return and I'd be able to stand up. All I had to do now was bridge the small remaining gap and roll straight to my target. Because I wouldn't have the strength to try again.

"He's here!" I heard someone's voice call when I'd nearly reached the backpack. I only had two rolls left but I couldn't finish them right away. I needed rest first. Jerking to one side again, I rolled onto my back and stared at the strange procession approaching — several dozen churchmen in different colored robes were moving toward us from the main building. The unique golden cassock immediately attracted attention. There was only one like it in the whole church. What had the High Priest forgotten at the academy? And why was he walking toward me? Roll! I needed my bag!

"What's wrong with him?" The crowd approached me just as I rolled over to the bag and even managed to throw my hand over it. Now I just had to get to the elixir, drag it to my mouth without spilling it, and drink. Just three little movements! Two hours of work, no more.

"Training," the cleric in charge of monitoring Fardi replied.

"The dark one disobeyed my order?" The voice belonged to Father Nor, but I couldn't pick him out in the crowd.

"The dark one only trained Fardi. There were no orders given preventing other students from practicing on their own in the vicinity of the Evil Engineer."

"Now there is," Father Nor ordered sternly. "The doomer Max has no right to study with the dark mentor!"

"Really, Father Nor, why so harsh?" The High Priest addressed this question somewhere to the right. Apparently that's where the wiry cleric was standing. Bring Max back to his senses. I understand that he has an elixir in his backpack? Help him."

A life-giving warmth spread through my body, returning control of my extremities. I rose to my feet and bowed in greeting to the congregation. Against the background of neutral, and even good-natured faces, Father Nor's expression stuck out like a sore thumb. Like a second, ever-disgruntled Evil Engineer.

"You should not restrict the doomer's desire to improve himself," the High Priest finished his thought. "If Max is certain that he can withstand the program we prepared for our young star, who are we to interfere with him? I believe that in a couple of days, he himself will understand the futility of his attempts and stop. Your influence is not needed, the situation will resolve itself. By the way, what is Karina Fardi doing in such an unpresentable form?"

"Warm-up at maximum power," the same monitor reported. "Per the dark one's orders, recovery elixirs are only permitted once they're in their own bed. We are not allowed to touch or aid. Only monitor."

"Hmm...sounds like the dark one. Always push yourself to the limit, otherwise what's it all for? Dear child, may I request your assistance?"

I turned around and gulped. The student Father Urg had called upon was Miralda Lertan. The princess and her retinue had come to watch Fardi suffer, but had caught the High Priest's eye.

"High Priest." The princess stepped closer and made a beautiful curtsy. "What assistance do you require?"

"Nothing that will sully your honor or be beyond your power. On the ground, as you can see, lies a sister of the Fortress. Karina Fardi must be delivered to her dormitory, carefully placed in bed, and — I emphasize — *carefully* pour a recovery elixir into her mouth. I don't think anyone in the academy could do a better job of this than you. May the Light go with you, dear child. Oh yes, and one more thing...You must not employ the help of any of your retinue, and every step will be monitored. One sideways glance toward Fardi, one careless or accidental movement that may harm her, one word against her, even spoken in a whisper, will be considered an attack on the church. If you, dear child, think that mocking a daughter of the Fortress will give you more authority, then I dare to dispel your illusions. Your punishment will be severe and you will not be able to avoid it. Have I made my point clear, or does the princess wish to object?"

I was as frightened as if my mirror had suddenly fallen. The good-natured old man had crushed Miralda into the dirt and walked over her in boots. The public humiliation was much worse than suffering the humiliation itself. What a blow to her reputation! And most unpleasant for the princess was the fact that she knew there was nothing derisive in the High Priest's request — simply providing help to a member of the Fortress. But the way he marked her boundaries and drew the line in the sand...it was beautiful.

"I will be happy to provide the Fortress with all possible assistance," Miralda said through her teeth, after which she lifted Karina in her arms like a weightless doll and, head held high, set off toward the dorms. Her retinue rushed after her, some ran past to clear the way, but Father Urg no longer cared. The High Priest had once again turned his attention to me.

"So it's decided. The doomer MAx has the right to work with the Evil Engineer. And at the same time, the dark one himself is within his rights to ignore Max. Father Nor, is it possible to train in the arena with such bracelets?"

"No, they would destroy whoever was wearing them."

"Then we have a dilemma. On the one hand, we have permitted Max to train, on the other, we have limited him. I propose we be consistent — for as long as the doomed soldier can keep up with Fardi, he will be relieved of his shackles. As soon as he surrenders, they will be returned. I trust you have no objection to this, Father Nor?"

"I'll have a talk with Dark Senior to ensure he gives Fardi the maximum possible load that she can handle over the next two or three days." Father Nor was clearly upset with me. Was it possible that a stone was influencing him to behave like this?

"If you so wish. However, I propose to move on to the issue we actually came here to resolve. Sir Chancellor, you've come just in time. The Fortress has decided to reward one quick-footed doomed soldier. It's not every day that we get our hands on an active member of the dark coven. Please take a look at this sheet. We need your help, Kimal. It's time to integrate the stones into Max's being and figure out just what's going on in the academy. A reliable source tells me that a servant of Magister Elor somehow wound up on campus. The only thing left to do is check every person at the academy in order to root them out. Every single one. Including your most secret and trusted confidants. When shall we give Max his new stones?"

Chapter 11

"SIT DOWN," Kimal Sarento pointed to a chair. The office, which was filled to the brim with strange devices, was located in the main building, but it was impossible to simply wander in. Several steel doors, a security post, no windows. A most secret room with secret devices. I looked around, captivated, hoping in vain that I could figure out which did what. I didn't even care that I must have looked like some rube experiencing the hustle and bustle of city life for the very first time.

Everything was terribly interesting, but completely incomprehensible.

"The process of integrating stones can be divided into three parts," the chancellor explained, taking the padded box containing the stones from the High Priest. "The first stage is preparation. The magic stones are processed in a particular way that allows them to interact with the person. The mechanism behind it is simple, but at the same time quite complex. I can't reveal the details, as you understand — academy secrets. But I can give you a peek under the veil of secrecy: this is the device used in the preparation process. We place the stone or, in our case, stones, into this special receptacle, give the order to our experts, and within a few minutes, we receive the results. Then comes stage two. This consists of the recipient — in this case, Max — using another device to place the stones within his chest. It sounds unsettling, I know, but in reality, there's nothing frightening or dangerous about it. The integration happens on a different plane than the physical. And finally, stage three is the direct installation of the stone into your magic field. This is carried out using a third device according to a predetermined algorithm. Nothing complicated. But! You, my friend, are not just an ordinary person — you have a dark essence. And here, gentlemen, is where certain doubts arise. As we all know, unlike all of us, Max is able to access his status bar, magic field, and other attributes that are inaccessible to us. If we act strictly by the book, there's a possibility that things will not go according to plan. In this regard, before we start the standard process, I propose to take a unique opportunity and test our ward's abilities. Father Urg, do you mind?"

"What exactly are you going to test Max on?"

"I want to test a certain theory. Some are of the opinion that dark ones can integrate stones not just without our devices, but without fire as well. That is, a conscious remodeling of one's ability field."

"Which leads us to some rather unpleasant conclusions," the High Priest contemplated aloud. "If the dark ones can insert stones at will, then their fields may be perfect. Reaching their highest potential."

"Which will affect the way we train our brothers," said Father Nor. "For now we operate under the assumption that if the dark ones have ability and enhancement stones, they act separately, in no way affecting each other. If the chancellor's theory is confirmed, we will have to rethink things. Nevertheless, I have my doubts — the younger dark didn't integrate *Amplify.* Either he didn't know how to do it, or wasn't given the opportunity."

"Which is why I suggest testing him. Father Urg?"

"Maybe I agree. Maybe Max really can integrate the stones independently. But who can guarantee that the integration process won't place the stones randomly, completely ruining the system we've created? One stone out of place is enough to render the whole project useless. If you'd like to run tests, you can do so after we've finished with our stones."

"As you wish." Kimal kept his composure. "In that case, you will need to wait a couple of minutes. Father Urg, would you be so kind as to pass me the stones? They must be prepared."

"I'm sure this is a stupid question, but could you loop me in on what exactly I'm integrating? Where, why, how? How will it affect my ability to kill dark beasts?"

"A reasonable request." The chancellor looked to Father Urg. "Max really doesn't have a clue what you're planning to give him?"

"The younger dark's task is to carry out the Fortress' orders, no matter how strange or unpleasant they may seem," Father Nor said, once again demonstrating his geniality. "The task will be given after the integration is complete."

"Father Nor, sometimes excessively severe measures do more harm than good," the High Priest said, softening the cleric's decision. "It won't hurt if we tell Max what's in store while the stones are being prepared. Whatever one may say, he's the one who will have to use these new abilities. Not me, not you. No matter how deadly a weapon may be, it still requires care and respect. Or else it will break. Think about it, Father Nor."

"Your field." A lean attendant approached and dispassionately held out a sheet of paper. A five-by-five grid with several filled cells with sets of numbers. Each number was deciphered below. I spent some time away from reality, trying to calculate my new prospects. Apparently the church had finally decided to make me not of this world.

Analyze — number of active facets: 4. Stone level: 1. Active ability. Range: 10 meters. Speed: 1

use every 30 seconds (60 without support stone). Mana cost: 15 (30 without support stone).

Spell Haste — a support stone that increases your spell casting speed by 2X. Every 5 gem levels, the speed factor increases by 0.5.

Reduce Cost — a support gem that reduces the cost of using a spell by 2X. Every 5 gem levels, the cost factor increases by 0.5.

Dark Essence — a support stone that allows you to study the parameters of Skron's dark beasts. Requirements: the presence of the *Analyze* stone.

Amplify — a support stone that increases the parameters of related ability gems by 2X. Increases parameters of paired amplification stones by 2X. Each additional stone level increases the coefficient by 0.5. Warning! Using this stone reduces mental defense against darkness.

"Um..." I said pointedly, raising a dumbfounded face to the High Priest. "*Amplify?*"

"Why are you surprised?" Father Urg was the very picture of kindness and grace. "The Fortress always adequately compensates those who put their life on the line for the church's cause. You were able to capture a representative of the dark coven, and thanks to your efforts, we identified ten converts hiding among the civilian populace. A deed like this must not go unnoticed."

"Striking my name from the list of doomed soldiers and reclassifying me as a living person would have been better," I muttered quietly to myself, but the High Priest still heard.

"It is all the better that you reminded me of your position. You very well could obtain your freedom with an *Amplify* stone. But only ordinary doomed soldiers who don't bear the 'dark' label may receive it. This method will not work for you. Even if you achieve the impossible and bring us ten amplification stones, it will not affect your status. You will remain a doomed soldier. A rich one, for we will pay for every stone you find, but a doomed soldier nonetheless. If you would like to return to the land of the living, you'll have to find another way. They do exist, I won't hide this from you, but you will have to seek them out yourself."

"What?!" I exclaimed, and would have jumped from my chair had the strong hands of the servants not held me down.

"Perhaps your merits do deserve further reward, so I will tell you of one method," the man robed in gold continued, ignoring my indignation. "There is a secret decree in the Zarak Empire, signed into action by the great grandfather of the current emperor. It says that if a doomed soldier is still alive ten years after his official registration with the Fortress, he will be pardoned. Unfortunately, throughout the entire existence of this law, we have never had occasion to invoke it, so no one else in your brotherhood knows about the decree, but it is certainly still in force. If you survive ten years, have found no other path to return to the land of the living, and remain faithful to the Light, you will be free. I give you the word of the High Priest!"

The indignation, which should have left, was stuck in my throat. Ten years! But what did this mean — ten whole years or ten years altogether? It was an enormous difference — and a lot was riding on it.

"But you didn't respond — why can't I use *Amplify?*"

"Sir Chancellor, I believe everything is ready. We may proceed to the next step." Father Urg could be even worse than Father Nor when he wanted to be! At the same time, I knew that if I continued to be indignant, they could easily cut off all my other escape routes, leaving me with this ten-year sentence. Alright, you bastards, you think you've won? Don't make me laugh! There was still the Evil Engineer, who owed me, no matter what anyone might claim to the contrary. I'd slam him against the wall and demand he tell me how he got free. I doubt he used a stone. But one thing was clear: no more sentimentality! No more resentment, cries of indignation, or other impulsive shows of emotion. The churchmen would use my every word against me and revel in their superiority. I needed to pretend that I'd come to terms with serving my ten years and then shake down the other doomers for information. If there was a price, I'd pay it. My life was more important. And I was not particularly happy with what was going on here, either. The stones were always described as beneficial, but what was this 'mental defense' it mentioned? How would it affect my mirror? I didn't want to become an ordinary doomer who had to face the dark beasts head on. I wanted to continue sneaking up on them and jamming my katars in their weak spots.

Warning! Launching magic stone integration process.
Would you like to interrupt, accept, or seize control of the process?

"Hmm...this is unusual." The chancellor frowned as the machine pressed to my chest began to hum curiously. "This has never happened before."

"I seized control of the process," I said, attracting the rapt attention of everyone assembled. "What? Did you really think I'd allow you to stick something inside me without a single word of explanation about what it's all for? Especially *Amplify*. A stone that the emperor's healer himself was willing to risk his life for! And you're simply giving it to a doomed soldier, knowing full well that you can't get it back. What is mental defense and why will it decrease if I implant myself with this stone? What will happen to my mirror? What do you expect me to do with *Analyze*? Why do I need *Dark Essence*? My dear fellow members of the clergy, let us share information and not try to use me as a pawn in your strange games. As evidence shows, I work much more effectively when I understand what I'm doing."

"So you've already received the stones and can install them at any moment?" the chancellor clarified. "The device is no longer needed? Let's see…it's true, the stones really are gone! We have proven what we set out to determine — dark ones can reconstruct their magic field at will. We aren't fighting madmen who received their stones by chance, but trained mages who are fully capable of wielding their dark abilities."

"This information must still be verified," Father Nor, as always, chimed in with his remarks. "Dark one, you must integrate the stones according to the scheme we've designed. Do it now."

"I will not!" I went for broke. "I've read the law. The Fortress can oblige me to perform any action dictated by any of its servants. From killing dark beasts to cleaning the toilets. But it must be a physical action I can perform, and not the mental process of integrating stones. I am ready to submit, to do what you demand, but only after I understand how it will affect me. Because new stones, especially those that reduce mental defenses, whatever that means, will certainly affect my performance in the rift."

"You will be punished," came Father Nor's icy tones.

"For what?" I raised a brow ostentatiously. "I'm doing everything I'm told. I'm sitting in a chair, submitting to the chancellor's device, and I'm ready to move on to the next one. The fact that something didn't work properly isn't my fault. I stand before you, innocent, Father Nor. I'm doing everything you asked, but for some reason, the integration process isn't working. I think Sir Chancellor must have done something wrong. Or the devices have been sabotaged. Or the stars are out of alignment. Basically, you can blame anything but me. And anything I may have said before was pure bravado."

"Do you understand what it means to defy the Fortress?" Father Urg smiled, but there was not even a hint of warmth. "Your words may hold up in court, but there is no court for doomed soldiers. Father Nor is right — you should be punished for your position. You must remember who you are. A doomed soldier. Without rights or free will."

Magic stone integration process interrupted.

Accept current formation or materialize for later use?

Five stones appeared before my eyes. Under the gaze of those gathered, I reached out my hand and took one of them, converting it back into material form. Then I repeated the trick with the others, holding out my open hand to Father Nor.

"I'm ready for my punishment. I'm ready for you to deprive me of everything, and maybe even my life. Ready to do any job, any orders, no matter how strange and stupid they may seem to me. But I will not allow my essence to be altered just because it is currently beneficial for the Fortress.

You do not have this right. As soon as it's explained to me why I need these stones in my field, they will appear there. But no earlier."

"Sir Chancellor, repeat the procedure. The stones will be integrated nonetheless. Even if we must render the dark one unconscious."

The blow to the back of the head was so unexpected that I passed out instantly, no warning. It was just suddenly dark. However, when the lights came back on, a familiar phrase was floating before my eyes:

Warning! Launching magic stone integration process.

Would you like to interrupt, accept, or seize control of the process?

My hands had been tied, evidently so I couldn't interfere with the process, so I had to materialize the stones with just my mind. One by one, the stones manifested before me and fell to the floor. No going back now, it was too late — I had drawn my line in the sand. It had to happen sooner or later, so why not now. It was time to defend my interests from a position of power. Even though I didn't have a lot of power to begin with.

"Father Urg, I need a persuasion specialist. Two hours of work with him and the dark one will do everything he is obliged."

"I believe we should think about what has happened here," The High Priest looked at me as if I had grown horns. "We shouldn't do anything rash. Although, I confess, I would very much like to. We had such a difficult time agreeing on the integration of unique stones and considered it a privilege to receive them, so we did not anticipate this reaction. It is completely unreasonable and, frankly, quite stupid. Five stones, upgrading all others to level three, turning a simple doomed soldier into a unique weapon against the dark beasts...However, our gift proved objectionable. Our actions, objectionable. Evidently, the Fortress itself has become objectionable to a doomed soldier who was granted too much freedom. I think we must take serious considerations. We will come to a decision as soon as possible. Escort the doomer Max to the room where he will await his punishment..."

(Magical academy. Father Nor's office)

"Who does he think he is?" Father Urg was practically shooting lightning from his fingertips, pacing in circles around the office. "Inexperienced little boy, barely torn from his mother's teat and he's already flexing his rights!"

"Don't forget where you are," Father Nor smiled. "In the magical academy, even the walls have ears. What will people think if they find out that the High Priest experiences negative emotions?"

"Ears? In your own office?" Father Urg sat on a chair and started spinning a pencil in his hands. "I would never believe you allowed this to happen."

"No, of course not, but I'm tired of watching you run around in circles. What do you plan to do with Max?"

"Plan to do with him? He should be flogged, and by someone with expertise. So we don't sit around for another week! Just think — to refuse a gift from the High Priest!"

"His stance is reasonable, logical and shows his maturity. And technically, he is acting fully within the law. It is unlikely that was able to do anything while he was unconscious."

"You should not be protecting him! The Fortress cannot suffer another Countess!"

"I fear that Max will prove much more unpleasant than the Countess," Father Nor frowned. "If you punish him physically, you will have lost. You'll be left with a broken doomed soldier, which are a dime a dozen in the Fortress. It's time to make a decision, Father Urg. Max needs a personal servant of the Light."

"Then do it yourself," Father Urg shot back at him, chewing over his words. "The doomer must be punished. One simply does not refuse a gift from the High Priest. The public wouldn't understand. What is your opinion, dark beast expert?"

"If you want my opinion, you should take the stones, call Max in here again and calmly explain why he needs *Analyze* and *Dark Essence*, and why *Amplify* will only make him stronger. But of course, we must not do this. The hit to our reputation would be too great. I suggest we put him to work in the field. There are seven rifts in the vicinity of the capital. We'll let him tag along with a beginner group. Let him cleanse a few rifts with them, witness the bloodshed, let him see the others die, and then he'll understand that he will not survive without preparation. And what's more, we'll hold him responsible for the deaths of the others. He still has a conscience, so this should dampen his spirits. After two or three rifts, we'll return to this conversation. And then we can deign to explain the purpose of the stones. Although I believe the loss of this team will make Max more accommodating, and he'll accept *Amplify* without further ado."

"How will we justify expelling a doomed soldier from the academy prematurely? Kimal Sarento will be opposed, and now is not the time to start conflict. I don't like the rift under the academy. Something must be urgently done — if there is a range there, that means the Riftmaster has already reached level fourteen. Within six months, chaos may be unleashed."

"That's why I want to send Max to the active rifts — he needs experience. Here, he won't be training anything but his mirror. And there will be no expulsion — only a punishment for refusing the gift of the High Priest. One lasting, say, three weeks. That's enough time for him to close two rifts. The doomer will serve his three months at the academy. Although you know my opinion — he no longer needs them. We're just wasting time."

"Have you considered what happens if no one

dies? What will you do in that case?"

"A beginner group closing three rifts with no deaths?" Father Nor looked at the High Priest in astonishment. "If Max manages to single-handedly cleanse the rift and saves the life of the entire group, then my opinions about his fate will have nothing to do with it. We have no control over Paladins. You will have to search for a new dark one and start his education anew, from scratch."

"Are you that sure of the boy?"

"I'm not even sure of myself, why would I suddenly put my confidence in a stupid boy who decided to defy the Fortress? But if I'm correct, then *Analyze* will only hinder him. You've read the archives."

"*Devour* is even greater a legend than Paladins." Father Urg used his hands to prop up his head, heavy with the weight of a thousand thoughts.

"That's why I propose we not be too hasty and act with consistency. First, we see if he can cope with a one-level rift. Then we'll send him to a two-level. If necessary, we'll go up to a three-level. And at the same time, we'll be able to find out what kind of map he managed to get his hands on."

"What say the Evil Engineer?"

"Nothing. He doesn't know what the map fragment is or why Max received it. I am inclined to believe him. I think it's time we find out what happens if you collect all five fragments. There are only four more rifts in the area indicated on Max's map."

"If my memory serves me, one of them is a four-level? Do you want to send it there too?"

"Consistency, Father Urg. Everything must be done in order."

"Fine. Then today I will assert my own will — I believe I know who to give Max as his personal servant. I am sure you will not approve the candidacy."

(Dark coven. Turb, Capital of the Zarak Empire)

"Are you sure it's safe?" Magister Elor carefully tracked the emotions of his senior acolyte.

"Yes, sir! The loss of our brother has not affected the coven's work. The organization was established according to all your recommendations — none of the twenty members knows any of each other's names or contacts. I am the sole possessor of this knowledge, but I bear the seal of Skron. If they capture me, my soul will be set free. The light ones can do whatever they wish with my body. I have good news for you, sir. We managed to deliver a living body to the academy and hand it over to your inside man. Two days later, we once again entered the academy and removed the body. Alive and unharmed. The academy guards suspected nothing. As soon as you decide to act, twenty bodies will be delivered to the desired point within three days. The main problem, as we see it, is the matter of transporting them to the rift. Here we are powerless — the couriers don't deliver there."

"My agent will get it done. They have access to the rift, and besides, the light's defenses don't affect him. Three days? This is good news. Perhaps because of it, I will spare your life, despite the obvious blunder you made with one of our brothers. Have you discovered how the light ones found the place?"

"Yes, sir. With the help of the very same doomer who destroyed our steel krona. He somehow forced our puppet to activate, and then it led him to the place it was created."

"The puppet returned home instead of dying and spawning new puppets?" Master Elor frowned. "I want details. Interview everyone who was there. We must understand why this happened. I think it's time to stop this doomed soldier — he's already crossed our path twice. It cannot be allowed to happen again. Tell my agent that the doomed soldier must die."

Chapter 12

"GET OUT!" The wagon door opened and I was set loose. The churchmen made quick work of doomers who stood up for themselves. Less than a day later, several servants of the Light came to me and, without explaining anything at all, removed the academy shackles, immediately replacing them with steel stocks on both my hands and feet. Moving with these adornments proved a difficult task, especially with my hands tied behind my back, but this didn't seem to concern the clerics. They were following orders from their superiors. I was escorted to the prison wagon and spent almost a whole day driving somewhere. Or they were just driving around in circles — there were no windows within the canvas covering, so I slept soundly the whole time.

I stepped out of the wagon and looked around. I had been taken to a small camp consisting of around twenty tents. The sun had already set, so that the area was illuminated by a lot of fires, around which both ordinary soldiers and churchmen sat. No scary buildings, secret prisons or bonfire in the central square. It looked as if everyone was preparing to cleanse a rift, not punish an impudent dark one who had decided to bare his teeth to the Fortress.

"Move!" I was shoved roughly in the back. The blocks made it impossible to keep my balance so I sprawled on the ground, puffing out my chest to protect my head. I instantly spun around and saw a short soldier with an ugly scar. Judging by his lack of a robe, an ordinary mercenary, which I immediately took advantage of. I was attacked, so I had every right to defend myself. That was the law. Swinging my shackled legs in a circle, I bent them sharply and used the momentum to fling myself to my feet and spring toward the enemy. The impact of my forehead on the bridge of his nose almost knocked me unconscious — circles swam before my eyes when we collided. But it achieved the desired result: the warrior, who hadn't expected such agility, flew to the ground as if he was diving for it. But I didn't stop there. Rising once again, I jumped, flipping in the air and landing on my blocks. The short asshole's grunt of pain was music to my ears. I thought I heard something crack.

They piled on me, dragged me around, and thoroughly stomped on me, but they weren't able to ruin my good mood. I had achieved my goal, and the next one who decided to shove me in the back would think twice. It was too bad I couldn't remember all the faces of the people who stepped on me. It was too dark. But the execution soon came to an end. Two thugs lifted me up and presented me to another mercenary. I couldn't see anything out of my right eye and my vision swam, but with my left, I managed to make out the insignia on his cuirass. Not just a mercenary — this was the commander of a group.

"What do you think you're doing, asshole?" he asked angrily.

"Protecting myself." My chin had done its job — my teeth seemed to be in the right place. That was good, at least. "According to the law of the Zarak Empire, doomed soldiers have the right to protect their own life. I was attacked in a cowardly manner, from behind. And as you can see, my hands are bound."

"Was a friendly shove worth breaking my man's arm?"

"He's lucky it wasn't his skull." I wasn't bluffing. I'd been ready to kill. "I missed. But no matter — live and learn. Next time I'll strike true. A fatal blow. Because I won't hold back and I won't miss again. I abide by the law. I won't attack first, but I won't turn away in fear and be the butt of every passing scumbag's joke."

"It seems there's been a misunderstanding." A cleric approached us. "The doomer Max was not given any information about where he was being taken or for what purpose, which is why he lashed out. But you should have a word with your men too, sergeant. From a technical stance, Max is right. He has the right to defend himself, and a blow to the back could be perceived as an attack."

"Max? He already has a nickname?" The mercenary commander frowned.

"The High Priest himself awarded him the honor," confirmed the cleric.

"Since when does the Fortress give nicknames to lunatics?" a voice sounded in the darkness, but it was impossible to determine exactly where it came from.

"This I do not know. If there are no other objections, I would like to take Max to explain his task. Walk with the Light, my brothers."

The mercenaries grumbled some more, but the Fortress' indisputable authority prevailed — we were left alone. When they released me, I really wanted to sit — my body ached. But I couldn't let this happen. I had to be unshakable, self-confident and ready to carry out any orders. No one would ever say that Max begged for mercy. The Evil Engineer had weaned me off of weakness.

"They'll remove your stocks now. In the letter Father Nor sent me, he specifically stated that I must warn you, Max: if you try to escape, you will be declared an outcast. The hunt will be on, and will only end in your demise. Final and irrevocable. By order of the High Priest, you have been punished with temporary excommunication from the magical academy. In three weeks, if you're still alive, you'll come back and continue your studies.

You are listed in the Fortress as an active doomed soldier, therefore, for these three weeks, you will engage in the standard work for your kind — destroying dark beasts. To begin, you and your group will have to cleanse a one-level rift."

"My group?" I singled out the most important words.

"Your group. A standard group of five doomed soldiers. Four nameless, and three of which do not possess magic stones. After you get to know the group, you will sign a contract to cleanse the rift, and you will have four days to complete it."

"Contract..." I finally lost the thread of the conversation.

"A contract is signed between the Fortress and the group of doomed soldiers, where the main stipulations are written," the servant answered patiently. "Time allotted, your share of extracted resources, the number of elixirs, cost of treatment, ranking points, penalties. The rift is small, so for everyone in the group but you, this is their first expedition underground."

"So you consider me a beginner?" I was taken aback. "Do they even know how to block out the dark influence?"

"All doomed soldiers wear solid steel armor to protect against the influence." The man was amazingly patient. "Your armor and weapons have also been delivered here. Tomorrow, you will be able to adjust it to fit your physique at the traveling blacksmith. The Fortress closely monitors the quality of the doomed legion's equipment."

"Why tomorrow? It's night now — the rift is open. Why not start today?"

"Because everyone just arrived on location today. They are tired, they need rest. As do you — you were bound and chained all day long, and you can hardly stand on two feet after the friendly greeting you received from the other mercenaries. The Fortress does not want senseless deaths."

"Remove the stocks, give me the katars, ten mana and recovery elixirs, and point me in the direction of the rift," I said. "I don't need armor or rest. The rift will be closed by morning."

"You cannot go into the rift without a signed agreement," the cleric said, not letting up. "Since you've already closed one rift, you have been promoted to commander of the group. Tonight you should get to know your team, determine their strengths and weaknesses, determine their weapons and equipment requirements, and tomorrow we'll discuss everything, delete some items from your list, add some others, and then we'll conclude the negotiations, write down all the conditions, and the next night you will go to the rift."

"Why such an elaborate form of punishment? I'm a doomer. My duty is destroying dark beasts and closing rifts. But there is no way I'll be able to determine my group's needs and then haggle for more favorable conditions with a representative of the Fortress!"

"Order is important in any process. Strict

adherence to established rules. Including in the cleansing of rifts. Every group commander goes through this process, you are no exception."

"What if I refuse to sign the contract? What then?"

"This possibility was also accounted for. Not including the day you arrive at the mission point and the day you leave the rift for the final time, you have two additional days...If, during this time, the rift is not closed, the group is recognized as incapable, unpromising and is subject to annihilation. In your case, this means that there will be five fewer doomers in the world. And yes, they won't let you into the rift without a signed contract. This is the rule of the Fortress."

"So they've got me surrounded," I sighed. Four days to clear one level? Will we be able to leave the rift during this time?"

"You may. You may choose not to go at all, but the consequences will be as I described. The doomed soldier himself chooses when and where he wants to leave this world. Either a guaranteed death here, next to the entrance to the rift, or below, where you have the chance of surviving until the next rift. Come, I'll introduce you to your team. Remove his stocks. And here, take a recovery potion. You'll need it now."

Several servants of the Light emerged from the twilight shadows. They removed the unpleasant steel shackles, but immediately gave me new ones — a steel hoop around my neck with a chain attached. The other end of the chain was held by a gloomy attendant pointing a cocked crossbow in my direction.

"As you understand, we have no reason to trust doomed soldiers. Standard Fortress procedure demands strict control over each subject. Of course, this rule only applies to nameless doomed soldiers, but Father Nor specifically indicated his desire to extend the rule to you. As recent events have shown, this is a perfectly reasonable demand. You are a danger to those around you. Follow me."

This new cleric never introduced himself. The one holding the chain started to pull, which forced me to move my legs. I think if I fell they'd just drag me along on the ground. Religious fanatics, what can you do with them?

The group was located in a tent standing separate from the main camp. There was no campfire, no one preparing food, no stories being told. When I went inside, the reason why became clear — all four of them had big metal necklaces like me. The other end of the chain was fastened with a large lock hung on a post dug into the ground. There was a latrine bucket nearby and two servants with loaded crossbows were standing by the wall. Every step the doomers took was under close surveillance, and there was none of the freedom that I had enjoyed during my campaign with the Countess' group.

"Attention everyone!" the cleric said loudly. "The fifth member of your group. A doomer named Max. He has already participated in a campaign to close a rift, so he has been appointed as your commander. Max, this is One, Two, Three and Four. It makes no difference to me who is which, deal with it yourself. Here's a pencil and a piece of paper. I expect a full list of your weapons, equipment, and other supply requirements by morning. Tomorrow night you're going to the rift. Brothers, leave them. The dead men need to talk. And just in case — whoever leaves the tent before morning will be destroyed on the spot."

The end of my chain was fixed to the post, making me feel like a horse, and then the servants left us alone.

"What, you really closed a rift? How old are you, pretty boy?" First to speak was a shaggy man who looked like an outright thug. Ugly face, ugly scars, unpleasant tone and manner of sitting. Gustav loved to call such people "beings unburdened by intellect." He was strong. Next to the other doomers in the group, he was a wolf among sheep. Dangerous, deadly, knew his own strength and, judging by where he was, enjoyed using it. The other doomers looked much more modest — chubby, rosy-cheeked — they looked more like sweet bun sellers than murderers who deserved a spot among the doomed.

"I don't get it — didja hear me? Hey pretty boy, you want me to whisper in your ear? I can do that for ya." The man didn't let up. "Or maybe you've got a kidney to spare for me? Don't worry — I'll beat the shit out of both your main kidney and your backup. Answer when your elder is talking to you!"

"Is it just me or is there a particularly smelly pocket of air in here?" I turned defiantly away from the meathead and toward my nearest neighbor. A man of about forty, completely unsuited for fighting dark beasts. And from the way his face blanched, he considered my behavior completely unacceptable.

"You're gonna bleed!" he growled menacingly and his chain clanked. I turned around, wrapping my own chain around my fist several times. It wasn't the best pair of brass knuckles I'd ever seen, but I didn't need them to be. This guy was strong, and possibly fast too, but I had an indelible advantage on my side — magic. It'd be bad for me later, but at least I'd finish here first.

The blow to my head was quick and, had it not met with my golden dome, could have easily rendered me a vegetable. The giant was used to solving his problems with brute force and had swung with all his might. The impact was so powerful that I was thrown to one side along with my dome, but the pain-filled scream was the signal that it was time to act. I remembered from last time that the shock collar would kick in after thirty seconds and I'd be turned into a weak-willed worm. Launching myself forward feet first, I landed with my heels in his kneecaps. Like Gustav had taught. Even the strongest and most resilient enemy wouldn't remain standing after such a blow. Things weren't looking too good for the hulk, who was cradling a broken hand. The massive body was still falling and swinging its arms, but I was already behind him, looping the chain around his neck. One end was rigidly chained to the pole, the other I wound around my hand and as soon as the man crashed to the ground, I put my feet on his back and pulled the chain toward me with all my might. Going hand-to-hand with a guy like this would be unrealistic — he'd obliterate me. Using magic in the tent also wasn't an option. Dark Spike would hit the other doomed soldiers and I wouldn't have time to heal everyone before I was neutralized. So I only had one option for protecting myself, at least for now. I didn't know what the churchmen were thinking, sending doomers like this into the rift. He was out of control!

The body began to twitch beneath me, but I didn't even think of loosening the chain. Even when the world turned upside down and I collapsed to the ground, convulsively gulping air, I still pulled the chain toward myself, finishing what I started. About five minutes later, when space stopped tumbling, I managed to get to my feet. One down.

"He...you..." the look the other three doomers gave me spoke volumes. These people weren't killers.

"He violated the doomer code," I replied calmly, unwinding the chain from the blueing neck. Just in case, I checked his pulse — nothing. "He attacked his brother. A member of his group. A commander. There's only one punishment for that: death. Instantaneous and merciless, just as the servants of the Light like it. Does anyone object to my reaction?"

"No." The doomers collectively shook their heads, and the one I had addressed earlier even dared to add: "It's actually good that you killed that animal. He was completely insane. He'd beat you for any little thing. Looking the wrong way, breathing the wrong way, pissing the wrong way — you get whacked. We've had to deal with him for two days now."

"Why didn't you kill him in his sleep?" I asked, causing the already pale-faced doomers to grow even more white. "Got it. One question, just so I know what I'm working with — why were you sentenced to death? You're clearly not just helpless little lambs if you're here."

"That's just the point," sighed the man. "I can't speak for anyone else here, but my situation is simply horrendous. I accidentally killed my partner. We were out celebrating a successful deal, had a little too much to drink, then had a little more and decided to play a game of chicken — who could lean out the window further. One leans out, the other holds his legs. My partner went first and I didn't hold back, and the court didn't care what state we were in. They didn't give me bail, and the law of the Empire dictates — a death for a death. So I was sentenced to the doomed legion. And I wouldn't have even gotten here without help from my partner's wife — she took over the whole business herself, apparently. I have no family...I really didn't want to die, so when they offered me the choice to join the doomed legion, I agreed without a second thought. I can't fight, I'm scared witless of dark beasts, I spent all of a day inside the Fortress and then they sent me off to the rift. And then this guy…well, that's how it went. The churchmen strictly forbade me from using my name on punishment of death, so now I am a nameless and rootless doomed soldier."

"You're Number One for now, we'll sort out the rest. What about you? Drunken revelries as well?"

The situation with Two was very similar to what happened with One. He turned out to be an embezzler. He worked as a clerk for the mayor and for ten years drew up false checks for himself. He didn't go overboard, so they didn't catch him for a while, but when a check suddenly showed up addressed to him, the gig was up. The mayor didn't defend him, and there was only one place the empire sent embezzlers: the gallows. But once again, just a few days ago, Two was offered the chance to live a little longer and signed up to be a doomed soldier. Spent a single day in the Fortress then was immediately sent here. No preparations, no experience, no physical data. The makings of a great rift warrior! At least I got lucky with Three — he possessed a magic stone and, according to the laws of the empire, had passed through a three-month course for "young warriors" at the academy. He didn't reveal the reason he had been consigned to the doomed legion and I didn't push. But despite all his training, this also turned out to be his first campaign into the rift — the man had been working under the surveillance of the servants of the Light for almost a month, absorbing the rules and customs of the Fortress, when he was suddenly called over and sent to die. Why die? Because the stone he wielded was *Fortify* — an aura that reduces incoming damage. The churchmen had boosted his stone to level three and had even given him an additional support stone to reduce mana cost, but this didn't change the overall picture: Three was also at the bottom of the food chain.

"Fantastic." All I could do now was raise my brows and stare off into infinity, trying to understand the Fortress' logic. Two completely useless doomers, textbook cannon-fodder. One more or less normal defender who could, at least, significantly reduce the damage my shield took. One melee fighter, now dead, who had forgotten what common sense was. And me, who had managed to earn a punishment from the High Priest himself. What a stellar team to close a rift!

"Does anyone have any requirements? Weapons, armor...wait! I'm being stupid. One — you said you had your own business? So I assume you know how to negotiate and defend your own interests? Negotiate contracts and all that?"

"Do I know how to negotiate? Young man, this is what I spent most of my life doing! I can't say I'm the best one around, I often had to make concessions, but it's certainly in my wheelhouse."

"Alright...Two, you were a clerk, and for quite

a while. You must be used to noting all the details, seeing the fine print and all the things people try to mask over with pretty words. We're going to have to sign a contract. I'm sure that the churchmen will try to slip a bunch of interesting little things in there, so that when we get out of the rift, we'll somehow still have to stay. I was never prepared for this, I'll definitely miss some important details and we'll come out on bottom because of it. And what's more, I can't negotiate. Your task is to carefully read the contract, find all the weak points, explain them to One, and if possible, to me as well, and then defend our interests."

"You're talking as if you plan to survive the day," Three remarked glumly.

"Not just survive, but receive our hard-earned ten percent of the extracted resources," I replied. "This is a one-level rift, we'll reach the final room in two hours. This is my task. You stand at a distance and don't get involved. Of course, it would be preferable if you stayed here, but your aura is just too nice to pass up. It may come in handy with the guards. I've never killed these monsters before. The Countess didn't let me in."

"You know the Countess?!" Three's exclamation of surprise was so sincere that I flinched involuntarily. So full of admiration, faith, hope.

"A week ago, I was assigned to her group to close a two-level rift. But, as I said, they didn't let me into the last cave, although I did kill the

Riftmaster. And yes — it was the Countess who initiated me into the doomed legion. Have you already gone through this process?"

No one even knew what I was talking about. Which made me think even more about the goals of the current campaign. Why had the churchmen sent these essentially useless people to die?

"We'll return to this issue after our first fight," I said, in any case. "What's important is that under no circumstances are you to get involved. You have your own tasks — negotiations, rooting out loopholes, the defense aura. Everything else is up to me."

"Is the loot also yours?" One immediately piped up.

"I think that's the very thing we should make clear in the contract," I said thoughtfully. I hadn't thought about it — I hadn't considered it before — I thought the Fortress itself was in charge of distributing the goods. "Who else has suggestions on what we should add? Come on, people, I need active participation — I'm not dying tomorrow night, and I advise you to try to do the same. Since the Light has brought us together for now, we need to figure out how to spend this time in a way that will benefit everyone."

"Why are you so sure you can cope with it? The Countess isn't coming with us." Three was obviously in a foul mood. Although he had been listed as a doomed soldier for four months already and knew how long people with his abilities generally survived.

"Is that not enough for you?" I nodded toward the lifeless body. "He was bigger, stronger, and more powerful than me. But there he is lying on the ground and I'm standing here talking to you. The same thing will happen to the dark beasts in the rift. See for yourself tomorrow. For now, we need to sort this out. Second, write down my requirements — I need my personal katars, ten mana and recovery elixirs. Steel armor...no, I don't need it, it will only impede my movement."

"You're going into the rift without armor?" Came their overlapping exclamations of astonishment.

"Believe me, this is the least strange thing you'll learn about me. Got that down? Great. Now I turn the question to you: what were you given to survive? Before we can figure out what you need, we need to understand what you already have. One, let's start with you."

In the morning, when the nameless cleric from the day before came for us, there was a surprise awaiting him. And not just one...

Chapter 13

"YOU CAN'T DO that!"

"Is it written somewhere that I can't?" One looked at the churchman as if he were an unreasonable child. "Is there some kind of Fortress rule that forbids us from taking baths and using the services of massage therapists?"

"No, but..." the servant closed his eyes, trying to maintain his inner peace. "Doomed soldiers are required to include only those items that directly affect their combat effectiveness."

"I don't understand your indignation," the First continued. "We'll return smeared in dark goo, we will need a thorough bath and recovery before the next task. It's not just a whim, Father, it's a hard necessity."

"Light be with you, you can have your masseuse and bath. But courtesans?! Are you out of your mind?"

"Once again, I ask, what Fortress law states that doomed soldiers, young and full of vitality, should not be allowed to let off steam in order to fully and completely concentrate on fulfilling their mission? We do not demand you pay for them — we will do that ourselves. It's just a matter of facilitating the meeting. I want to note that this has a direct impact on group morale. If we know what awaits us upon our return, not a single dark beast will be able to stop us from running to the arms of a beautiful woman. Again, for rehabilitation. Both physical and mental."

The cleric fell silent. He hadn't been prepared for this kind of presentation. He had expected a young and inexperienced novice who could be trained to do absolutely anything. But as soon as the crowd descended upon him and I stepped aside, our monitor's mood plummeted straight to the bottom of the rift. Because One immediately started to demonstrate the superiority of a man who both knew how and delighted in bargaining over simple schmucks like me. We were intentionally vague in terms of our requirements. Again, at One's suggestion. He also suggested including some of the items that any normal person would strike off the list at once. The bathhouse, massage, courtesans, Kaliman tobacco, Shurgan wine...what frivolities didn't we come up with in an attempt to slip in our basic requirements under the radar: sharpened weapons, amulets to guard against a fatal blow. The latter Three insisted on — it was always good to have a "second life" at hand. These amulets were considered rare and were expensive, so we didn't even have the money to buy them. Prices started at a thousand gold apiece. And that was the family and friends discount.

"Alright, we'll leave out the massage." One began making concessions. "We'll try our best to recover on our own."

"And there won't be any amulets," the cleric said. "If you need them, you can purchase them at the Fortress. As well as fitted armor — for your first task, you go in with what you have been given. Those are the rules."

"Purchase at the Fortress? No problem. When will they let us in? What items are in stock? What discounts can we expect? What form of payment?" One jumped on this new information.

"Weren't you taken to the store before coming here?" the cleric wondered. "It's mandatory protocol."

"We not only haven't been there, we didn't even know it existed. And Max hasn't been to the Fortress once."

"The general store is the foundation of doomer life," the cleric said, and then paused to think. "Everything outside of the standard equipment can be purchased there. Amulets, various elixirs, weapons, armor, even magic stones. Payment is made with ranking points. The sooner you complete the rift, the more points you get."

"Well, there isn't a word about it in the

contract." Two flipped pointedly through the pages of the agreement. "How much will we get if we close the rift in one day? Where does it say?"

"This is written in the rules of the Fortress, which you certainly should have read by now. Unless..."

"Unless we were never even informed that these rules exist," I finished his thought. "They didn't inform us about them, they didn't demand we read them. Evidently the Fortress has violated its own rules by sending out unprepared and unequipped doomers who haven't even completed their initial briefing? I wonder what the Countess will say to that. I'm sure she'll enjoy this information. And I think it's worth informing the High Priest. Whenever we next meet."

"What occasion would the High Priest have to meet with a doomer?" the cleric frowned. We had pulled the ground out from under his feet and he was clinging desperately to anything he could.

"Over the past two weeks, I've had two meetings with Father Urg. I have no right to divulge the content of our conversation, but have you read Father Nor's letter? Do you think the High Priest would personally punish a doomed soldier he didn't know? So I'm sure that as soon as my exile is over, I'll have an audience with him once more. Where I will ask him why the Fortress is neglecting its obligations while demanding its orders be fulfilled. Alright, we're getting off topic, I'm clearly asking the wrong person. So how many points will we get per rift?"

"Every member of the group receives one hundred points for the first level of the rift, three hundred for the second, six hundred for the third and a thousand for the fourth. Level five and higher are rated individually, depending on the number of group members."

"So that means I already have four hundred points in the ranking system? I closed a two-level rift, they even gave me my reward. But for some reason I was not informed about the points. Can you give me an idea on prices? How much does an amulet cost that will block lethal damage?"

"Three thousand," he responded automatically, causing us all to gasp.

"And how will this ranking system affect us overall?" asked Two. "It can't just be points we use to buy things, you said we were ranked."

"The higher a doomer's rank, the more difficult the tasks he's given, but the more indulgences he is allowed. Even including lightening his surveillance."

"So if you spend points in the store, you lower your rank?" asked One, to which the cleric nodded. "What's the point? You sit at the bottom of the ranks, you keep your head low, you're only sent to one-level rifts. You survive and never know suffering."

"The ranking system is the basis of the doomed soldier's existence. The higher the ranking, the fewer additional orders the doomer receives. Those who exceed five thousand points never have to do the cleaning and tidying or provide for the others. For example, you will be given armor, but you won't be able to put them on yourself. This requires assistance provided by low-ranking doomed soldiers. Cleaning up after the horses, emptying chamber pots — all the work of low-ranking doomers. Moreover, the brothers in the Light strictly monitor the fulfillment of these tasks. But if you think this sounds glamorous, I will warn you: every six months, thirty of the lowest-ranking doomed soldiers are grouped into a team and sent to clear a two-level rift. The more industrious earn all the map fragments and piece it together, and this earns you a higher ranking as well. They are, of course, provided with everything they need for the task, but few return. The law is harsh, but it is the law. The Fortress does not tolerate freeloaders."

"It appears we're striking amulets and armor fittings from the list," said a white-faced One and made a few notes. "Then we'll return to the massage. We won't sign without it."

"There will be no amulets or armor fitting," the churchman confirmed, took the sheet from One, skimmed through it again, and then sighed resignedly. "I have no issue with the rest. If you close the rift, you will get everything you require. But I would like to make it clear right away that the payment will come from the gold you're due. The Fortress does not pay courtesans. Alright, have we come to an agreement?"

"Actually, we've only agreed on the basic conditions. Exactly as you requested. I, however, have a few questions." Two smiled and handed the agreement to the churchman. "I made a few small notes on sections that raised some concerns for me. And in light of all of the above, we must include a bonus for successfully closing the rift. Despite what anyone may say, we're novices who have been sent to die. And without providing for our basic needs. If this is the case, there must be some bonuses in the contract to ensure that this misunderstanding doesn't happen a second time. Am I right, everyone? See, they're all nodding."

"Bonuses, how could I have forgotten!" One jumped on the topic.

"There will be no more items added!" The churchman suddenly stood up. "You've gone too far!"

"Who said anything about new items? Ranking points will be sufficient. First, we were not given access to the store. Our commander has four hundred points; I'm certain he would like to purchase something useful that would help us on our campaign. This is a flagrant violation and, so that it does not happen next time, I propose to add one rift level to our final points. That is, on paper, we will have closed a two-level rift. Do you consider these concessions a fair compensation for turning a blind eye to the infractions? I think Max may even reconsider mentioning it to the High Priest. Why would he, if the church is ready to pay for its mistakes?"

The servant of the Light stood in thought for a long time. I didn't think he had any say in such things, but suddenly he sighed heavily and nodded.

"Very well. We must write everything down in order to clearly substantiate everything in the paperwork. I agree that there was a clear violation of the rules."

"Excellent. So we've dealt with the first issue. Now onto the second — an even greater transgression. We were not acquainted with the rules of the Fortress. We, doomed soldiers! The only document dictating all our activities! It's not even a violation — it's a pure crime. I believe that the internal security service should investigate this issue thoroughly, find the perpetrators and punish them, but we are again ready to meet the Fortress halfway. All it will take is increasing our points by one more rift level. And when Max meets with Father Urg, he will have nothing to say about the rift. Because for a doomed soldier, it will be an ordinary campaign unworthy of remark."

"A three-level rift? Have you completely lost your sanity?" The cleric finally lost his composure and flared up. "A thousand points for a one-level rift?"

"A thousand points for the Fortress' critical mistake," One corrected him. "I believe I recently heard an excellent phrase that beautifully characterizes our current situation. The law is harsh, but it is the law. Or do the laws of the Fortress work only in one direction, and the servants of the Light may choose not to comply? I really hope this isn't the case. Otherwise, how would you be any different from Skron's minions?"

"Don't you dare!" hissed the cleric. "Don't you dare compare us to those dark beasts who sold their souls in exchange for power!"

"Listen carefully, Father…um…fine. Listen carefully. There was no comparison. By the way, what's your name? We've known each other for a full day already, but I don't know how to address you. Is…"

One didn't get the chance to finish his sentence. The tent flap opened and admitted another person into the tent. A pretty girl around my age with a cute little button nose. Her face reminded me of someone, but I couldn't say who exactly. Judging by her well-manicured, aristocratic hands, she also had a nice figure, but I couldn't appreciate it underneath the shapeless white robe that hid all her charms. A girl in a cassock. Was that even possible?

"I beg your pardon, Father in the Light, I came as soon as I could," she said apologetically. Her voice matched her appearance — pleasant and melodic.

"There is no issue, Daughter of the Light, you are not late. We are just discussing the terms of the contract and the bonuses that must be added."

"Bonuses?" the girl looked with interest at the sheet with our requirements. "These are requirements. Stupid ones, of course, but it's not for me to judge Max's group. Where are these bonuses and why are you discussing them? Oh, forgive my tactlessness, I forgot to introduce myself. Am I correct in assuming you didn't give the doomed soldiers your name? Very wise. So, gentlemen doomers, my name is Sister Alia. Stress on the 'i.' The High Priest has appointed me to be your group's conservator. Now any questions concerning your relationship with the Fortress can be directed toward me."

"Um..." We all had the same reaction. No one had expected this turn of events. I think for many it was a discovery that the Fortress contained more than just men.

"Why are there only three of you? Where are the other two?" asked the girl, ignoring our confusion.

"One of them is resting, the group decided not to take him to the meeting, and the other was sent to the Fortress," said the cleric calmly.

"How did he die?" the girl frowned, knowing perfectly well the only reason a doomed soldier would be sent to the Fortress from a mission.

"As I was told, he refused to obey the rules. Attacked the commander. Behaved unacceptably and aggressively. I didn't investigate further — this is your diocese, and you determine the reasoning behind such an act yourself. Perhaps I should excuse myself. Doomers, it was...interesting speaking with you. I have never negotiated such a contract before."

"Please, sit," the girl said, and the cleric, who had made to stand up, obeyed. "Finish what you started, then you can be free. You should have presented me with the signed contract. There is no reason to shirk your responsibilities, Father in the Light. This is not the path to follow."

"We've already come to an agreement. You saw the requirements, all that remains is the issue of the thousand-point bonus."

"Is that so... Perhaps I should hear the reasoning behind such generosity on the part of the church. I don't think it will cause undue delay to explain to me why the Fortress must pay the price of a three-level one for a single-level rift. And what I'm most interested in is how you came to that idea. Begin..."

The girl looked young enough, but she had a vice-like grip. The way she quickly cut to the heart of things demanded respect. It was she who reminded us that Three was actually trained and had all the necessary access, and had even visited the store (the main reason why we didn't take the mage with us to the meeting. So that the nameless churchman did not lay eyes on him), so One had to work his linguistic magic again to turn the emphasis back on me, as the commander of the group with four hundred rating points. The conservator had nothing to say about this — apparently she was aware that I'd never visited the Fortress.

"What the brothers and fathers in the Light have done is a blatant violation. Unacceptable. I fully agree with your decision, I only ask you to carefully indicate this point in the contract. As I understand it, you will be handling this?"

The girl looked at Two, making him squirm.

The beauty had a heavy gaze. But what alarmed me most of all was that Sister Alia was already familiar with each group member's skillset. First impressions are often misleading, but I got the impression that the girl was smart, well-read, savvy and had been given extensive powers. If that was the case, she couldn't help but realize that the three men in our group were absolutely unfit for the rift. But this didn't concern her. What she cared about most was the wording in the contract.

After a couple of hours, everything was in order: we corrected a few points, added our conditions and bonuses. Sister Alia and I signed two copies of the text, concluding the first official agreement between Max's group and the Fortress.

"When do you plan to start?" the girl asked. The question made sense — from the moment the treaty was signed, my group had six days to destroy the Riftmaster. Four in the rift and two additional.

"Today," I replied. "The sooner we start, the sooner we finish."

"In this case, the group needs sleep. Take them to their tent and make sure that none of the mercenaries are hanging around today. Leave Max with me, I need to talk to him alone. Thank you for your help, Father in the Light, and farewell. There is business that awaits you at the Fortress. Brother in the Light, wait outside and see that we are not disturbed. You can pick Max up after we talk."

The tent emptied out rather quickly. My chain

was attached to an ordinary bed, so that if I really wanted to, you could lift the leg of the bed and free myself. But once our conversation started, it completely swept any thought of escape from my mind. The girl activated some kind of stone and a magic dome formed around us.

"It's called a protective canopy," Sister Alia explained. "Now no one will be able to hear what we say. This stone is extremely rare, it is given out only to the top tiers. Those who are appointed personal servants of the dark ones. Yes, Max, I know who you are and, as you must understand, I am your servant from now on."

"If you thought that would clarify things, you are mistaken. Now I'm more confused. I don't know what a personal servant is or why I need one."

"They warned me that you hadn't undergone the mandatory training, so we'll have to start from scratch. As you know, the purpose of the church is to fight the dark creatures in all their manifestations. Both in the form of beasts and in the form of converts. But sometimes the dark ones do not succumb to the influence of Skron and remain in the Light, despite their status. There are very few of them, but they have always been there, from our first confrontation with the darkness. The highest hierarchs of the church perfectly understood the importance of cooperation with such dark ones, but not everyone shared this opinion. The overwhelming majority wanted to destroy the dark ones, seeing them as a future threat. Which is not unwarranted — more than half of the dark ones end up going over to Skron's side eventually. The temptation of the dark side was too great and there were too many promises of easy power. And then a special organization of servants was created. Those who stay in constant contact with the dark ones until the end of their lives and are confidants in all Fortress affairs. The servant knows everything about their dark one. Everything. I know the stats and composition of your magic stones, I know that you possess one of the five map fragments, two of the twelve *Amplify* fragments. I know how you became dark and that you are a dark mirror with the ability to ignore dark beasts up to the third level of the rift. I know everything the Fortress knows about you. The reason personal servants are different is that we report personally to the High Priests, and other churchmen have no power over us. Over us or our dark ones. If we make a pact, a lifetime pact, you will follow only my orders. None of the servants of the Light, including the High Priests, will have power over you."

"Lifetime? Sister Alia, allow me to let you in on a terrible secret, as my confidant — I am going to do everything in my power to cease being a doomed soldier and to escape the Fortress' influence. I have a clear-cut plan, and I intend to enact it."

"I'm afraid that you're misunderstanding the very essence of the matter. A doomed soldier may stop being a doomed soldier, but he will never stop being a part of the Fortress. Even if you become the founder of a new Valevsky family or kill off Duke Odoevsky and his entire family, you will still remain dark, our agreement will remain the same, and you will have to fulfill the tasks I assign. No matter how strange and dangerous they may seem to you."

"So once again, the game only has one true player?" I chuckled, trying to quell the anger rising in my chest. "I owe everything, the Fortress owes me nothing?"

"My job is to help you grow, progress, and become stronger. I will defend your rights in the Fortress as my own, fight for every little thing, down to your women of easy virtue, if you need them. But this kind of care will cost you complete transparency. You will have to tell me everything about yourself. I mean everything. Any notifications that pop up before your eyes, any new additions to your taskbar, anything you don't understand about the rift or about life. I must become your second ego."

"But I still don't understand why I need all this." I looked into Sister Alia's eyes, trying to find an answer. "Why should I open up? Because you're a beautiful girl and I'm a young guy who's supposed to shake his tail feathers and strut around like a peacock?"

"I wasn't appointed to this position because of my appearance," Sister Alia's voice slid into cold metal tones. "And not because I'm a girl your age. I have been serving the church since the age of three, when my father first brought me to the service. Over the past fifteen years I have been able to prove myself capable of more than just a coy smile, sitting off on the sidelines, waiting for men to resolve their issues so that I can clear their dishes away. I have proven to everyone that women can fight dark beasts on equal footing with men, perhaps even better than some."

"Then I am extremely confused. The Fortress is turning up the heat, sending me on a mission with an obviously weak group, trying to foist unknown stones onto me, punishing me for any question I ask, sending me an extra monitor, regaling me with the news that even if I cease to be a doomed soldier, I'll always be a part of the church. Did I forget anything? And despite all this, I'm supposed to happily share all this information with you because...what? Why would I do this? Because you said so? Because it's my civic duty? Because doing otherwise violates the laws of the Fortress? Even though the Fortress itself doesn't comply with these laws. And she said she was going to fight for me...get your own affairs in order before you meddle in mine. May I go? I need to sleep — I've got a hard night ahead of me. As you know, I haven't fought a guard yet. I have no idea how to destroy them, and, of course, no one will teach me how to do it. Or does anyone in my group have experience with this? Even purely theoretical?"

"I will not justify the actions of my brothers in the Light. Just as I will not accuse them of breaking the law. This is not my domain. I can only say that the highest hierarchs are not always able to act as they please. We all have roles that we can't escape. There is the doomed soldier and there is the Fortress, and there are established customs dictating the relationship between them. You are the Fortress' most valuable resource, but they cannot acknowledge this, otherwise the more orthodox brothers in the Light will rebel. And they're in the vast majority. Have you thought about how people come to the church? Why they hate the dark beasts with all their hearts? Because they have lost everyone they love to the darkness. They see people like you as you see the relatives of the Duke of Odoevsky. How many words have you shared with Karina Fardi? And how many times have you promised to kill her? Roles, Max, everyone must play the roles that are expected of them. That being said, you were sent to your first rift with the best doomed soldiers the Fortress had at its disposal. They tested your combat readiness, consigned you to the list of doomed soldiers before you even graduated from the academy, protected you from the imperials demanding blood for your participation in the incident at the Chescony ball. The Fortress has protected you in every way possible for the entire three weeks that you've been a doomed soldier. Yes, you are being punished. Sternly, ostentatiously, but how much harm have these punishments really caused you? The fifth level of the rift? Where you trained your mirror for three days and saved the Evil Engineer's life? Or depriving you of the opportunity to continue training with him so that he can increase the workload? Which, again, gave you the chance to improve. The stones...I was a witness to the meeting concerning this issue. I saw with my own eyes how Father Urg defended his position, while nearly all the orthodox heads of the different regions were adamantly against giving a dark one more power. The High Priest had no right to explain the features of each stone to you, because there were other eyes and ears around. By law, you were supposed to accept this gift with gratitude, instead you were sent into exile. Here. To a single-level rift. With a group that seemed perfectly matched to you: a negotiator, a lawman, a mage with a protective aura...There was also a melee fighter, but for some reason you wrote him off immediately. We know perfectly well that you are already capable of closing single-level rifts alone. If they really wanted to punish you, they would have sent you to a two- or three-level right away. That would be a real punishment. But what are you left with instead? You'll close the rift, get the second piece of the map, a third fragment of *Amplify,* a thousand ranking points, and a slew of privileges that most doomed soldiers would never dream of. But your main issue is with the hoop around your neck and the chain that binds you to this bed. The leg of which, I would like to add, you could break with one sharp jerk. Was I aware of this? Naturally. But why do I turn a blind eye? Because of my role, Max. Everyone plays their part. The cleric that met you reports to one of the orthodox heads of the region. He's already in a hurry to report to his leadership that there have been no concessions made to the dark one, that Father Urg isn't singling you out and really did send you to the rift. May the Light be merciful to me...I really didn't want to justify the Fortress' actions, but here I am launching into a monologue. I'm not asking you to trust me now. I'm not asking you to open up. I understand that it will be a long process. It took Father Nor almost five years before the Evil Engineer began to trust him. But I want you to realize that I will be a part of your life from now on and until your last days. Or mine, if I die before you. We can't rule that possibility out either."

"Father Nor is my mentor's personal servant?"

"For more than ten years now. Everyone knows that when you say 'Evil Engineer,' you mean Father Nor. Until now, there have been only four personal servants in the world. One for each officially recognized dark human in the church. I'll be fifth as soon as we make a deal."

"If we do make a deal," I muttered, trying to process the girl's monologue. Somehow it didn't seem to fit what was really happening to me. "Just a question. Will I be the only one sharing information? Or will I be given the knowledge on dark ones that the Evil Engineer and others have told the church? The maps, *Amplify* fragments — I already know about them. What else do you have? Surely there's more."

"I will answer in due time. First of all, not 'if,' but 'when,'" Sister Alia corrected me. "There is no other way for you to fulfill your mission. Do you want to avenge the murder of your entire family? Until you have a personal servant, the Fortress will not let you go free."

"But you won't help me?"

"Why not? At this point, the Duke of Odoevsky is your main target. Once that is over, you can focus on other, much more significant things. I cannot use the Fortress' resources for the sake of killing a civilian, but I am ready to assist you in everything else. Personally, I don't care if you kill the Duke Fardi or not. If you wipe out their entire lineage. What's important is that you handle the missions given to you in order to destroy the dark beasts. For instance — the nocturnal guild will put out a hit on the duke for five thousand gold. Not for just anyone, of course, but I enjoy a privileged position. They will listen to me. Save up the amount you need and I'll help you take the first step toward your current goal. As for information on dark humans, you will receive everything that the Fortress has. That is, everything the Dark Engineer and the previous dark ones of our empire have told us. The other dark humans belong to other dioceses, our High Priest has no power over them. I repeat once again, Max, from now on we are bound until the end of one of our days. And now it's not my problems or your problems. They are our problems that must be addressed. Think about it. I think our first conversation was fruitful. When you close the rift, as I have no doubt you will, we will return to this topic again. I will give you our contract and I want to immediately warn you that no one can be involved in negotiating it. It's just between me and you. Between the doomed soldier and the Fortress. Between the dark one and his personal servant of the Light. One piece of advice before you go into the rift — take a two-handed sword with you. You can clear your way to the guards with the katars, but you'll need something more powerful to finish them off. Good luck on your upcoming mission. Now rest, you have hard work ahead of you. In the next three weeks, you must close at least four rifts — a single, two doubles and a triple. It's time to find out what happens when all five map fragments are combined."

Chapter 14

"IS EVERYONE READY?" Despite the team's comical appearance, I didn't dare smile. Three steel-armored doomed soldiers followed behind me like a chain gang heading toward the chopping block. They knew full well that they couldn't do anything on their own in the rift. Even the spears and swords that the churchmen had given them would be no more than toothpicks for the dark beasts. A nice after-dinner treat.

If the steel armor really could protect against the dark influence, it didn't do a very good job. My trio began to show the first signs of fear as soon as we began our spiraling descent. The further we went, the stronger it was. A merchant, a clerk, and a burgeoning mage who had never encountered any dark beasts in their lives, so they were simply mentally unprepared for the sensations that any doomed soldier has to live with. I had to stop and even double back to have another conversation with them. I felt like I'd explained everything beforehand, but theory never comes anywhere close to practice. You can't teach someone to smell red. Everyone has to experience this first encounter on their own.

"It doesn't seem possible." Big drops of sweat were running down the One's pallid face. He didn't even try to wipe them off — it was pointless. "We're wearing steel armor!"

"Thin, not well fitted to your body, with holes the size of fists." I stuck my fingers between the cuirass and the armpiece to demonstrate. "And I definitely have some questions for the doomed soldier who tightened the belts. It seemed like it was his first time. Let me redo them. Maybe it'll make things a little easier for you."

"Mine too." The wave of fear was nearly making Three's teeth chatter. "Are you so calm because of your block?"

"That's right. But don't worry, you'll learn how too," I assured them. "Here the main thing is practice. The more you go into the rift, the faster you'll adapt to the local climate."

"You mean to say, if I take this weight off of me, I'll seize up, but it'll get better faster?" One immediately tried to find a way to "cheat the system." "If we're going to have to go through it all anyway?"

"Honestly, I'm not sure," I said pensively. "In theory, the steel armor should provide some sort of relief. Otherwise those without magic would never be able to enter the rift at all. If you remove it now, you'll have no barrier between your body and the dark aura. Even if what you have now isn't that sound."

"Help me pull it off," said One. "You're right, each of us has our own job to do today. Yours is to defeat dark beasts and close this Skron-cursed rift. Ours...mine is to grit my teeth and learn how to survive. Learn to pass through the rift without armor. If I understand correctly, in a two-level rift, even the first level will be complete torture. Either I learn to block the influence now or I'll never learn. Take it off."

"Why though?" I still didn't understand. "Your only specific task in these rifts is to survive."

"And what then?" Two chimed in. "Let's say we close four rifts. Everyone is happy, everyone is satisfied. But then after three weeks, you go back to the academy and we return to the Fortress. It's unlikely we'll be there for long before they send us to work again. One is right — we need to learn how to block the influence of the dark ones. I'm not talking about beasts yet — I haven't seen them in my eyes, I have no idea what they are capable of. But I have to find out what I myself am capable of. Help me undo my armor too. It's just getting in the way."

"Madness." Three threw back his visor and looked at his brothers as if they were fools. "Even the best doomed soldiers pass through the rift in suits of armor. This is the law. Nothing else will protect you from the aura of the guards."

"No one's forcing you." One pulled off his gloves and I thought I saw his face grow even paler. "I'll say it again. What I'm doing, I'm doing purely for myself. No call to action, no campaign. And I'm not tossing the armor, I'll carry it with me. I still have to hand it over at the end so they'll sign off on it. They're bureaucrats, really, and not churchmen. If you would have told me in my past life that the Fortress requires every move it makes to be certified by two or three signed documents, I wouldn't have believed you. Stupid and wasteful. Something smells fishy."

"Fishy?" It was Two's turn to frown.

"Just think about it: what's the church's main mission? To fight the darkness in all its manifestations. Both beasts and converts. Isn't it obvious that if this fight is for the fate of the world, the Fortress should be getting the best equipment? Weapons, armor, elixirs, stones? But what actually happens? They gather hordes of doomed soldiers — that is, former criminals — and send them to close rifts. Sorry, what? Where are the specially trained heroes who can single-handedly take out a five-level rift? I'm not talking about Max. He's still young and has only been a doomer a little longer than we have. But what about the rest? Where are the hundreds of mages eager to destroy the darkness? I mean, where is the army? Where are the aristocrats that used to stroll imposingly along the Wall? Isn't it obvious that if all our forces were combined, we could close all the rifts once and for all in a matter of months? I've never asked this question before — I didn't need to in my business. But it only leads me to one conclusion: someone in the Fortress really doesn't want the rifts to be closed. For them to disappear."

"Your own kind would kill you for thinking such thoughts," Three muttered softly.

"What difference does it make who else wants to kill me?" One waved him off and pulled off another glove. "The darkness, the churchmen, the doomers?" The result is the same: a dead merchant who did something stupid. But I cannot fail to notice the peculiarities in the things that are happening to us. They're too...superficial, or something. It's strange that you don't see this yourself."

"The thing is, we *do* see it," Three said in the same quiet voice. "That's why I'm here with you. I had exactly the same questions as you, and I had the imprudence to ask them. I...I was trained as the personal squire of a respected aristocrat. They even granted me a stone. My former master ordered me to stay near his son, so that he was always in my aura. But I didn't even last a year...I started asking questions, like One. Why are aristocrats sent to the Wall? Why is there no army there? Why can't the dark beasts be finished once and for all by simply invading their lands? My young master was only ten years old, he could not answer these questions, but he was able to ask his father. I was tried quickly and without the right to pardon. If not for my aura, I would already be dead."

"Somehow you don't look like a squire," I said doubtfully. "Not the right physique."

"I wasn't required to carry weapons or armor. My task was to constantly be near the young master, to teach him to read and write, history, and society. I am a teacher. That's why they gave me a protective aura. I had good prospects for becoming a mage, if I had kept my mouth shut. New stones, abilities, boosts, money...But now all this is in the past. The clergy walked all over me. My back is striped with flog marks. Everyone was trying to find out where such seditious thoughts came from in the mind of a simple lyceum teacher? Who put them in my head? There was no question of any objective consideration of the case. The Fortress hates being asked uncomfortable questions."

"The way you're talking, you'd think the church is collaborating with the dark ones," Two remarked maliciously. Everyone smiled bitterly, but not me. They noticed: "What? It's just a joke to defuse the situation!"

"That's the thing, it's not a joke... According to the Fortress's official position, I'm a dark human."

My teammates gulped so loud that the Riftmaster himself probably heard it.

"Looks like I'll have to open up a little too," I chuckled. "Since we're working together, it's only right..."

My story didn't take long to tell. We were in no rush — we had the whole night ahead, and I didn't think it would take me much time to pass through the rift. So I recounted my adventures from the moment I turned eighteen to how I was put in a group with them. Without too many details, of course, but without excessive secrecy either. I even mentioned the conservator. Let them know what kind of beautiful lady would now be keeping our company.

"Eliminating an entire lineage?" Two frowned. "That's a strong move. Plus, evicting all those people…they do sometimes carry out complete cleansings, but never with so much enthusiasm. As One has already said, there's something dirty going on here. Have you tried talking to the clergy?"

"Like it would make a difference."

"Maybe it would, maybe it wouldn't, but the alternative is coming to terms with your lot in life and agreeing to follow any order given by a higher authority. Maybe it makes sense to make a request to the emperor? Like, 'I, Baron Valevsky, refuse to accept the share that has fallen to me, I ask you to consider the case again, because I consider the actions of Duke What's-His-Name to be unlawful.' You can give your dissenting opinion."

"I'm certainly not going to accept my lot in life," I said firmly, and Three grinned.

"Throughout your story, you mentioned taking revenge on the duke three times, but not a word about restoring the Valevsky name. Is there no better revenge than returning your name to the general registry? For aristocrats in the upper classes, death is preferable to dishonor. To defeat. That's what you need to fight for, not to someday meet the duke and finish him off. I'm sure the clergy will do everything to protect the duke from you. At the same time, they'll feed you with fairy tales while you dance to their tune and follow orders. Two is right — you need to start with a letter to the emperor. Ask for indulgence, mercy, restoration. One letter, two, a hundred — sooner or later you will either be rapped on the head and reprimanded, or the letter will end up on the table of the monarch. And who knows what will come of it? Why did the duke close off your lands?"

"They closed off the land so that it can recover," Two explained. "Five to ten years of ordinary farming, twenty to forty years logging, or more — these are special forests with rare animals. But there are a lot of agreements to go through. If the Valevskys had ordinary cultivated land, the closure is well justified."

"Well, we did have forests," I frowned. I had never seen the Duke's attack from this perspective. And I couldn't bear to think about it now.

"Then we return to our new group motto: Something's fishy here! You, young man, would do well to decide what your ultimate goal is — either revenge, despite the fact that you won't be allowed to get anywhere near the duke, or restoring your family. Always wanted to work for aristocrats. Why are you looking at me like that? Why not dream of a time when we are no longer doomed soldiers?

Max dreams, why are we any worse off than him? If you think only about the negative, this negativity will consume your life. We need to stay positive..."

"Let's take care of the rift first, then we can turn our minds to more joyful things," I suggested. "I agree that my behavior over the last three weeks might not have been the most prudent. Apparently my education was lacking..."

"The third son of a provincial baron?" Three looked at me strangely. "It's amazing that you can read and write at all. Usually they spend all their resources on their first son, leave a little for the second. The fate of the third and beyond is the Wall and heroic death in the teeth of the dark beast. Why breed competitors? You're still lucky. My master had two younger brothers — they only began to talk at the age of six. The middle one, as far as I know, was still given a governess, but the younger was simply handed over to a mentor to make a warrior out of him. That's it!"

"So let's finish our conversation." I shut out the steady flow of revelation washing over me like a wave. "Remove your armor and go down to the caves as soon as possible. Don't touch the beasts — according to our contract, they're not ours. If you manage to catch up with me and can cope with the influence, then we'll talk more about what happens if we survive. Including how to escape the fate of a doomed soldier. Yes, it's possible, and I know of several ways. But first, the rift. I'll be waiting for you downstairs..."

I must confess that my partners had given me

a lot to think about. So much that I almost forgot to put up my mirror when I entered the first cave. Not even almost — I forgot! My golden dome of protection sparked, throwing back the rapse that had fallen on my head. I automatically moved my hand forward, piercing the creature mid flight, and only after did I realized that something was wrong. Dark beasts shouldn't be jumping on me. I had to stop and deal with the situation. Only later did I curse myself with every swear I knew — at first I had really thought it was something wrong with the rift. Maybe I really should adopt that new motto: "Something's fishy here!"

Putting up the mirror, I went to conquer the rift. I encountered no more problems. The beasts died, one after the other, not even knowing what destroyed them. The first three caves were inhabited by simple kronas. Only from the fourth on did magical beasts begin to appear. And not a single elite creature with a golden aura — I thought they must have considered this rift too shallow. But here, I was also mistaken — I met an elite lurge in the twelfth cave. I suspect this praying mantis alone would be enough to shred several groups to cabbage. After making sure that only one guard remained ahead, I decided to return to the group.

"How's it going?" Amazingly, the trio of round-faced men had managed to crawl all the way to the seventh cave. They hadn't gone in — they didn't have the strength to do so. That's why they crawled. But they did so confidently and with purpose, helping each other along. Upon my arrival, the group reacted with a unified sigh of relief, at once transforming into three shapeless amoebas, unable to remain upright.

"How do people survive under such an influence?" Three croaked. Of the three, the teacher seemed most collected.

"Habit, nothing more. The longer you stay in the rift without armor, the less it will affect you. Soon, you won't notice the dark aura at all. So I suppose we need to do what I should have done at the very beginning of this campaign. Stand up. Come on, come on! Stand up! Don't stagger! We'll hold on to each other. Great."

With much grief and toil, I managed to raise everyone to their feet as they leaned against each other. The men staggered, but stood. Approaching One, I put my hand on his shoulder, waited for at least some reaction to my presence and said, as the Countess had said to me just recently:

"Do or die. Die, but save. The blood debt is sacred, for my life is your life, and your life is my life. Welcome to the family, Brother One. I will notify the doomed legion that we have a new brother."

The businessman's eyes brightened. Something similar to gratitude even appeared in it, but I didn't stop to consider it. I had two more speeches ahead of me...

"Now you are officially doomed soldiers, and not just some people sent to the rift to die by the Fortress. In any case, the other doomers will consider you one of their own until you prove otherwise. And one more thing...I suggest you do the impossible and crawl to the last cave. The guard is the most dangerous opponent on level one. If you can get used to its influence, the first level of any rift will seem like a cakewalk. In terms of auras. I can help drag you there, but it's better if you do it yourself and find a way to deal with the horror your body is experiencing. So, group! Heed my command! We cling to each other and take one step forward. On the count of three! One. Two. Three! Great! Rest five seconds and repeat! Once. Two. Step! Again!"

I never thought that I would turn into Gustav. I thought that my destiny was to carry out the commands of wise commanders, to have fun and spend my life in the arms of magnificent heartbreakers, but never to hover over three adult men, any of whom could have been my father, and to ruthlessly demand they comply with my orders. Shouting. Sometimes hitting. Cheering. Shouting again, on repeat, until their bodies obeyed and their legs moved. And just their bodies — judging by the crazed, horrified looks of the whole trio, their minds, if they remained, were buried somewhere very deep. However, something kept my group moving forward, despite the growing influence of the guard. Nobody was going to give up, as if everyone knew that their lives going forward depended on how far they could advance now.

The last cave was the hardest of all —

everyone's legs gave way and the men fell to their knees as soon as they entered the room. I had to lift them back up with a groan.

"We'll wait here. Stand and wait! Nobody falls down! Everyone is waiting! Do or die! Die, but save! The blood debt is sacred! Repeat! Do or die! Die, but save!"

Three hours! It took three hours before the Three began to repeat after me! I was hoarse, repeating the same phrase over and over again, but did not give up, trying to get through to their conscious minds. Five minutes later, Two joined us. One needed an extra half an hour, but soon he began to mutter too. So we stood, hugging each other and repeating the doomer code:

"Do or die! Die, but save! The blood debt is sacred!"

"Take a break!" I ordered, and the group collapsed onto the rocks. There was no more chance of any conversation. My partners could only take frantic, gasping breaths, trying not to look at the last passage. All of the nightmares that flooded their minds emanated from there.

Leaving the group behind, I moved forward. The guard was terrifying. A three-meter barrel-shaped body stood in the very center of the room, spreading its huge wings. The eyes located around the entire perimeter of the body could follow everything that was happening in the cave, and four thick legs were ready to carry the monster forward and crush the enemy at any moment. The creature did not react to my appearance — my mirror was still up.

It soon became clear that the katars would be completely useless. The most I'd be able to do is poke a small hole in the opponent, which would irritate it even more. Taking a step to the side, I frowned as my mana level jumped down by one. A few moments later, it happened again — another point.

A brief assessment revealed that I lost one point of mana every four seconds, and without any colorful effects. It just vanished. Apparently, this was part of the guard's aura, which is why they didn't let anyone approach without armor. An aura that bleeds you dry. There was only one guard, so the aura was weak — only one mana point.

I moved slowly around the perimeter of the room, deciding what to do. The creature paid no attention to me, as if I didn't exist. Once I reached the opposite end of the cave, I peered behind the "screen" — the cube-shaped Riftmaster was hard at work, preparing a projection of a krona.

The temptation to enter the cave and deal with the final creature was so great that I could hardly resist it. I didn't know what the guard would do in this case. Maybe it would go mad and rush through the caves, crushing my entire group like cockroaches. First, I needed to protect my men as much as I could.

I returned to them and explained my plan. No one had any objections. All three of them knew they were useless in open combat against the monster, so we all returned to the first cave, where

I helped them put on their steel armor again. It would provide at least some protection from the creature's aura, if it decided to go crazy. And only after I was convinced of the relative safety of the group did I return to the guard cave.

The barrel-shaped monster hadn't gone anywhere. It stared blankly in all directions, making no attempt to stop me, so I made it to the Riftmaster's chamber with no problems. I moved closer and hesitated. The krona being manifested before my eyes was almost complete. The projection was already fully formed and now seemed to be gaining power. Mass. Energy. I couldn't find the exact word, but the general idea was that the master was somehow transferring a part of its essence to the beast. The projection began to flicker, preparing to incarnate a new monster, and the best thing I could think to do was bring my katars forward. The steel slid easily through the incorporeal being and I witnessed the mystery of its birth — the creature suddenly gained density. The body fell to the floor. It's hard to stay upright when your vital organs have been run through with sharp steel. I expected an outburst of rage from the guard, some reaction from the Master, but nothing happened. A new projection simply appeared — this time a lurge. The Riftmaster continued to vacantly weave its children, completely unconcerned with their survival.

"Die." I directed my fist at the Master's heart and activated the katar. A short blow, and familiar inscriptions appeared before my eyes:

1 of 5 location map fragments obtained. Total: 2 out of 5.

1 of 12 *Amplify* Shards obtained. Total: 3 out of 12.

Turning toward the cave with the guards, I prepared for battle, but again nothing happened. One minute passed. Another. There were no huge stomping feet, no whirlwind, no menacing wingbeats. Complete silence. I looked around the corner — the guard continued to stand in the center of the cave, indifferent. Not a single movement. It didn't even breathe. I stood like that for several minutes, and then it dawned on me — my mana was no longer being drained! The aura that had been bleeding me dry was no more!

Gaining courage, I got up close to the dark creature and swallowed. The three-meter body was overwhelming in size. I didn't have any idea how to destroy one of them on my own. It was unreal!

I touched the guard's wings. They looked like a dense fabric impregnated with something viscous, like the stuff they used to make waterproof tents. But this thought flashed through my mind in a second before my thoughts were immediately occupied by something else. More precisely, the notification that appeared before my eyes:

Enhancement obtained. No predetermined

**choice, enhancement chosen randomly.
Elemental Resistance +1**

As soon as I finished reading the last line, the hulking mass of the guard lost its integrity and collapsed on the stones, dragging me along with it. There was no pain, no spasms, nothing at all had happened to my body upon receiving the last boost. The gruesome death that my mentor had warned me of didn't happen either. Apparently I had more questions for the Evil Engineer…

(Former territory of the Valevsky Barony, during Max's group's first campaign into the rift)

"Alright, this is the place," said Count Baileymore Fardi, the Duke of Odoevsky, making a wide, sweeping gesture.

"I am grateful to you, Duke, but I must reiterate — you need not have taken the pains to accompany me personally," Brother Zwarm, a red-robe, nodded and got off his horse without waiting for a reply.

"My duty is to help the Fortress in all its affairs," the duke did not let up, dismounting after the churchman. "Including to ensure the comfortable journey of its representatives to the evicted lands."

"You were very wise to allow the peasants to harvest before you plowed the land. Is this where Max was initiated?"

"The shore, the pit, the fire, stunted trees."

The Duke of Odoevsky listed the main landmarks. "Everything is as stated in your letter. One request — do not speak the name of the doomed soldier in my presence. I am far less than pleased to know that somewhere out there is a person who has sworn to destroy me and my entire family, and I have no way to influence the situation. I will not hide — if it were my will, I would cut this doomer down before he even left the academy. I don't want my daughter to have any problems in the future."

"You have nothing to worry about. The Fortress will protect you and your daughter against any of this doomer's attempts to harm you," assured Brother Zvarm. "Besides…Yes, this is the place — it was here that the power surge took place. Thank you Duke, we've seen everything we need to see. My brothers will finish clearing the territories, after which we will leave your company. The Fortress confirms that the actions of Duke Odoevsky were carried out in strict adherence to our worldly laws. And yes, about the doomed soldier. Even if he somehow managed to survive at the academy, he won't last a day at the Fortress. Even with the patronage of the High Priest. Too many heads of too many different regions are opposed to seeing this beast within the Fortress walls. Father Dvar is one of them."

Baileymore Fardi nodded his thanks and made a subtle gesture. A squad of underlings stationed nearby disappeared into the forests without a sound. The churchman was lucky that he hadn't dug deeper than his authority allowed.

Otherwise, the master's order was unequivocal: the Fortress must under no circumstances find out about the existence of three rifts actively developing in these lands. The time had not yet come.

251

Chapter 15

"GREAT LIGHT, WHAT A BEAUTY!" One lilted blissfully, immersing himself up to his neck in warm water. A naked courtesan (I couldn't bring myself to call her a beauty) clung to the man, persistently giggling and whispering something in his ear.

"Oh yeah, it was worth it," said Two, blowing clouds of smoke. The Kaliman tobacco had cost him nearly his entire reward, but he couldn't deny himself the pleasure. Near him, as well as near One, Three, and — why deny it — myself were four naked happy endings. The relaxing massage was long over and all our basic needs had been met in separate booths, so for now, we were simply enjoying the company of our...well, frankly, somewhat frightening lady friends. Next to my stars Lana and Dana, they didn't even compare. But...we simply did not have enough gold for more. The tobacco, wine, sauna and massage treatments were too expensive. Capital prices, what could you do?

"That's your time, gentlemen." The manager approached us. "Would you like to extend your visit?"

No one did. The giggling gals vanished behind closed doors, and four stern servants of the Light peeled off the walls. Less than a moment later, a steel hoop with a chain appeared around the neck of every doomed soldier, the other end of which ended in the hands of his servant. Rest time was over, time to face the hard reality of our everyday. Our clothes hadn't had time to dry properly, so I had to put them on wet. But clean. After the bath, I felt like a completely different person — alive, healthy, capable of doing the impossible, just to get the opportunity to come back here again. Even without the courtesans. I wouldn't stoop to such lows again.

We were led into a closed cart, the standard mode of transportation for doomed soldiers. The only difference between this and the trip from the rift to the capital was that this time, we weren't alone. Sister Alia came with us.

"Where to now?" One asked cheerily. "The next rift?"

"The Fortress," she replied, continuing to fix her steely gaze on me. Let's just say our little meeting after my return from the rift hadn't gone very well. At all. As soon as we stepped outside and declared the rift closed, a team of collectors rushed inside, but rather quickly one of them ran to Sister

Alia with a report. Actually, this was the moment our relationship really deteriorated. We were stopped, forced to strip naked, the doctors even checked in places where no decent person should ever have to check. They made me drink several liters of water and immediately induce vomiting. The churchmen were obviously looking for something and believed that one of us had it. But no one found anything, and this infuriated everyone. The rift had only one level, and as such, there was little to be extracted, and the Fortress was counting on something particular, unique. But it wasn't there. In the end, the girl came up to me and tried to ask about how everything went, but even I felt the innuendo in her words. She was not at all interested in how I managed to destroy the Riftmaster. She was interested in something else, and I had begun to get an inkling of what. Some particularly valuable ingredient from the guard. And she was trying to tell me about the special bond of trust between a personal servant and a dark human? She could shove it with her conspiracies.

To make a long story short, a few hours later we were loaded into a wagon and taken to the bathhouse, where a cleric in a blue robe issued our reward. Six gold. They didn't even give us the mana or recovery elixirs. And all the gold pieces were immediately handed over to the manager of the bathhouse. We even had to chip from our own savings to cover the costs. Quite coincidentally, everything together cost twenty-four gold pieces.

And most of it was spent on Kaliman tobacco and Shurgan wine. The best that could be ordered by ordinary imperial citizens.

The doors of the wagon closed, and the whole thing started to sway. We were off.

"Stand against the door!" Sister Alia ordered sharply, glancing at my three companions. I didn't know what they saw in the girl's eyes, but they all turned white and the order was carried out without the slightest hesitation or delay. Grasping me with her hand, the conservator pushed me as far as possible toward the opposite wall and activated *Protective Canopy*.

"We don't have much time, so I'll be direct. Rift Guards yield one of the rarest ingredients needed to create enhancement elixirs. It's called yem. The extraction technology is kept strictly secret and the knowledge is possessed only by select servant collectors, who are always present at any rift closure. There is always yem. It is a fundamental truth. But today this truth has been called into question. The collectors could not find any among the remains of the guard. For the first time in the entire existence of the Fortress, from what I know. But I need to check the archives. The report detailing this situation has already been placed on the table of the highest servants of the church, who are extremely displeased with your existence. The High Priest approved the plan for your three-week excommunication from the academy, and nowhere within it was it written that you should visit the Fortress. However, that is where we are now going — Father Dvar, the head of the security service, wants to personally find out why the most valuable ingredient was not extracted from the rift. Extraction and further processing of yem are the basis of the Fortress' financial stability. The sale of enhancement elixirs keeps the church afloat and provides its warriors with everything they need. But there was no yem found today. I cannot change our route — you'll end up at the Fortress anyway. I believe there will be several assassination attempts on you. Not directly by the clergy — the hierarchs definitely won't approve this now. They'll bait other doomers to attack you. You must survive. Your group will be allocated a separate room — don't leave it unless necessary. Try to stay within the sight of the servants of the Light. If, at some point, you notice there's not a robe in sight, you must leave immediately. Don't tell other doomed soldiers about your position. What happened at the rift, Max? Why did the guard look like that? Why didn't the collectors find the yem?"

"I need to send a letter to the emperor, can you help?" I asked, pretending that her impassioned monologue had completely passed me by."

"Letter?" Sister Alia scowled as if she'd heard the impossible.

"A letter. I want to write a petition for reconsideration of my case. I consider myself and my family innocent, the accusations of the Duke of Odoevsky are false, and the trial that took place is biased. To be honest, I haven't worked the exact phrasing out yet. Only the fact that I must write the letter."

"No one will permit you to send it," said Sister Alia. "You're a doomer. Property of the Fortress. A being whose name has been stricken from the list of the living."

"Now we've cut to the meat of it. When I need help, you start denying. When you need information, you push your questions on me. Weren't you talking about mutual cooperation, conservator? I don't see anything of the sort."

"I repeat, Baron Maximilian Valevsky no longer exists. He died. Officially. If a paper signed by a deceased person reaches the emperor's office, it will be sent to the archive. Or burned. And this is if it reaches him at all — for doomed soldiers, a sheet and a pen cost more than Kaliman tobacco and Shurgan wine. The fact that you were able to frivolously use writing materials at the academy is an exception to the rule. But even there, the servants of the Light have a strict order to count the number of sheets and record everything in their reports. You won't be able to write a letter, let alone send it."

"That's why I need your help. Remember you told me you could hire an assassin? That means you can ensure I have the opportunity to write a letter, after which it will appear in the office of the emperor. Marked "urgent." Give me this and we can have a normal working relationship. As for the warning about the Fortress — thank you, I will remain vigilant."

"So you won't even give me a hint about why there wasn't any yem found on the guard?"

"For now, my answer is, 'I have no idea what you're talking about.' But that could change if I get what I want. Guaranteed. With extra confirmation. Take the canopy down, it's nothing my team can't handle."

Sister Alia shot me an irritated look, but complied.

"Two, we have a problem. According to our conservator, they won't even consider a letter written by a doomer. Any ideas how we get around this?"

"I'd need to read the literature." The legal expert returned to his seat and looked at Sister Aliya. "The Doomed Soldier Code, all laws pertaining to Doomed Soldiers, and perhaps the laws concerning rehabilitation. The latter is the highest priority. I think we need to start from there. How can I obtain these things?"

"You have a second rift in front of you, you can order whatever supplies you please. If you can prove that it is pertinent," Sister Alia said in a lifeless voice. "Today, you'll be acquainted with the rules of the Fortress, which indicate the main points of the relationship between the doomed legion and the church. Anything outside of this you'll only obtain for an additional fee."

Two grimaced in displeasure, but did not dare express it.

"Maybe we can still try to find a way to

cooperate?" I suggested. "My group knows who I am and why you are assigned to me."

"Your group will be disbanded as soon as you enter the Fortress." Sister Alia's voice did not change. It remained just as cold and lifeless. "It's not registered, people have been assigned to rifts, but no one expected us to return to the Fortress before we were done. You can go to the next rift as part of another group. I have a task and I am going to complete it. On the list of variables I must consider is the doomed soldier Max, but not his group."

"What do I need to do to ensure our group remains intact? Even after we reach the Fortress?"

"Register. But that's practically impossible. First of all, these doomed soldiers haven't even officially been listed as part of the brotherhood. Secondly, a group cannot consist of people who are not officially listed in the Fortress. That pertains to you. Once a week, the group is required to accept or refuse a task. In three weeks, you will return to the academy and remain there for two and a half months. It's ten weeks. Ten unaccepted tasks, each of which reduces the participant's rankings by five hundred points. They will be killed before you get to the Fortress."

"Why can't I close one rift a week? It won't take long."

"Because now you are being allocated rifts that are several hours away from the capital. In three weeks there will be no such indulgences, and the rifts may be at the very outskirts of the empire.

A few days' journey. The law forbids you from leaving the academy for more than three days."

"Practically impossible and impossible are two different things," noted One.

"They are," Sister Alia agreed, never taking her piercing gaze off me. "But I don't understand why I should care about your fate? You are not my assignment."

"So you need something from Max, but he refuses to give it to you?" One continued his thought. "And you're playing hardball and trying to pressure him through us?"

"One more word like that out of you, doomer, and I'll kill you. You have no right to speak to a representative of the Church of the Light in that tone ."

"I beg your pardon for my tactlessness," said one, blanching, but he clearly wasn't about to surrender. "I forgot myself and overstepped. Although...as far as I remember, I haven't put my signature on any paper acknowledging that I've been told the Fortress rules. How could a simple doomed soldier know the principles of communication with the servants of the Light, if these very servants did not even bother to acquaint the doomed soldiers with these restrictions?"

"Don't test my patience, doomer." Sister Alia didn't even bother to turn in his direction.

"But still, to finish the same line of thought — Max has the information you need. You have opportunities that we don't. Maybe it makes sense to meet each other halfway and give everyone what they need? We give you information, you give us the codex of laws and register our group? If you are assigned to Max as a point of contact with the Fortress, maybe it makes sense to make concessions and show that this relationship can bring not just a chain around the neck, but also benefits to both parties? That you're not just a stick, but can be a carrot as well?"

"Suppose I really can keep the current group composition, and that I even know how to assign you to the closest rifts to close." Sister Alia's voice suddenly gained emotion. "Suppose I help you get the required laws, and even deliver your useless letter. What will I get in exchange? Another snort from Max and the words 'I have no idea?' I've already got that. As long as there's no signed agreement between us, I am only the conservator of the group, nothing more."

"You will get information on what happened with the guard and why you didn't find what you were looking for," I said decisively. "I agree with One. Before we start to trust each other, we need to learn to cooperate. Let's try it."

"I need to know this before we get to the Fortress," Sister Alia stated peremptorily. "I need to understand how to build your defense. The fact that the Fortress lost such valuable resources may be forgivable."

"What assurance do I have that you will keep your end of the deal?" I asked.

"My word. You won't get anything else."

"Alright then, your word. Let's try to trust one another. Should I relay the information privately, or may I speak in front of present company?"

Sister Alia finally deigned to look at the other three doomed soldiers. She thought for a while, then said:

"The choice is yours. If they become part of our contract, then the same rules apply to them as to you. Except that they are ordinary doomed soldiers."

"Just a question. I may be in possession of a stone. The High Priest has already warned me that it's useless to me, but what about my team?"

"You didn't listen very attentively." Here Two came to the rescue. "Whatever you can't do, we can't do, no matter how you ask. Until we have information about you and what the Fortress wants from you, we are useless doomed soldiers. But as soon as we gain access to this information, a dependency will form. I don't mind sitting out again. We don't want any more problems in the future."

"We agree," One and Three said.

"Set up the canopy," I nodded, inviting Sister Alia to another round of private meetings. "Okay, I won't play hard to get and ask what you want to know. I'll tell you everything. I didn't kill the guard. I didn't fight it at all. I used the mirror to pass through to the last cave and found myself in the Riftmaster's lair. While there, I killed a krona that was being manifested and closed the rift. The guard had turned into a huge, harmless carcass of meat. When I touched it, a message appeared stating that I had received a random enhancement, since I didn't bother to select the parameter to be improved in advance. After that, the guard carcass lost its integrity and crumbled to the floor. That's it."

"You can't pass a guard," Sister Alia frowned. "We've tested more than once. It got to the point that the creature simply blocked the passage to the Riftmaster with its body."

"I had my mirror up. The dark beasts saw me as the same creature as them. That's why they let me through."

"What did you get? What enhancement?"

"I believe this is outside of the scope of our agreement."

"Max...don't start. We can go the long way if you want. Don't forget — the Evil Engineer has *Analyze*. He only needs to look at you to determine your full list of your buffs. Including new ones. What is the point of hiding something that can be easily revealed?"

"Elemental resistance," I responded after some thought. My mentor really would see the new enhancement, she was right. There was no point in hiding this information.

"A ten-percent increase in resistance," Sister Alia nodded knowingly. "A useful addition. The Light itself guides you. If you can boost this parameter to one hundred percent, then fire, cold and electricity will have no effect on you. Open the options in your taskbar and try to figure out how you can make an informed choice of enhancements. Chance will not always work in your favor."

"You mean you're not going to reprimand me for unauthorized treatment of guards?" I frowned. Not the kind of reaction I expected.

"Max, we are in the same boat. My goal is your development. Physical training you can handle on your own, so mana and resistance are a priority. Resistance even more so — while you can wait six months for the mana and boost it with a standard elixir for a reasonable price, enhancing your elemental resistance costs crazy money and is not accessible. Too many rare ingredients are needed to make the potion. So I'm rather pleased that the Light sent you the right enhancement. Is this all?"

"Absolutely. There was nothing else new or special about the rift. I received the third fragment of the *Amplify* and the second piece of the map."

"Could you go past all the dark beasts without killing them?"

"All the way to the Riftmaster? In theory, yes. In practice — we'll have to see. Don't forget that in two-level rifts, Wardens start appearing — exclusive beasts. Red beasts react rather strangely to the mirror, as if they see me as a direct competitor. They are aggressive."

"You can kill the Warden, it's not essential. What's important is that we look at the others — how first- and second-level beasts will behave if you only kill the Riftmaster. Will they freeze up like the guard? Become aggressive? No one has ever conducted an experiment like this, so the Fortress is fully prepared to pay for your participation."

"I can't take my group with me. If the dark beasts become aggressive, they'll simply tear them to shreds. Does the Fortress really need senseless sacrifices?"

"I understand. We'll cross that bridge when we come to it. Your main task is to survive until then. I wasn't bluffing when I warned you about the assassination attempts. For many, another dark human, and one we don't fully understand, is like a slap in the face. They want to get rid of you, and the missing yem will just be an additional argument against you. But we'll deal with this issue later, when we reach the second rift. As for your group, I will make sure that you are registered. Have you accepted them into the brotherhood?"

I nodded.

"Rightly so. Regarding the code of law...I need to speak to the High Priest on the matter. This point concerns not only you, but also your entire group. I understand your desire to find freedom. Let's think about how this can be accomplished. For now, while you are a doomed soldier, it is easier to control and protect you. If you suddenly resurrect yourself, the laws of the empire will apply to you. In all their diversity and focus on the highest aristocrats. Are you ready to face Duke Odoevsky on his territory? Soon we will reach the Fortress, where we will have to split up. If you want to save your group, you will need to do the following..."

The briefing dragged on — Sister Alia demanded that I repeat her instructions word for word. She only took down the canopy after our wagon had stopped.

"Hurry!" The door opened, and one of the churchmen peered inside. Our conservator jumped out, and the doors immediately slammed shut, preventing us from enjoying the beauty of the Fortress. The cart swayed again and dragged forward, but just a couple of minutes later it came to a halt once again. For good this time.

"Don't lag behind. Stick together," I ordered as I got out. From the inside, the Fortress looked like the courtyard of an ordinary castle — tall stone walls with guards, a main complex, a bunch of small buildings around it, people hustling and bustling. There was even a training ground not far from one of the walls. Inside, several dozen people stripped naked to the waist were practicing their spear work.

"Follow me." We were met by a greeter cleric in a white robe. Sister Alia had warned me about this ahead of time, so there was no issue. Climbing the stairs, we entered the main building and found ourselves in a huge hall. No — an enormous hall! Several dozen wooden tables divided the hall into three areas, The first and largest was designated for doomers with a rating below a thousand. It was dirty, noisy and overcrowded. The second, where we were taken, was intended for doomed soldiers with a rating of one to ten thousand. There were fewer people here, and the tables were clean. The third, the smallest part of the hall, was enclosed by screens. The doomer elite. Each of the sections had its own corridor which led to private rooms. Ten people per room in the first tier, five in the second and individual rooms for the third.

"This is Max and his current group, the ranks have been updated," the greeter introduced me to a bald man sitting at the entrance to one of these 'compartments.' Also a churchman He opened his notebook, flipped through to the very end and made a few notes.

"Access confirmed. Your tokens." Four metal badges with the number "2" inside appeared on the table from nowhere. Actually, not quite — three identical badges and one with a name. Below the number 2 was the nickname "Max." It looked a lot like a dog tag.

"Fasten it to your chest and do not remove it while you are within the Fortress walls. Has the group already been formed?"

"We're going to the administrative office right now," I explained. "We need a separate room for Max's group, four people. I'm the commander. Can we proceed to registration?"

"You can do whatever you'd like," the bald servant of the Light replied blankly. "I have a note that at three o'clock in the afternoon you are all expected in office one-twelve of the administrative building for briefing and familiarization with the rules of the Fortress. Don't be late. Questions?"

"No questions," I replied for the group and

dragged them away. The conservator had told us the registration office was in a separate building, so we had to hurry — we had less than forty minutes left before our introductory briefing. Sister Alia specifically explained that we must register the group before we sign off on the rules. Because that was the only way to cheat the system and register a group under my control before I left the academy.

But we didn't even make it out of the main mess hall. The road was blocked by a huge fellow, both one and a half times taller and wider than me.

"So you're the doomer Max who closed the rift with the Countess? I don't like your face, kid! It's too sugary sweet, you look like a girl. That won't fly around here. We'll have to fix it. I, the doomed soldier Tiger, require your presence in the ring for hand-to-hand combat training. Follow me, the fight will take place now."

There was silence as everyone waited for my reaction. And most unpleasantly, the man bore a personalized badge with the number 1 on his burly chest. Sister Alia had been mistaken — it wasn't some third-ranked player who came after me, who I'd have every right to ignore. And not even a warrior on the same level as I was, who I might have to listen to, but didn't have to follow orders from. But no, my opponent was a top-ranked doomer. One who, according to doomer law, had every right to command all those below him in rank. Including me.

Chapter 16

"HOW TEMPTING," I chuckled. "Training with someone who could kill me with a single punch. Why not? We only live once, right? Except…I'm afraid you don't have the right to invite me to practice, Doomed Soldier Tiger. I'm not in your league. Of course, you could break the Fortress rules and attack — even beat up a simple person like me, but I'm afraid to even imagine what the clergy would do to you. I only know one thing: if you touch me without my permission, there will be one less first-rank doomer in the world."

"What are you blabbing about? You have a badge!" Tiger frowned.

"Well, guess what! Dear servant of the Light, could you please clarify one small detail: can the venerated Mr. Tiger here beat me up before I go through the introductory briefing?"

Amazingly, the bluff worked. The bald cleric,

who monitored the passage to the second compartment, measured us up with an indifferent look and said:

"Until the doomer Max has his introductory briefing today at 3:00 p.m., he is subject to the rules of the empire. Not the Fortress."

"He passed through the rift!" Tiger barked angrily, but the churchman didn't care anymore. He returned to his notebook.

"No problem, I'll wait. One hour won't change anything." The enormous man stepped aside to let me through, but I wasn't going anywhere.

"Where are you going, apparently-not-so-venerated Tiger? I haven't released you yet."

The murmur that had risen in the hall subsided at once. Obviously, no one expected such a quip from a beginner, especially addressed to an older brother.

"I do like the idea of training, but there's one thing I don't understand — in which rift do you find beasts that will engage in hand-to-hand combat? Are you really a doomed soldier, or circus strongman waving his fists for the amusement of the public? You want a training session? No problem — let's train. But let's make it a real workout and not a tea party. One on one, any weapon you, armor or magic we can find is permitted. Steel is welcome. To make it easier for you to choose, I'll tell you about mine — I'll take a training spear and no armor. We're training for the rifts, right? So I'll fight you the way I fight my way through the rifts. The goal is to break the opponent's spirit so he can no longer stand on his feet. If someone gets hurt, this is their problem. Means he didn't train well enough. Better to find out here and now than in the rift, where you'd risk the lives of the rest of your group. This is a training session I'll gladly attend — in ten minutes."

"Twenty gold says Max beats the shit out of Tiger," sounded a familiar voice. I turned around and saw Gimlet not far away. The mage from the Countess's detachment nodded affably and raised his hand. "Father Kurch, record the bet. Who will risk their gold and bet against me?"

"I will!" a voice rang out, and the huge hall turned into a humming beehive. Everyone rushed to the churchmen who controlled the entrances to the different areas of the hall. Apparently, these bald and completely indifferent servants of the Light played every role for the doomed soldiers.

"You have ten minutes," Tiger spat at me with vitriol. "I'll be waiting for you at the arena."

"I hope you know what you're doing, boy." Gimlet came up to me. "Tiger is a very dangerous opponent. One of the best fighters. You won't be able to ride him like a dark beast. He wields a spear — not as well as Rabblerouser, of course, but at a fairly high level."

"We'll see." I shook his outstretched hand. "I urgently need to see the administrator, then get to the arena. Can you show me where it is?"

"Registering a group?" Gimlet looked at my group and sighed heavily. "You're even weirder than I thought. Come on, I'll show you where everything is. Bring your men with you too — their badges need to be corrected."

There were no others who wanted to block my way, so after a couple of minutes I was standing in front of a churchman dressed in a blue robe. As far as I noticed, they were the overwhelming majority within the Fortress walls. Everywhere I looked, there was blue.

"Registered." The churchman fiddled with the papers for a short time and finally put a large round wax seal at the bottom of a thick sheet of paper. "The group of doomer Max, consisting of four people, has been created. The group's current rating is 1,000 points. Give your badges here — you need to put your identifying mark on them."

In the next room was a jeweler's machine, with which the servant of the Light rather deftly scrawled the name of our group on our dog tags. The still nameless doomed soldiers finally had some sort of identification. And within the Fortress walls, as Three had whispered in my ear, that meant a lot.

"Our arena," Gimlet said, leading me to a building located behind the main complex. People were already crowding at the door, waiting for the spectacle. Apparently, it wasn't every day that someone challenged the Tiger and insisted on full contact. I looked at the huge clock tower — there was still half an hour before our introductory briefing. We couldn't be late. Sister Alia would not forgive me such misconduct.

"Alright, the sooner we start, the sooner we

finish," I said, going inside. If you didn't know what kind of building it was, you would never have guessed that a room similar to a rift cave was hiding inside. Multi-level stadium seating stretched around the entire perimeter and the doomed soldiers were flooding in, swearing and fighting over the best seats. There was no mention of any tickets. The first tiers, as I noticed, were designated for those with the number 1 on their badges. Among those gathered, I noticed the Countess — a beautiful and dangerous woman. She was talking with Rabblerouser and gave me a fleeting nod of greeting. Tiger was already in the arena, and for a moment I felt a sharp pang of panic. My opponent was a warrior clad in perfect armor, a master at wielding his spear. This became clear from the way the man deftly twisted the spear around him to stretch his arms. Great idea, by the way, too bad I was late. Unlike my opponent, I'd have to fight with cold muscles.

One of the servants of the Light approached me and removed my collar. According to the conditions of the duel, we were allowed to use magic, so there should be no restrictions. A similar procedure was carried out on Tiger, thus demonstrating that my opponent had magic. Okay, let's keep that in mind for the future. Reaching down to touch my toes a few times, I went to the weapon rack and took the spear, feeling its balance point. Compared to the monster Tiger was wielding, it looked like a toothpick. And how else would a training spear look compared to a combat spear? My katars had been taken away after the rift and clearly no one was going to return them, while the enemy was using the full arsenal available to him. It was a dream for him, not a duel!

"Ready?" I turned to the Tiger, sweeping my spear in a circle. "Do you remember the conditions? We fight as long as you stand on your feet. We stop only when you admit defeat. Is that acceptable?"

"You die today," came his response. Calm. Emotionless. Tiger really was an excellent warrior who knew his business and knew how to control emotions. Trying to piss him off was useless — I'd sooner lose my temper than this bastard.

One could ask a quite reasonable question: why did I remain calm, despite facing such a formidable opponent? The reason was actually simple: my mana was at its max and I had four additional vials on my belt. Whatever kind of warrior Tiger may be, he'd be fighting two opponents — me and himself. A spear was not a sword, the doomer Tiger was not Master Hwang, so it wouldn't be possible to break through my defenses quickly. The memory of training with Rabblerouser was still fresh in my mind, but much had changed since then. First and foremost, I had changed. No matter how naive it may sound, I really had become both stronger and faster. In my hands, even a training spear was now a deadly weapon, capable of many things. It was time to see firsthand how well the Evil Engineer taught me.

I moved first. I didn't see any point in wasting time. My state of combat meditation, which had saved me more than once during battles with Karina Fardi, had become something so near and dear to me that I didn't even notice I had slipped into it. I just started moving exponentially faster than before. Assuming that Tiger was not inferior in speed to Rabblerouser, I pushed myself to the limit of my capabilities right off the bat. And for good reason, it turned out. Despite all my speed, Tiger still managed to attack me. Deflecting his attack, I didn't care that the tip of his spear wasn't pushed far enough aside — let my *Golden Dome of Protection* deal with such trifles. Sparks flashed and Tiger's spear, as expected, was pushed to the side, which allowed me to continue moving and make a precise lunge, aiming for his head. The enemy didn't have a lot of weak points — his head, knees and elbows. Everything else was so well protected that this useless piece of iron that someone had called a training spear had no chance of breaking through.

The blow was considerable — the sound of the hit resounded throughout the entire arena and the recoil nearly knocked the spear out of my hands. Jumping back, ready to repel Tiger's counterattack, I hesitated — instead of chasing me and leaning on me with all his inhuman strength, the man remained in place. Frowning, I began to slowly spiral toward him, closing the distance, ready for any nasty tricks, but for some reason there were none. Tiger simply stood in one place, spear pointed forward. Not even in my direction. A few steps, and I was standing a meter behind the enemy. The tip of my spear rested on his back, but he did not even think of defending himself. Just stood there like a statue. I pushed a little, pushing the Tiger forward, but instead of taking a step, the enemy began to fall forward, so that in a moment, with a deafening roar, he would collapse in the sand.

Rolling the huge form onto its back, I pulled off the helmet with difficulty — the dent where my spear had landed was huge. The visor had gone from convex to concave. Entirely concave. I even had to "borrow" Tiger's knife to cut off the straps fastening it to his head. Tiger's face was covered in blood. His nose and jaw had been crushed, as if from a direct blow with a sledgehammer. There was not a hint of consciousness in his rolling eyes — it was amazing that the doomer had managed to stay on his feet with such wounds. No longer in the mindset that I'd been in just a few moments ago when I thought I'd have to finish him off, I activated the healing aura and took out one of the three recovery elixirs, slowly pouring the contents into my torn mouth. I had no desire to kill Tiger.

"Healer!" I shouted, only now noticing the silence that hung in the air. "We need a healer, now!"

Finally, the air began to hum with the sound of human voices. Several churchmen pulled me away from Tiger and he was carried away somewhere. And they took the spear I'd used with them. I began to slowly move toward the exit, but Rabblerouser's voice made me stop.

"When did you learn to move like that, dude?"

Turning around, I saw the Countess's full team. Even Flask, who habitually reeked of alcohol, had come to watch.

"I don't understand the question," I answered in bewilderment. I didn't feel as if I was doing anything special. Yes, I was pushing myself to the max, but before Karina Fardi, it had been like walking to another empire on foot.

"You were moving so fast that you were practically a blur," the Countess said.

"I really had to strain to track your movements," Rabblerouser confirmed. "You were working at my speed, boy. We haven't seen you for a week, what has happened since then?"

"He has matured," Flask said. "Become stronger, more powerful. As if he's gotten two or three enhancements during this time. Humans can't make that kind of progress without magical intervention."

"Do you care to share the secret of your progress with your brothers in misfortune?" Gimlet winked. "Tiger didn't even have time to use his abilities."

"I don't know what you're thinking, but I haven't done anything special," I said. "That's just what I worked on during training at the academy, putting everything into one blow. If you watched the fight closely, you saw that Tiger struck first, but my defense deflected his spear and upset his balance. There was an opening and I didn't miss. That's all. No secrets or surprises. As for the speed, you haven't seen how the aristocrats in the academy move. I'm a tortoise compared to them."

"That's like comparing assholes and oranges," Gimlet chuckled. "Aristocrats are strengthened with potions every six months from the age of six. We only get them if we're lucky."

"Enough chit chat," the Countess stopped him. "Max, I'm coming to you with an offer. My squad needs a fifth fighter. Join us. We saw you in the rift. In the arena too. I think that you're a worthy warrior, despite your age. Judging by the current rankings, you've already managed to close a three-level with someone else, so you know what creatures we have to fight. A rift has been discovered near the Wall. The intelligence data tells us it has at least seven levels, but it's likely eight. As far as I heard, a large-scale battle is planned in a month that will involve the regular army and high aristocrats. If we delay, the Riftmaster will dig down to level ten within a couple of years, and then we will lose this territory. Rifts with so many levels cannot be closed. Come over to my group — we'll get it done together. So our likelihood of survival is greater. Don't forget, we're in the top rank."

"I appreciate the offer, Countess, but I'm afraid I must refuse. I already have a group and I'm not going to throw them aside just for the chance to work with you."

"Your group is useless. They're not warriors.

They'll just weigh you down."

"You shouldn't judge those you don't have the slightest idea about." My voice was cold as steel.

"Are you telling me they were the ones you closed a three-level rift with?"

"What difference does it make how and with whom I passed through the rift? Again, I am grateful for the offer, but I have to refuse it. I have obligations to my team and I'm going to fulfill them."

I no longer had any desire to communicate with the Countess. What was strange — she was a legend and having a place by her side would be a great honor, but I was certain it didn't interest me at all. Why? Who knows?

"I looked at the ratings," said Rabblerouser. "Max got four hundred points for our rift. And a thousand for the one he just passed through. Just like the other three. They're also in rank two now."

"They're the same as you?" The Countess frowned.

"No. Ordinary doomed soldiers. Don't you think this may not be the best place to have this conversation? Too many ears around."

My remark was quite fair — a rather impressive crowd had indeed gathered around us. The people were wondering what the Countess herself could be discussing with some unknown little boy.

"You're right, it's not the place. Alright, Max, I understand and accept your position. May luck always favor you."

"May luck always be on your side," I answered, but my words flew into the woman's back. The Countess did not wait for a response.

"Your reward," a churchman in a blue robe appeared next to me and handed me a heavy purse. "Forty-two gold pieces. Ten percent of all bets were placed against you."

I accepted the award, keeping my eyebrows in place with difficulty. Forty-two gold! I had earned nearly three months of Gustav's salary in just one performative fight. Of course, the fact that it ended so quickly had made me tense — I thought that the battle with Tiger would drag on for at least ten minutes. And certainly wouldn't end after just one hit.

No one else tried to block my way, so at exactly three o'clock, my full team was standing outside of office one-twelve. The only thing that could be said about the briefing is that it took place. The Fortress' rules differed little from what Three had already told us. Don't go here, don't look here, don't think about this. A doomed soldier is a slave of the Fortress, and it is impossible to change this for the rest of his life. Nevertheless, there were also some interesting points: rewards, access to the store, concessions in the choice of tasks and other things that made life a little easier. As I put my signature on the paper to signify receipt, I thought about how they must have tempted Tiger to call me to training. Much of the document was dedicated to doomer rankings and the relationships between them. An open challenge to a duel between ranks was punishable by fine. Moreover, this rule worked both in both directions — even if the lower-ranking doomer challenged a higher-ranking one. Since officially, it was I who challenged Tiger to the arena and offered different conditions than his, we would both be punished. The punishment itself depended entirely on the will of the rank's conservator and could be anything. Up to and including flogging. This was also practiced in the Fortress — Three had already regaled us with several stories of incidents that had occurred during his previous stay here. The only thing that saved me from punishment was the fact that I hadn't signed to signify my familiarity with the rules before the fight. Formally, I still didn't know that I shouldn't challenge a doomed soldier of a different rank to a duel, so Sister Alia, if she really is my representative in the Fortress, should easily prove my innocence. In general, it seems like I'd won, and I'd even gotten gold for my efforts, but I derived little joy from this.

I spent the rest of the day in the room assigned to my group. I didn't even go to dinner, so as not to provoke a new skirmish, and my group brought me a tray full of food. Doomers were allowed to eat anywhere within the Fortress.

"What are we going to do?" Three asked as the lights-out gong sounded. After ten in the evening, none of the doomers were allowed to leave their rooms. The punishment for disobedience was death. This was strictly enforced by the clergy. Those who fought dark beasts must be well-rested, well-fed and ready to break into the rift at the first call.

"Honestly, I have no idea. We just sit in the room and wait," I replied. The conservator never appeared, I was not summoned anywhere, there was no punishment for beating Tiger, no other provocations took place. This wasn't the life I had come to know — it was a cakewalk!

"You broke something with that duel," One grinned. "The ones who called us here clearly expected a different outcome. I talked to the people here — Tiger regained consciousness, he was healed, but he doesn't remember the last two days. You hit him hard. They say that when he was told that he had challenged a doomed soldier from rank two, his face went slack, as if this was incredible news to him. Which means he hadn't even heard of you two days ago. I'm sure those same churchmen arranged it, who else."

"I visited the store," Three said after a long pause. "What can I say...with our thousand ranking points, there's not much to do there. Ability stones start at a thousand and go up to infinity. Same with support gems. Fitting armor to size costs five hundred units, normal weapons — three hundred, mana elixirs are ten, recoveries are fifty. I won't even mention the enhancements and amulets. Nothing below two thousand. The prices here are exorbitant, of course."

"We have two doubles and a triple in front of us," One started thinking aloud. "That's another thousand eight hundred ranking points. Two thousand eight hundred total. Enough to buy a decent stone. Can we haggle?"

Three began explaining something about the catalog, but he was interrupted almost immediately — suddenly the door to the room opened and a disheveled Sister Alia appeared on the threshold.

"Things with big teeth right behind me! Run!" the conservator ordered, throwing my katars at me. I caught the weapon and was already on my feet. Sister Alia's behavior was so out of the ordinary that the excitement swept over everyone. As such, no one had anything, except for the purse of gold that I had received for my battle with Tiger, so we got dressed and in ten seconds we were ready to go.

"Follow me! Don't fall behind!" Sister Alia ran out into the corridor and rushed to the exit as fast as she could. We huddled behind her, sincerely hoping that the churchmen on duty would speak to her before firing their crossbows. However, there were no servant guards in place. Even the bald monitor who had seemed rooted to his chair was also absent.

"What happened?" I caught up to Sister Alia at the entrance to the main building.

"Questions later!" she threw back at me as she ran and pointed to the wagon, the doors of which were open. "Get inside, alive!"

No one wanted to argue, and after a couple of moments we settled on the seats inside. Immediately a silent churchman appeared, fastening steel collars on us and chaining us to the wagon. Even during our escape, the servants of the Light did everything according to the book. Sister Alia climbed inside with us, and as soon as the doors closed, the wagon started off.

"Not a sound!" ordered the girl and peered through a small crack into the darkness. Several times we stopped and some unintelligible voices were heard, but each time we were let through without checking the back. Finally, Sister Alia peeled herself from the peep hole and sat up straight. The girl was visibly shaking, so we had to wait for the conservator to calm down and explain what was going on. Where were they dragging us to at this time of night? It took almost an hour for a response. All this time, Sister Alia sat with a deeply pensive look, as if she were solving the most complex equation in this world. Having come to some solution, the girl looked at us and said:

"Tonight, the highest authorities of the church decided that the dark doomer Max is too unpredictable and potentially dangerous for the Fortress. Of the nine heads of regions, nine people voted to kill you. Now the decision is up to the High Priest. He may accept this decision or offer his own. But in order to go against the heads of the regions, Father Urg needs to present iron-clad proof of your worth. The single and even triple rifts won't count — they're closed by ordinary doomer groups. You need to do something so incredible, so that even the orthodox heads will not dare to look in your direction with pretensions of murder. You must become valuable to the church, and I could only think of one way to do that. We're going to the Wall."

"To the eight-level rift," I muttered. "Sister Alia, tell me, what difference does it make how I die? A rift this big is impossible for me."

"You have time to adapt to the influence of the dark ones. Regulations do not apply to rifts of this level. Moreover, you all will have to go inside. They'll reach us by morning and anyone who remains outside the rift will be immediately arrested. I acted at my own peril and risk, pulling you out of the Fortress. They will definitely punish me, and most likely, they will deprive me of my dignity and relegate me to the ranks of the doomers, but I could not do otherwise. Max, if you really want to return your family name to the list of the living, you must close this rift at all costs. You have no other choice."

Chapter 17

"SOUNDS LIKE A SET-UP," I said doubtfully. "If the hierarchs have already sentenced me, what will prevent them from carrying out their decision after the rift?"

"I don't know," Sister Alia responded truthfully. "Max, if you had stayed in the Fortress, your execution would have taken place this morning. If you close the rift, there is a chance that the hierarchs will change their mind. Just a chance, but as long as it's there, I must do everything in my power to keep you alive. The others must see what I do, you are important to the Fortress."

"If you want to save my life, let me go," I said. "I'll assume another name, run to the Kaliman Empire, start fresh."

"No!" The girl was even taken aback by the suggestion. "You're a doomed soldier! The fact that

I pulled you out of the Fortress without the consent of the High Priest does not grant you freedom. I am still your conservator, you are still a slave of the Fortress. And the decision of the highest hierarchs of the church will not affect this in any way."

"In other words, you're acting purely in your own interests, using us as a bargaining chip. If everything goes well, you'll get the honors and accolades. If not, they'll simply scold you and remove you from your post."

"Honors and accolades?" Sister Alia laughed bitterly. "You weren't listening, Max. They will punish me in any case, regardless of the outcome of your campaign. Close the rift or not — it won't affect my fate. Given my clearance level and knowledge of the inner workings of the Fortress, the church will have only one option: defrocking and execution. Because it would be too dangerous to conscript me to the doomed legion — I know things ordinary people shouldn't know. This is the price of not being burned alive today. And I'm ready to pay it! Yes, I'm ready — I already paid it! I traded my life for you to have a chance to survive. So do not accuse me of self-interest and greed. Up until my last breath, I will remain a faithful servant of the church. If the rift does not change the attitude of the higher hierarchs toward you, you will follow me. This means that this is the will of the Light, and we must accept it with sincere joy."

I kept my mouth shut, trying not to look at

the flames of fanaticism burning in her eyes. You couldn't fake that — the girl really believed in what she said, and was going to fulfill her mission to the last. I looked at my group. They were gazing, dumbfounded, at the conservator, as if they were seeing her for the first time. Sister Alia's behavior came as a surprise to everyone. Nevertheless, One could not resist asking:

"Why should we go into the rift with Max? To hide from those who will follow us? For what? We are enacting the will of the cleric assigned to us. We're doing what you say."

"I understand and... And I apologize for my behavior. In fact, I shouldn't even have taken you," Sister Alia answered after a long pause. "I...I wasn't trained for this, so I just panicked, going against the will of the council. If you had stayed in the Fortress, the maximum that could be done to you was to lower your rank. But now you have to go with Max into the rift to demonstrate the unity of the group. The only chance for you to survive in our current situation is to sign a cleansing contract and pretend that you are trying in every possible way to fulfill it."

"A seven, maybe eight-level." One felt himself on solid ground once it had turned into a business negotiation. "This is an unregulated rift, so the ranking should be higher than usual. Let's count. One hundred for the first level, three hundred for the second, six hundred for the third, one thousand for the fourth. Total: two thousand, strictly according to the regulations. How much should the fifth level cost? I think three thousand, no less. Especially since Max will close it alone. The sixth is five, the seventh is ten. In total, we'll have earned twenty thousand ranking points."

"That's if there are seven levels," I remarked sullenly. "They suspect there may be eight. They use entire armies to close rifts like that, and half of them don't see the light of day again."

"If there's an eighth level, that's another twenty thousand. In total: forty thousand points for Max's group." One really did have a way with words. "What do you say, Sister Alia? Is this a reasonable reward given our current situation? If this is our reward, we are ready to fulfill any of your strange orders, even breaking away from the Fortress this late."

"Forty thousand," the girl repeated thoughtfully. "Yes, that's quite a decent figure, so they won't ask questions. We'll put it down. The last time they closed an eight-level, the survivors were credited with thirty thousand."

"Someone has closed an eight?" I asked.

"Twelve years ago. The combined forces of the Fortress, the army and the aristocracy. Three thousand doomed soldiers went into the rift, thirty-two people came out. A dark day for the Fortress. After that incident, it was decided that we wouldn't allow rifts to grow that large. It's the local servants of the Light's fault that we missed this one. They overlooked it. Especially so close to the Wall. Are you interested in anything other than rankings?"

"Wine, tobacco, bathhouse, and a massage," One began to list. "Courtesans. Only this time from Red Rose. Does that sound feasible?"

"Considering that you'll be the ones paying, entirely." Sister Alia was not easily embarrassed. "Is that all? Can I draw up the contract?"

"I would like ten more individual training sessions with the Evil Engineer and Ursula de Vrath, as well as ten chabre crystals."

The look Sister Alia gave me spoke volumes. So much anger and frustration! Apparently, the conservator knew perfectly well what chabre was used for, and silently showed dissatisfaction with the fact that I kept silent about the symbols. But I easily held her gaze, confident that I was right. I didn't owe anything to anyone, especially the Fortress. The girl pursed her lips, cast a fleeting glance at the group, and then said:

"Chabre must be processed before it can be used. The crystals themselves are useless — you cannot use them to activate a symbol."

"It feels like we've involuntarily heard something that we had no right to hear," Two moved toward the wall. "Are you going to activate your dome of silence? I don't want to end up under fire."

"I am not yet a personal servant to a dark human, so after the first rift I had to return the *Protective Canopy* stone. There are too few of them to distribute to just anyone."

"Then maybe you shouldn't discuss your affairs in our presence?" suggested Two.

"No one is planning to." Sister Alia looked at me again. "In order to apply it to a symbol, the chabre must be processed in a special way, turning it into paint. You can't buy this in the Fortress store, so you can specify it as an additional requirement. Just one question, Max...just one. What symbol?"

"No comment," I replied, going on the defensive.

"So be it," the girl nodded. "I hope you can find common ground with your next personal servant. Does anyone have additional requirements? No? Okay, as soon as dawn breaks, I'll draw up a deal. Now I recommend you sleep — we have a long way to go and there won't be many stops."

"If we're going to be hiding in the rift, we'll need to think about food," said One. "How about stopping by a store?"

"Excellent idea, but I don't have any money with me," said Sister Alia.

"I do," I said, showing her the purse I'd received from the churchman. "A bunch of gold, which is unlikely to ever come in handy for me. One is right — you can't mess around in the rift without food and water. Are you sure we're being chased?"

"Absolutely. At first, they will look for you at the academy, then they will discover the wagon gone and they will raise the alarms. It won't take much time to put two and two together — Father Dvar is reputed to be a man of common sense. If

I'd had a little more time to prepare, I would have taken care of the food so we wouldn't have to stop. So we'd have a better chance of making it there first. But you're right — you can't go into the rift without food. Everyone, let's rest."

What else could be said about our hasty escape? Only that it lasted two days. There were a minimum number of stops, and purely to satisfy physiological needs. They changed horses a couple of times, but they didn't even let us out of the wagon then. And the stops were short — the conservator barely had time to buy us a mountain of food. I also had to fork out the gold for the change of horses, but it meant that the wagon moved at a decent speed toward its target. We weren't particularly interested in shooting the breeze, so we slept for most of the journey. Finally, toward the end of the second day, when the sun had already sunk below the horizon, we stopped.

"We are here, sister." The cleric who had unquestioningly obeyed Sister Alia's orders opened the doors, releasing us to freedom. Rather, only the girl was released, we were led inside by our chains. The cool night air was invigorating, and I took several deep breaths, chasing away the smells of the stuffy cabin. Such a small enclosed space was not the ideal place for five adults to pass two days together comfortably. Especially without the opportunity to wash.

Space was suddenly torn asunder by a prolonged howl, putting everyone on high alert. Even the horses became agitated and the churchman could hardly calm them down.

"There are things coming out of the rift," Sister Alia explained. "Going in search of food for their Master. This was actually how the rift was discovered — dark beasts attacked a village a few kilometers to the south, but didn't kill everyone. The Wall is not far, so the survivors managed to reach it. They didn't set up a patrol, but everyone within a radius of five kilometers was evicted. Now no one will stop us. What are you doing?!"

"Heeeeeeyyy!" I shouted at the top of my lungs, attracting the dark beasts' attention. "Take it off!" I said, pointing to my collar. "Before we go down, we need to secure the area. So there's nothing staggering around on the surface. In the morning they'll rush back and attack my group while I'm busy with the creatures on the lower levels. Do we need that? I think not."

"You should warn us about things like that in advance," Sister Alia said with displeasure, but gave the order for me to be released. And then she took in a lungful of air and shrieked with all her might, startling the horses once again.

"Now they'll definitely come," Sister Alia grinned. "The Evil Engineer taught me that trick. 'The call.' The dark beasts think that I'm an important member of their community, and they will rush to save me as fast as they can. You have less than a minute."

"Did you study with the dark one?" I was surprised.

"Of course. In order to understand the dark

ones, you must become a dark one yourself. Even if just for a time. The Evil Engineer taught me a lot in the time I was given with him. Moreover, Father Nor gave me full carte blanche. The dark one was as open with me as he generally is with the Fortress."

"I wouldn't have guessed you graduated from the Evil Engineer's course."

"Not training, just information. He gave me knowledge about the dark ones, the specifics of their species, their features. Everything classified as top secret. If we were a team, I could have passed all this on to you, but now it's too late to discuss it. You'll have to deal with your next personal servant. Oh, our guests have arrived. Max, go greet them."

Ten common kronas answered Sister Alia's call, and it took all my skill to keep them from eating our horses. Seeing the helpless animals, the dark beasts seemed to go into a frenzy, rushing forward without regard for losses and injuries. There was one I couldn't save — the attack was too savage and vicious. When the last krona was destroyed, Sister Alia raised the lantern high, showing us the darkening entrance to the rift. The light of the blue crystals that shrouded the caves did not penetrate to the surface, so we'd have to walk in the dark for a while.

"Don't waste time. I've got a premonition we don't have long — soon, a servant of Father Dvar will arrive. They won't listen to anything any of us say. If you start to resist, they will simply kill you."

"Take the food and weapons, and follow me!" I ordered, and the three doomed soldiers began to pull the bags purchased by Sister Alia from the wagon. I had no idea what was in there, but they looked pretty heavy. Even here, the clergy did not make concessions, only removing my team's collars at the entrance to the rift. There was no point in commenting on such fanatical adherence to the laws of the Fortress, so we pressed on toward the descent. Seven or eight levels. Sheer madness.

"Max!" Sister Alia shouted before we had completely disappeared. "Try not to kill dark beasts unnecessarily! Only red ones! Let the rest live! This should work in your favor!"

"What do you mean, 'don't kill the creatures'?" asked One, as soon as we reached the first cave. "How else can you pass through the rift?"

"Just like this," I grinned, put up my mirror and entered the first cave. There were only three kronas here — we'd already destroyed the others on the surface. I walked up to the beasts and, without thinking twice, sat down on top of one like a horse. Turning toward the group, I saw three gaping astonished faces. Their mouths were agape as they watched me work with the dark beasts. After three quick jabs, I had cleared the cave — there were no nasty rapses to be found.

"Something like that," I approached the group, noting with surprise that the men backed away as I approached. "Stop it, you guys. You knew how I kill beasts. What's with the reaction?"

"Knowing and seeing are two different things," One shook his head and even took several deep breaths, trying to stop himself from trembling. The businessman was frankly shaking with fear. And it wasn't emanating from the dark beasts, but from something much more dangerous. In this case, me.

"Riding a krona like a horse…I wouldn't have imagined it in my wildest nightmares," Three agreed. "So the beasts don't pay any attention to you at all?"

"Not at all. Although no — the exclusives smell something. I have to fight them. The rest just ignore me."

"Okay, I understand." Two also stopped shaking. "Terrifying, of course, but at least now I understand it. But why shouldn't you touch the creatures?"

"When I killed the Master in the last rift, the guard became docile. They believe that by leaving the monsters intact, they can save a lot of resources extracted from them. That's why the conservator asked me not to kill the beasts, so that the extraction will be even more fruitful and work in my favor when considering my sentence. But I think the first three or four caves still must be cleansed. If we're really being chased, the clergy might risk going down after us."

"Really? You doubt the girl's words?" One gave me a strange look.

"I doubt even my own words," I grinned. "A

certain dark human once taught me that you can only trust one person in this world — yourself. Everyone else will use you as they see fit. The fact that there was such a commotion around us leaving the Fortress may make it seem like the truth from a distance, but it may just be an attempt to tug at my heartstrings with the unenviable fate of our conservator and start cooperating with her."

"Do you have the leverage to bargain with the Fortress?" One grasped the main point right away.

"You should always have an ace up your sleeve. If I sign a contract with Sister Alia, formally I will have no reason not to give her and the church all the information about myself. Of course, I have no idea how they will enforce the conditions of the contract, but I don't really want to test them."

"The *Truth* stone," offered One. "A rare gem, but they use it to help the trade guild verify that contracts have been completed, if any disputes occur. A prerequisite for the use of this stone is the existence of a signed contract. In this case, it is always possible to prove that some party has not fulfilled its obligations."

"That's why Sister Alia didn't want any of you to be present at the signing of the contract," I chuckled bitterly. "Because it's always easier to fool the young and inexperienced than the veteran negotiators."

"You may just be flattering me, but I don't mind," One smiled contentedly. "I have a proposal about the cleansing. What if you don't fully clear the second cave? You can do more than just ride the beasts, right? For instance, you could put them in a far corner while we move from the first to the third?"

"Why would I do that?" I didn't understand.

"When the churchmen come down here, they'll see a living creature in the second cave and will think that we've all been eaten. Or that we'd become the same as you and gone deep into the rift, ignoring the dark beasts. In any case, this should slow down the chase. And no one will touch us for a while. And you'll be back by then."

"A reasonable thought," I agreed, surprised at One's forethought. I hadn't even considered this option, but it could work. Would the red robes come down into the rift? Yes, they would. Would they risk attacking two or three creatures? Not sure. So we needed to try."

It took me no time to clear the third and fourth caves. I made quick work of the second as well, leaving only three kronas alive. Actively pushing with my legs, I forced the creatures to move to the wall farthest from the passage. Nodding to One, I prepared to attack the overly rowdy kronas, but this wasn't necessary — the attack zone of ordinary beasts was considerably smaller than the size of the cave. Pale with fear, but decisively enough, the businessman tiptoed along the wall and disappeared into the safe third cave. He was followed by Two and Three. I had already dragged the backpacks and weapons in there and my group didn't have steel armor, so after a couple of minutes the third cave was filled with hysterical nervous laughter. We'd made it! We passed through the cave with the dark creatures, and now the churchmen would have to rack their brains to find us!

"Alright, sooner we start, sooner we leave," I said, checking my katars.

"Take some food," offered Three. "There's no way you'll pass through seven levels in just a couple of hours."

"It'll take me longer than that," I agreed. "My current limit is level three. In order to move lower, I will need to adapt to the dark influence. Crawling in much the same way as you did during the last rift. It took me almost two days to securely hold my mirror at level three. Light knows how long it will take to get through the fourth and below. Maybe two days, maybe a whole week. I wasn't lying when I said I still couldn't close this rift. It will take a lot of time."

"Then take a whole sack," pushing the duffel bag toward me. "The other three will definitely be enough for us."

"Before you take it, we should look through them," Two said, opening the backpack, pulling the contents out and placing them directly on the stone floor. "Do you know what Sister Alia bought? I don't. Maybe Max doesn't have a drop of water in his backpack? Or vice versa — he has all the water, but not a crumb of food. No need to rush. A couple of hours won't make a difference."

Two turned out to be right — my bag

contained all the jerky our conservator had bought. And not a drop of water! We had to divide all the food equally. If there weren't four of something, it went to me by default. When we were done, I packed my food into my backpack and after walking a few steps, I stopped with a warning finger to my lips. Voices were heard from the side of the passage to the second cave.

"There are three dark beasts in here! We won't go any further!"

"Do you see any bodies? Blood?"

"It's all dark in here. There was a battle, I counted twenty dead creatures, but I didn't notice any human bodies. Maybe they were eaten?"

"No 'maybes!' If there are no bodies, then they have moved on. We go out and block the passage. No one is getting out of this rift alive."

The voices subsided, and soon the rift plunged into its usual silence, broken only by the rare growl of a beast. We exchanged glances. There was nothing left to say. We had no way out now. Either I finished off the Riftmaster, or Max's group would cease to exist.

"Whatever happens, I'll be back in five days. The fourth cave is empty — you can use it as a restroom. Enjoy your time as much as you can and don't deny yourself any pleasures.

Shaking hands with everyone, I threw my backpack over my shoulders and slowly walked into the depths of the rift. Suddenly, my body began to ache, as if after a full-fledged training with the Evil Engineer. My body knew perfectly well what I would have to go through, so it began to prepare in advance for the difficulties. Stopping, I took out a bottle of water and took a sip. Judging by the voices, Sister Alia had spoken the truth. We really were being chased. Maybe I should start trusting her a little more? No, I needed to talk to the Evil Engineer first. If anyone could be trusted in this life, then it was only the dark one. The light had yet to prove that they were on my side.

Chapter 18

GREAT LIGHT, WHEN WOULD I die?

I sat in a cave on level five, stared down at the hole in the floor that led to the floor below, and realized that I could not find the motivation to move on. The lower I went, the more time it took for the body to rebuild and stop perceiving the surrounding space as hostile. It took me almost two days to move from the third to the fourth level, three days to go from the fourth to the fifth. For two hours now, I had been sitting by the passage to the sixth floor, but all I had achieved in this time was passing out several times. The lower I went down, the heavier the dark aura was, as if something new was added to it with each level. Here, at the threshold between floors five and six, I simply turned into jelly. A sort of shapeless mass dreaming only of how to leave this place. It was good that I had already thought to eliminate the dark beasts in this room. I couldn't really move, so I had to use *Dark Spike*, since there weren't too many of them.

When my vision started swimming again, my internal clock suddenly reminded me that I had promised the group to return in five days. It felt like high time to make good on that promise, because the longer I sat in front of the passageway, the worse it got. I knew perfectly well that I was doing everything all wrong. Instead of blocking the dark influence, as Father Nor had taught, I'd grown accustomed to it, simply rebuilding my body. If I knew how to properly construct a mental wall, like all the other mages, I was sure that the transition between levels would not become such an issue for me. But if I ever attempted to return to the rage that had allowed me to survive in the very first rift, I would have to say goodbye to my mirror. Because it would be very difficult to go back after that.

"Screw it," I muttered as I crawled from the cave. That was enough, I needed a break, at least for a couple of hours. Otherwise, I'd just go crazy before I reached the goal. I only managed to pull myself to my feet once I'd reached the next cave, and only with help from a krona. This rift turned out to be populated mostly by dogs. Through all five levels, I'd only encountered five lurges, and only three caves contained rapses. The rest of them were all those dog-like beasts with pillow-shaped bodies.

The retreat proved much easier — my legs

bore me away from the terror of level six themselves. The bag full of food was practically untouched. It's hard to eat when you feel sick. And I had to haul it everywhere with me. For some reason, I had no doubt that as soon as I moved a couple meters away, the eternally ravenous beasts would immediately deprive me of my entire food supply. The kronas were constantly glancing sidelong at me, craning their necks curiously. They clearly smelled the dried meat.

As Sister Alia requested, I did not touch the dark beasts. The only exceptions were in the caves with a passageway between levels, which I completely cleansed. This rift turned out to hold a lot of surprises — while the first and second levels were like what I'd already seen under the academy, from the third on, there were stark differences. The beasts became larger, new crystals appeared on the walls, and each cave held three or four elite monsters that had undergone metamorphosis. They were still kronas, but with additional spikes, growths, and even armor! One of the kronas I found was covered in something hard to the touch, very similar to metal armor. The fifth level held a menagerie of magical and elites — not a single common dark beast was found among their ranks. But I was glad for one thing — I still hadn't met any exclusives. I had no desire to fight them now.

I realized that something strange was happening when I reached level two. A few caves before the passage to the first floor, I heard the sounds of battle. The metallic clangs and explosions couldn't be anything else. Speeding up, I ran through another cave and stopped, amazed by the scene before me.

The Countess's group were fighting dark beasts and suffering a crushing defeat.

At first glance, it didn't look so bad. The four warriors were huddled behind their shields, driving the particularly spirited kronas with spears as they tried to break through the barriers with their paws. But that was only at first glance. Once I noticed the details, they made me grimace. Flask was barely moving. He hung on Gimlet and there was a huge pool of blood forming underneath the healer. Gimlet wasn't throwing fireballs, although half of the kronas in the cave were charred. It looked as though the mage had run out of both mana and elixirs. Rabblerouser and the Countess were lunging with their spears, aiming at kronas, but their movements seemed to be sluggish. As if the group had done nothing for the last couple of days but fight the creatures. But even that wasn't as dangerous as three rapses hanging from the ceiling. In what seemed like an act of spite, this seemed to be one of the few caves where the ceiling saboteurs lived. And now the creatures were slowly approaching the group, remaining completely invisible to them. The attack happened before I could yell to warn them. Three magical rapses flew down, crushing the doomed soldiers under them. Those who weren't expecting the attack simply trembled and collapsed. As if on cue, the kronas circling nearby rushed forward to finish off the pitiful humans, but the beasts weren't so lucky.

They were too slow.

I don't know where I got the strength, but as soon as the rapses separated from the ceiling, I rushed forward, wringing out all my remaining energy. I must have moved even faster than in my battle with Tiger. The doomed soldiers collapsed to the floor, the kronas fell on them from above, but didn't even manage to get a bite in before I cut their lives short. The three rapses did manage to tear through their armor, even reach flesh, but no more than that. Three quick blows and the beasts were twitching in death throes. I didn't bother to finish them off, switching instead to the kronas. The dark beasts still didn't see me as an enemy, and they paid dearly for it. After a few moments, everything was over, and the only beings left alive in the cave were human.

"What in Skron's name are you doing here?!" I asked, activating the healing aura and tearing Flask's helmet off. From the injuries, it looked as if the kronas had inflicted three terrible penetrating wounds on the healer, two on the thigh and one in the shoulder. But the doomed soldier was lucky — they didn't seem to hit his arteries. Otherwise, how could he still be breathing? Pouring two recovery potions down his throat at once, I assessed the condition of the others. Rabblerouser wasn't moving — the dwarfish man was unconscious. The Countess was stirring, but her movements were uncertain.

Of the entire team, only Gimlet looked more or less healthy. In any case, he was able to sit down without assistance.

"Do you have a mana potion?" he asked in a hoarse voice. I silently handed him one vial, pushing the dead krona off the Countess. This helped — the woman was able to roll over and sit up, leaning on Gimlet. Rabblerouser needed a little more work. He'd gotten it as bad as Flask. It was amazing how he managed to stand, hold a shield and jab his spear at the same time. The last recovery elixir went to him, after which I returned to the Countess, holding a vial of mana in my hands. The healing aura actively absorbed mana, but there was no way I could switch it off. If I did, Flask and Rabblerouser might not survive.

"Did you forget something here or what?" I repeated my question once I was sure I saw consciousness in the Countess' gaze. However, the answer came from Gimlet:

"We came after you. The Fortress' order is to deliver the doomed soldier Max, dead or alive. Alive is preferred, of course, so that you can later be burned at the stake for the audience's amusement."

"My team..."

"Has been sitting in a cell for the past two days. Same with your conservator. Fifty teams were driven in the rift to find you. And ten of them have already been sent to their eternal rest. You know, Max, if I didn't know you, I would have thought that you were the very embodiment of

Skron, that's how excited the churchmen were."

"You forgot to say the phrase, doomer," the Countess croaked. Her voice betrayed that she wasn't feeling well, but I couldn't do anything to help except maintain my healing aura. The recovery potions had run dry.

"If you mean 'You owe me your life,' I'm not going to say it," I replied. "I have other things to worry about now."

"Either say it, or we will be forced to attack you," the Countess insisted. "A doomed soldier cannot attack someone to whom she owes a life debt. You read the rules of the Fortress."

"I did. I read them quite thoroughly, paying special attention to the part where it says that a doomed soldier has the right to make his life debtors die in his place if he himself has been sentenced to burn at the stake. You didn't come here to pave the way for me with daisies, right? You came here to drag me outside to face my fate. If I make you my debtors, you will go to the chopping block instead of me."

"Either you say the phrase, or we attack," the Countess pulled the spear closer to herself. "I don't need any favors."

"You know where you can shove it?" I said, getting angry. "Right up a krona's ass, that's where. I'm not saying anything. You want to attack, go ahead. The ball's in your court. Gimlet's mana has been completely restored. I'm not going to fight back. Although…you know what, you can actually shove off! Countess, you and your crew owe me a life! And in payment of your debt, you will now leave the rift and tell the man who's in charge of this whole operation that I've already reached level five. And it'll take me another two weeks at least to make it to the end of the rift. I'll go myself. No need to drive the doomers in here. In two or three weeks, I'll close this Skron-damned rift myself."

"*You* close the rift?" The Countess marveled. "By yourself?!"

"And what's more. Be sure to tell whoever is in charge that the more doomers kill beasts now, the less loot the Fortress will extract from the rift. And it'll be significantly less. Did you get all that? Gimlet, hoist them up and drag them out. Once you step out of the rift and deliver my words, your blood debt will be considered paid in full. That is my decision."

"So two or three weeks?" the mage asked, helping the Countess to her feet.

"I have no idea. I got stuck between the fifth and sixth levels — the dark influence there is simply monstrous. I think it will take me five days to adapt to the sixth level, a week to the seventh and maybe even a month to the eighth. I just don't know. I don't have experience passing through rifts this deep. But I can guarantee that I'll do it. I will close this rift. No need to drive people here to be slaughtered. No need to waste resources."

"There he is!" someone shouted. I turned around and saw a familiar figure. Tiger and his team entered the cave.

"Tiger, stop!" Despite her condition, the Countess managed to take a step, standing between me and the new doomed soldiers. "We're leaving the rift!"

"Leave. I'll take this freak out and get my reward from Father Dvar."

"You don't understand — all doomed soldiers are leaving the rift. You are leaving with me. That's an order."

"You have no right to order me!" Tiger practically screamed.

"Would you like to challenge me, junior?" The Countess's voice was steely. "Let's do it, here and now. Even in my current state, I'm ready to accept the invitation. I'm giving you ten seconds to make a decision. Either you attack or we leave. No other option."

"Father Dvar will know that you let Max go!" Tiger said with hatred, but retreated. A huge brute bowing before this miniscule woman? Who was she, this Countess?

"I'll pass your message along to Father Dvar, Max. But the final decision will be up to him. If he decides that we have to come back in to get you, we will."

"Let Father Dvar talk to Sister Alia. She will explain to him why I'm not killing the dark beasts and what's going on. I need time. At least two weeks."

"I heard you. We're leaving. Tiger, help my men. They need to be brought to a healer..."

Trying not to lose sight of the big man

throwing me loaded looks every now and again, I reached the passage and practically ran through several caves before I stopped and caught my breath. My heart was pounding in his chest, threatening to jump free and go in search of a new owner. Sister Alia had been as open with me as possible — she had acted independently, without the consent of the High Priest. It was unlikely that the head of the security service himself would be here. Our idea of using the cave filled with kronas as a decoy hadn't worked. No one thought that the Fortress would drag fifty doomed soldier groups to the rift at once. Even if I closed the rift, I'd still be arrested. The only question was, would the appraisers be able to clear the rift before I burned or not?

Maybe it made sense to take the guards on myself? Escape the rift, attack the churchmen, break through the doomed legion, flee the empire, change my name, maybe even my appearance? Live a simple life? Become a peasant, catch fish, cultivate the land...would I be able to break through the army of doomed soldiers? In theory, yes. But it was unlikely that there were just doomed soldiers here. There would also be a huge crowd of monitors. Clerics with crossbows. No matter how strong my defense was, it was unlikely to be able to withstand a volley of three dozen crossbows. Even if it could, I didn't want to test it now. And there would certainly be some sort of guards at the exit. Maybe I'd be enveloped in a web of steel as soon as I emerged from the rift. No, they could attack at any moment, even in the Fortress. I wasn't going to just stroll calmly to the stake. And until they dragged me there, I needed to fight for my name. That meant it was time to return to the passage to level six. I hope that reason would prevail and Father Dvar wouldn't risk useless sacrifices. I needed two weeks.

At least I hoped I'd get it done in two...

Level six bent to my will in four days. There were considerably fewer magical dark beasts, almost all the monsters were elites, and in one of the branches I even managed to find an exclusive. The krona exuding a red aura immediately jumped up as soon as I entered the cave. The creature obviously did not appreciate my presence. A barrage detachment of elite dark beasts rushed to intercept me, not letting me near their "master," so I had to stop short. I didn't intend to leave such prime loot for the churchmen. They'd have enough guards. And I was very curious what I could obtain from a level six red beast. It wasn't everyday that people got to descend to such depths.

For starters, I cleared the neighboring cave. I needed a place where I could sleep peacefully. After resting as much as was possible within the rift, I went back to the exclusive. The elite kronas reflexively ran up to me, trying to push me out of the cave, which was only to my advantage. One by one, the creatures fell onto the rocks, never to rise again. Twenty blows — twenty extinguished golden auras. The red krona was clearly beginning to get agitated as I took a few steps toward him. It got to the point where it bore down, ready to pounce and smash me into the ground, so I had to be proactive. *Dark Spike* flew into the creature's snout, blinding it for a few moments, and before it could get its bearings, I was there. But my ensured victory was interrupted as the protective dome surrounding the creature deflected my katars to the side, and so aggressively that my shoulders almost flew out of the socket! The dark beast had the same protection as I did!

To say I was in shock is an understatement. All I could do was to jump far back, preparing for an extended battle, but the krona did not attack. It stayed where it was, except that the further I retreated, the calmer it became. When I went out into the corridor, the creature completely turned away, staring at some other point of interest. Sitting on the corpse of the elite, I thought about what had happened. *Dark Spike* had flooded the place with darkness, predictably failing to break through the defenses. Then I attacked, but the steel ricocheted, almost tearing off my arms. Was I ready to continue? Of course not! Now I was useless. Destroying a beast of this caliber would require significant buffs to *Dark Spike*. I didn't want to get close to the red krona. It had too many additional spikes and ridges; it looked too intimidating. What conclusion could I draw from this? Quite a disappointing one. The creature, which was unique on level six, was probably found in droves on the eighth, or maybe even the seventh floor. It was clear that something needed to be done about my weapon. The exclusive monster's protective dome intercepted my swing half a meter from the body. My blades were not long enough to penetrate further and reach vital organs. I needed a sword...the question was how to carry it with me so as not to disturb the dark creatures once again. Damn, what was I thinking? They're stoking the fire for my execution outside, and here I am thinking about weapons!

Just in case, I sat in a nearby cave for some time, making sure that the red creature would not pursue me. The beast probably felt like a hero. A competitor appeared, tried to attack, but was thrown back and kicked out. Would it be worth catching up to me and punishing the insolent? It certainly made sense, so I should wait to meet the exclusive creature without unnecessary witnesses.

Everything seemed to be going well — nothing was pursuing me. Now I just had to kill one elite creature in each cave to make sure that the red monster was the only one with a support stone that blocked steel. The other dark beasts died without further ceremony. None of them had the same protective dome as the exclusive monster. This made me feel better — I could destroy the enemy knowing it was unique. These weren't being mass produced on level six. But this discovery paled in comparison to what I found when I reached the descent to level seven. There was no Warden, which meant only one thing: there weren't seven levels in this Skron-cursed rift, as they had thought in the Fortress, but at least eight. Damn!

I only met the Warden eight days later. Crawling, because I could no longer stand on my feet. Level seven turned out to be...Let's just say that there were no magical creatures at all. Only elites. Almost every other cave was home to an exclusive creature, ten in total on the level. I had to edge along the wall under the close supervision of the army of henchmen. By the end of this journey, I couldn't even stand on two feet. The influence of the seventh level red monsters was simply horrendous. And I didn't even check how well they were protected! I just didn't have the strength for it. The rift had driven me to the edge of sanity and by the time I crawled to the last cave, I had nearly lost my mind. I was pushing myself forward on pure instinct with no idea what was happening around me. I didn't clear the penultimate cave — I wasn't sure that I could manage the red monster and its large army. As a result, I was left in the passageway between two exclusive kronas, dreaming only of how not to die. Although I was still making progress — I no longer lost consciousness. Yes, it was bad, terribly bad, but not so bad as escaping to dreamland and allowing the dark beasts to devour my body, tormented by the dark influence.

I could only move freely after another two weeks, and I have no memory of the first five days — they passed in a fog. I don't even think I ate during that whole time. And there was no thought spared for personal hygiene. All I could think to do at the very beginning was to pull off my still clean pants and put them aside, and change position every three or four days, since the corridor was quite long. When I was able to move more or less normally, I tumbled bare-assed into the Warden's cave. Something strange was happening to my body. I couldn't stand. My muscles just didn't obey, no matter how hard I tried. I had to crawl on my hands. The krona did not like my presence, but didn't attack first. The red beast had no minions, so no one pushed me out. Assessing the position of the creature and the descent, I crawled in the usual way — along the wall, keeping as far as possible from the monster. It didn't take its eyes off me, but didn't interfere, even when I crawled to the descent. What was striking was the slight increase in pressure. The feeling in my chest intensified, my stone-filled head became slightly heavier, and I completely lost control over the lower part of the body. Everything below my chest, I no longer felt. However, this did not prevent me from sliding down to the last level, and, seeing two red beasts, quickly crawling away toward the wall. And at the speed of a wounded snail. Nevertheless, the creatures did not attack me. They only made sure that I did not linger in their cave. Second cave. Third. Tenth. Each of them had two or three red monsters, and without a retinue. At the eighth level, there were only exclusive beasts.

I ran into problems in the last cave — eight guards drained my mana by ten points every four seconds. I only had one elixir and eighty units left in my mana bar, so I didn't have the chance to do a test pass. Clenching my teeth, I crawled forward at the same sluggish speed, praying to the Light that I would have enough strength and time. I had to drink the bottle immediately, and as soon as the mana level dropped to zero. I had no right to spend a precious resource on restoring my protection. The bar briskly filled to the brim, only to immediately decrease by ten units. The eight guards created such a monstrous aura that my level two stone struggled to cope with it.

I made it. With seconds to spare, but I still made it. After passing the barrier, I stumbled into the room with the Riftmaster. It was not much different from its kin and was in the process of creating a krona. To reach the central part, I had to crawl into its cube. Rolling onto my back, I raised my hands with difficulty and flexed my fingers as usual, activating the katars. The steel blades rushed forward, and the moment they reached the target, I was drowning in notifications. But the pressure proved beyond my strength and my consciousness flickered out. Dreamland met me with open arms as the notifications burned in front of my eyes like red-hot iron:

1 of 5 location map fragments obtained. Total: 1 of 5.

1 of 12 *Amplify* shards obtained. Total: 4 of 12.

3 of 100 *Devour* shards obtained. Total: 3 of 100.

Chapter 19

(Office of the High Priest. Fortress. Ten days later)

"THANK YOU, FATHER Dvar. You did everything right. Father Frass?"

The gray-frocked man rose from his seat, completely unfazed by the unfettered gaze of the highest hierarchs of the church. Until quite recently, meetings like this were held at the Fortress once every two or three years, at most. That being said, it was quite difficult to get the High Priest, nine heads of regions, as well as all the highest hierarchs of the Fortress in one room. Everyone had urgent matters to attend to and adjusting to the others' schedules was nearly impossible. In any case, that was how it used to be. But now, such unprecedented times were upon them that these general meetings of the highest hierarchs of the church of the Zarak Empire were taking place for the second time in less than a month. And both times for the same reason: to decide the fate of a dark doomed soldier named Max.

"There is no darkness in him," Father Fras reported curtly and sat down. The gray robe had done his duty.

"Father Pruch?" The High Priest suppressed a smirk. He had gotten used to such behavior from the darkness monitor long ago, but the heads of the regions, who considered themselves decision-making hubs, snorted in displeasure. Having ascended to the top ranks of the church, they expected respect from every servant of the Light and considered any scornful attitude as a personal insult. But Father Frass didn't give a damn — even priests were afraid to touch the darkness monitors. They were a separate caste of the untouchables with which interaction seemed impossible.

"The final analysis of the contents of the rift will be ready only in a month," the blue robe got up from his seat and handed over a pile of papers to his assistants. Servants ran around the office, passing the financial report around. "However, we are ready to give a preliminary assessment right now. Please read the report, I will answer any questions."

"Is there some mistake here?" Priest Zwat, head of the central region, was the first to voice his doubts. "Sixty-four yem? How is this possible?"

"There is no mistake here, Priest." Unlike

Father Frass, the financial manager tried to please everyone and everyone, therefore he bowed almost every word. "It was a level eight rift, containing eight guards, each of which held eight yems. Apparently, one for each level, but without stats it's hard to say. One rift closed by the dark doomer Max gave us a third of all the yem we recovered last year. Which was considered our best yield in the last few decades."

"What is a tram?" Priest Lusk, head of the northern region, saw an unfamiliar word.

"Material that was considered a fairy tale for several hundred years, therefore excluded from the general list of resources received. It is obtained only from exclusive creatures on level eight. It doesn't exist on the upper floors."

"Father Gron, we need an explanation." The High Priest addressed the owner of the black robe. The Fortress Explorer grunted as he got to his feet, his mind wandering elsewhere. The meeting tired and infuriated the man, who wanted nothing but to return to the laboratory as soon as possible and continue his experiments.

"According to the archives, tram is meant to increase the quality of magic stones, endowing them with new properties and improving current parameters. All this requires careful study, but even now it can be reliably stated that with the help of tram, mage stones can be made at least twice as powerful. And without investments in levels and facets."

"You're saying all these figures indicating the

number of extracted resources, which are impossible under normal conditions, are actually real?" Priest Zwat pressed.

"Quite right," Father Frass confirmed. "That's why we need time to complete an accurate assessment. The lower the level, the more materials are extracted from each dark beast. But the resources are trifles. A nice bonus. Please direct your attention to the final pages. Magic stones of an elite, and even exclusive rank. I combed through the archives — there has never been such a haul in the entire history of the Fortress."

"And the dark human did all this?" Priest Zwat couldn't believe it.

"The stones and resources were obtained by servants of the Light trained to butcher intact dark beasts. There are only four such people in our empire, which is why it took so long. Passage through the rift usually entails total destruction of all creatures, so we had to make due with just the scraps. What the doomer did has fundamentally changed the approach to closing rifts."

Silence hung over the office. The regional priests studied the materials provided, trying to keep their emotions in check. What they saw really changed a lot. However, not everyone managed to maintain equanimity — with each sheet he read, the face of Priest Lask broke into an increasingly satisfied grin. The rift he was holding the report for was located in the northern region. His region. This meant that according to the laws of the

Fortress, thirty percent of all extracted resources or their equivalent in gold belonged to its diocese. Which almost immediately made Priest Lask one of the most influential regional heads. Few could boast of having such resources.

"What do we do with the dark one now?" asked Priest Zwat, setting the report aside.

"He's still unconscious," said Father Dvar. "The accelerated pace really wrung him dry, he's practically a mummy. Critical exhaustion. We'll keep him alive, but we won't bring him back to consciousness. We'll do this when the council sets a date for his execution."

"That is to say, he won't be able to close any more rifts like this?"

"It is not known for certain, but there is an assumption that his condition is due precisely to the speed with which he closed the rift. If the dark one has more time to adapt to the levels, then even deeper rifts will no longer be an obstacle for him. A nine, maybe even a ten-level. The only question is how long it will take him to adapt. It took him several days to adapt to seven, two weeks to level eight. If the progression continues, the transition to level nine, or rather — a safe transition to level nine may take several months. The tenth may take years. It's all too uncertain — we have not encountered this before."

"I ask that only the heads of regions remain in the office," the High Priest said, and after a few moments only ten people remained in the room.

"Before we open the vote, I would like to add

something." Father Urg looked at each regional head. "All of you are trying to prevent rifts deeper than level four from forming in your lands. Because it takes too many resources to close them. But what if this is no longer the case? All of you know perfectly well what needs to be done to add an additional three or four levels to the rift. What if now, this becomes your main headache? Just six months, and everyone will be the possessor of an eight, and even a nine-level rift."

The High Priest once again took the financial report in his hands and leafed demonstratively through it.

"Priest Lusk, what about your thirty percent?"

"With that alone, the northern region will finally be able to buy materials and restore the destroyed sections of the Wall. What I have been asking the Fortress for the past six years will finally come to fruition."

"You are fully aware of the church's financial situation," Father Urg continued. "The Empire is mired in its own contradictions, in which there is no place for battles with the dark beasts. But for the first time in many decades, we have a chance to be reborn. Get stronger. Impose our will on the empire. The only question is, what are we willing to do for this? I propose a vote. Raise your hand if you believe that the dark doomed soldier Max should go to the stake, no matter what benefit he may bring to the Church of Light."

Four hands immediately shot up — the

orthodox heads of the southern, southwestern, southeastern, and western regions were not swayed from their original opinion. Dark humans had no place in this world.

"I ask those who agree that the dark doomed soldier Max should stay alive to raise their hands."

Four more hands. Three northern regions and an eastern one. Regions where the influence of the dark beasts was especially acute. Especially in terms of the number of rifts found annually.

"Priest Zwat, there can be no abstention on this issue." Father Urg looked at the head of the central region. The most influential of all the other priests. A man with longstanding designs on the head of the church of the Zarak Empire.

"On the one hand, I agree with my seniors," Priest Zwat nodded to the southern leaders, causing them to smile with satisfaction. "There is no place for darkness in this world. On the other hand, I am haunted by the contented face of Priest Lask, as well as the problems in my own diocese. There are too many of them to ignore. I believe that the dark one should benefit the Fortress. Let him tirelessly run from rift to rift, unable to even raise his head. However, High Priest, the will of the council was ignored. The fire has been stoked for a long time. Someone should be punished, and in such a way that there is no longer a desire to demonstrate his own will. The will of the supreme council of the Church of the Zarak Empire must be the law for all servants, regardless of their background. The woman who once bore the name

Sister Alia must be punished."

"I have no objection to that," the High Priest nodded. "Tomorrow, at three o'clock in the afternoon, there will be a public execution of the offender by burning. May the Light have mercy on her soul. I consider the issue with the dark doomed soldier Max closed. From now until the end of his days, he is part of the Church of the Light. Today we will send him to the academy to complete his studies. Prepare the rifts, regional heads. In three months, the Fortress will begin the process of revival."

(Academy medical unit, next morning)

The world acquired color reluctantly, lazily. At first, I saw only light, then a haze of different colors, and only then did my hearing return and thoughts began to swim through my head.

Where was I?

Concentrating with difficulty, I was able to make out the hospital room. An exact copy of the one in which I repeatedly woke up at the academy. Everything was clean and white. Something squeezed my throat, making it difficult to breathe, and I instinctively stretched my hands to remove the obstacle. I couldn't — my wrists were bound. As were my legs, and even torso. Chills went through my body. They had chained me up so that I wouldn't run away. So, it was still an execution...alright, I was breaking out of here. I wasn't giving up like that!

"He's awake!" came a male voice, and soon I saw Magister Smalog's face. The academy healer looked tired, haggard, but quite pleased.

"Very good," he said. "Just fantastic! Untie him quickly, I want to see if Max can walk."

After a couple of moments, I felt relatively free and even breathing became easier. I was helped to sit up, and finally I was able to finally look around. It was not just similar to the ward I'd woken up in several times before. It *was* that ward! I'd woken up in the academy!

"Can you stand, or do you need help?" asked Magister Smalog.

"I'll try," I replied, looking doubtfully at my feet. They seemed to have shrunk by half, turning into thin reeds. As had my arms — the muscles I'd grown so proud of were no longer there. It was as if I had been dried under the scorching sun for several years before being restored to consciousness.

"What happened to me? Why do I look so strange?"

"Ten days of unconsciousness, plus critical exhaustion of the body," the doctor explained, and nevertheless helped me to my feet. They trembled but held my weight. "You drove yourself hard, Max, worse than a racehorse. I recommend bed rest, taking it easy, and plenty of food over the next two or three weeks, but who am I to argue with higher authorities? The first two recommendations they dropped, so only the food remains. Actually, here it is — bring it in. You don't have to look at me like that — you have to eat it all if you want to get back in shape. And even then, I think it won't be enough."

My surprise was not feigned — the servants carted in three large trays, bursting with plates filled to the brim.

"How long have I been here?"

"They brought you in today. Previously, you were in the Fortress, I had to go there every day to monitor your condition. Today the High Priest gave the go-ahead for your final treatment, and I have to admit, it was hard work. Bringing you back to consciousness after what you've been through has been quite difficult."

"What about my team?"

"I'd prefer you refrain from asking me things I don't have the slightest idea about. My job was to keep you alive. Why you were in such a state and why you were kept in the Fortress is not a question I ask."

"Perhaps this is my domain," a voice rang out and Kimal Sarento entered the ward. Magnificent and radiant, as always. "Will you leave us, Magister?"

"I really have nothing else to do here. He's all yours, I did my part."

The healer and his assistants left the room and my stomach growled treacherously, sensing the proximity of food.

"Eat," the chancellor smiled. "You can listen with your mouth full."

"The chancellor was wrong — it turned out to

be impossible to listen and chew the way I did. The first tray was empty so quickly that I didn't even notice it. The contents of the second tray filled the stomach, and only once I reached the third and final tray could I approach the meal with all the grandeur of an aristocrat — I could eat it without turning into a ravenous animal. I would never have thought that my body could react so aggressively to food.

"A healthy body with a healthy appetite," Kimal Sarento smiled, watching me eat and slowly loading me with information. It was only after I had begun the third tray that he told me what had happened during my ten-day absence from the world of the living.

"The fortress has recognized you as an integral part of the church and has agreed to spare your life. Max's group is in the Fortress, they have been cleared of all charges of fleeing, the agreement to close the rift has been declared fulfilled, and, as far as I know, each has received forty thousand ranking points. This is quite enough for the group to sit idle in the Fortress for a couple of months and wait for your return. The level eight rift has been officially registered to you, so from now on, you are a hero among all doomed soldiers. Near your bed, there's a whole pile of letters with requests to join your group. You have a vacancy, and the doomed soldiers are ready to fight for it. You will deal with this yourself."

"What about our conservator?"

"Here, I'm afraid, the news is not as happy.

The Council of Priests decided to punish her for her willfulness. Today at three o'clock, there will be an open execution by burning. According to the decision of the council, you are a mandatory participant at this event. In order to remember what disobedience to the higher hierarchs leads to. Me, Father Nor, and you are leaving for the Fortress just after dinner."

"Can she be saved? Trade her life for something else?"

"I'm afraid that is no longer in our power — the decision of the priests cannot be changed. This is the unity of the church. So today we will see the death of a smart and — I won't shy away from the word — a beautiful girl. It's a pity, of course, but this is the will of the Light, and we must accept it."

"According to the contract, I have the right to ten individual lessons with the Dark Engineer. I would like to speak to him before we leave for the Fortress."

"This is impossible — the dark one is at the Fortress now, analyzing everything that was pulled from your rift. The list of magic stones alone is impressive. Are you aware that they extracted stones similar to yours? Three *Golden Domes of Protection* and two *Steel Resistance*. The High Priest and I have already been arguing about who has the primary research rights."

"That's what I wanted to talk about as well — level eight creatures have unpleasant defenses. My katars can't reach their bodies. And they ricochet."

"Actually, that's why we insist on studying

the stones. It doesn't stop with steel, as they say, but these specifics are beside the point. You will spend the next two months at the academy and, if we can come to an agreement, in the rift. I went down to the fifth and ninth levels, and they contain too many exclusive dark ones. I'm afraid the Evil Engineer is right — the rift below us has reached a dangerous depth, and this problem needs to be urgently addressed. My campaign, of course, significantly slowed down the Riftmaster — it is now actively restoring the dead creatures, so we have another six months to a year. But then the rift will have to be closed. It seems to me that two months will be sufficient for you to do this. Any resources you need are completely at your disposal."

"Can the academy exist without a rift?"

"Why not? This is already the fifth academy building built over a rift. Not far from the capital, another hole in the ground was found. Construction around it has already begun — in a year, the academy will move to a new territory. Since the Fortress has recognized your right to exist, we have the opportunity to develop you. What do you think about upgrading all your stones to level six? It will improve you greatly."

"Won't the Fortress be against it? The High Priest, as far as I remember, had some plans of his own regarding my development."

"That was before your confession," the chancellor was unfazed. "Now you are a full member of the Fortress with your own rights and duties. And the right to buff your stones, as well as install new ones, if necessary. No one has taken this from you. Plus, you don't have an official conservator now, so no one has the right to restrict you."

"Is that why you're here? Persuade me to upgrade the stones before the new conservator arrives? But why do you need this? Why fortify someone who is leaving the academy in two months?"

"I believe I've already explained this, but I'll reiterate: I need to close the rift. With your help, this process can be simplified several times over. Both in terms of resources and in terms of human lives. The investment I'm about to make is negligible compared to the cost if the rift has to be closed with the help of the army or aristocrats. Under an agreement with the doomed soldiers of the Fortress, they will not be allowed into our rift, even if a metamorph appears here. But you are not yet a doomed soldier — you will only become one in two months. Therefore, I am willing to pay for you to complete this task. And I'm willing to pay well — buffing your stones and giving you additional ones, if needed. I even reserved an elixir for you on the brink to further improve your defense, attack or healing. All for the sake of victory."

"And I need to act here and now, before my new conservator arrives?"

"Officially, you are still unconscious," Kimal Sarento's smile was disarming. "You will be returned to consciousness right before your trip to the Fortress. We have three hours to discuss our case. And the main question is whether you will take it. Like it or not, there are fourteen levels. Your current limit is eight. Although, it seems to me, eight levels in a normal rift would be equal to ten, or even eleven of ours. Nevertheless, in any case, you will have to learn to adapt once again, which is what brought you to this state in the first place. But, as I said, this time you will have all the resources of the academy at your disposal. Both in terms of recovery and weapons. I have some ideas on how to upgrade your katars so they can pierce the golden dome."

"Two months?" I looked at the chancellor and he nodded. "Okay, I'm in. What about buffs?"

"Follow me," the chancellor peered out of the ward like some kind of conspirator. "Don't fall behind! Three hours may not be enough to upgrade your stones to level six! There is not a second to lose!"

Upgrading stones to the sixth level…it sounded daunting, and it turned out to be much worse than I imagined. The levels increased according to the Fibonacci sequence. One elixir for the first level, one for the second, two for the third, three for the fourth, five for the fifth and eight for the sixth. I had five stones, each of them were level two, so in order to get to the sixth, I had to drink ninety elixirs! Ninety! I have never drank so much in my life. At some point, I even thought the liquid would start pouring out of my ears, especially after my fairly heavy breakfast, but it all worked out in the end. It was completely absorbed into my body without residue, leaving behind only a phantom heaviness.

When it was all over, I leaned back in my chair, exhausted, and opened my ability field. Yes, now I was starting to look like a real mage. Level six had brought my stones unprecedented power. *Golden Dome of Protection* allowed me to block a lot of damage without losing mana and, it seemed to me, would easily cope with the aura of one or two guards. *Dark Spike* had transformed into a formidable weapon, increasing the amount of damage dealt by almost tenfold. The radius of *Healing Aura* increased and, judging by the description, could also deal half as much damage as *Dark Spike*, while still managing to heal. *Damage Reflection* and *Steel Resistance* didn't change that much, but now I was sure that even Magister Hwang would have a hard time coping with my increased speed and damage reflection.

"I won't offer you the magic stones now," the chancellor said as soon as I finished examining the new parameters. "First, get used to the current changes, figure out what you're missing, and we'll discuss it in a more relaxed atmosphere. The main thing is that we managed to improve you. Now not a single conservator will be able to prevent this. Come on, it's time for us to leave. You can't keep Father Nor waiting."

The cleric, who was standing not far from the open carriage, looked up at us. I took a few steps and suddenly stopped in my tracks. Great light, how had I not noticed this before?! Those eyes, the shape of the nose, the structure of the lips...Swallowing, I looked dumbfounded at the chancellor then at Father Nor, and back at the chancellor. It could not be! This kind of thing just didn't happen!

"You didn't know?" Kimal Sarento was surprised. "Strange, they are quite similar, like two peas in a pod. And the Fortress should have informed you."

"Sister Alia is Father Nor's daughter?" I asked in a whisper, for some reason.

"Precisely. And in two hours they will burn her at the stake. After all, she had to go against the decision of the Council of Priests to save your life. The Church cannot forgive this."

Chapter 20

"DO YOU PLAN TO GO to the Fortress like that?"

Father Nor's greeting was discouraging. I expected anything but a comment on my appearance. I was wearing the standard doomed soldier hunting uniform that I had worn to close the previous rift. Clean, ironed, perfect for the trip.

"I confess, Father Nor, you even have me second-guessing," said the chancellor.

"For the next two months, the doomer Max is a representative of the magical academy of the Zarak Empire. And he has to look the part. You have five minutes to get yourself in line with the academy's requirements."

"So that's what you're on about...yes, there is a grain of truth in what you say. Change, Max. The academy uniform is on your nightstand. Try to hurry — we mustn't be late."

Father Nor's piercing gaze might have pinned

me down, but I had already developed an immunity to such gazes. Who hadn't wanted to take my life over the past month? If I cowered under every unpleasant look, I wouldn't have the nerve to survive. Nevertheless, I did not try the churchman's patience and ran swiftly to the doomer den. Both my roommates were home, which was strange — it was time for dinner. Running up to the bed, I began to take off my clothes, when I stopped, staring at an unprecedented spectacle for the academy. Several dozen huge bags stood against the far wall.

"Is that all food?" I asked in surprise.

"Everyone's gotta get their kicks somewhere," my tall roomie shrugged. "As it turns out, the students simply cannot live without sweets, but not everyone has the opportunity to order. Where have you been? We started to think something bad had happened."

"And how long will this go on?" I couldn't take my eyes off the bags. Twenty-one bags! This is madness!"

"Are you talking about the food? We're going to distribute it all today — this batch was delivered in the morning. We got it all honestly — your share is in the nightstand. If not for your gold, none of this would have happened. And so…when we get to the Fortress, we'll have something to buy weapons and normal armor for ourselves. And we can try to establish a business there. Do you think doomed soldiers would be in the market for some good food? Or is the food better there than here?"

"Madness," I muttered as I started to change. It was only now that I could smell the cloyingly sweet aroma of fresh buns. "Gold is useless for doomed soldiers. Your main purchases are made with ranking points."

I did not wait for a reaction and ran out of the house. Their behavior seemed so strange to me that I even managed to ignore the gaze of Father Nor as he tried to burn a hole in my head the whole ride there. Where had the two robbers suddenly gotten a windfall of cash? Twenty-one bags of rolls...there weren't enough students in the academy to eat all that food! But the gold in the nightstand was quite real — ten round coins that could warm anyone's soul. Things really seemed to be working out for them, and they seemed happy with their lot. It still seemed crazy to me...

From the outside, the Fortress resembled a real fortress. High stone walls, towers, which for some reason could not be seen from the inside, a deep mote in front of the walls. A real castle within the city. The drawbridge was lowered, letting in a crowd of people. The fact that a demonstrative burning would take place today had been announced publicly, and the townspeople hurried to see the spectacle. Not so rare within the Fortress walls, but quite rare for them to admit the public.

"What an interesting phenomenon," the chancellor said, pulling me out of my own thoughts. Following his gaze, I saw a storm front on the horizon. The dark sky was terrifying — it seemed that Skron himself hid in the clouds, sending bolts of lighting to the ground. They sparkled, but the sounds did not reach us yet. Too far. Incidentally, a thunderstorm this time of the year was quite rare. It was the sunny season.

There were more than enough people in the central square of the Fortress. The bonfire occupied an honorable central location, and not far from it there were several tiers of seats for the highest hierarchs. Of all those present, I knew only Father Dvar in his unchanging red robe, so I looked with interest at those who had a certain power in the Fortress. Gray, blue, black robes. But it was the purple ones that caught my attention the most — nine people sitting around a golden chair. All the regional Priests had come to see the execution of Sister Alia. Or, as I understood it, just Alia. Her title had been stripped and she was now an ordinary person.

"We are given places of honor in the front row," Kimal Sarento pointed to an empty space literally ten meters from the fire. A scowling Evil Engineer was sitting next to our spot. Our eyes met, and I realized that the dark one was angry. Very angry. And the reason for his anger, surprisingly, was me. However, the dark one didn't say a word even when I took a seat next to him. He essentially pretended that I did not exist. I didn't care — I didn't beg for friendship. I needed answers to some questions, and the dark one would give them to me, even if he openly hated me.

"Max, you have a different seat," an unfamiliar churchman suddenly appeared next to me. "I will lead you there."

The chancellor and Father Nor stared at the servant of the Light in surprise, but remained silent, not daring to protest. I followed the man, and with every step my surprise grew. I was led to the central stand. There, where the main figures of the Church of the Light were located. Passing by the priests my guide pointed to a place near the golden throne. Still empty. The High Priest was in no hurry to be in the public eye.

"You will sit here for the duration of the event," the cleric explained, and took a seat on the other side of the golden throne. Only now I noticed the badge on the minister's chest indicating that he was the personal assistant to the High Priest. A buzz went through the ranks of those assembled — everyone was discussing my appearance and the spot I assumed. The High Priest had singled out a doomed soldier? There must be a reason.

Keeping a stony face, I gazed up past the top of the wall. The cloud was getting closer. Thunder was already beginning to rumble, the wind had risen, and there was a fresh smell in the air. However, it seemed that the storm would pass the capital by — the cloud was drifting to the right.

"His Excellency, High Priest Father Urg!" a loud voice sounded, and most of the people rose from their seats to greet the head of the church. Only the heads of the regions remained seated, but even they stood up and bowed when Father Urg took his seat.

"Let the cleansing in the name of Light begin!"

the High Priest said, and the gaze of the assembled people turned toward the distant building. The doors opened and Alia was released. The girl walked by herself, confidently, with her head held high, as if, despite the fact that she was about to be burned, she felt victorious. After all, the one she had sworn to protect was still alive.

"For disobeying the decision of the Council of Priests, Sister Alia is sentenced to be cleansed by fire!" the voice of the herald sounded, which caused a hubbub to go through the crowd. How was it possible that someone went against the highest hierarchs? To the stake with her! The herald continued to add fuel to the fire: "A sister in the Light decided that her opinion was more important than the opinion of the regional heads, and that her actions could be justified. By the decision of the council of the regional heads, supported by the resolution of the High Priest, the Fortress unanimously recognizes sister Alia as unworthy of her dignity. Let it be so!"

Cleansed by fire. What an interesting veiled name for the execution. The Church remained true to itself, trying to distance itself from death as much as possible. The clergy put up a ladder, and Alia, still with her head held high, climbed to the top of the huge wood pile, allowing herself to be tied to a pole. Noticing me, the girl even found the strength to smile, although her pale face perfectly demonstrated her true feelings. Alia was Terrified. Scared as all hell. But she didn't want to show it. Those who had sentenced her to such a terrible fate would not have the satisfaction of seeing her beg for forgiveness and pardon.

"This isn't right," I whispered, evidently too loudly. Father Urg heard me. The High Priest turned in my direction, prompting another wave of whispers.

"Everything that is happening now is done by the will of the Light, Max. And, of course, your perseverance. You abandoned Alia, which doomed her to such a fate. If you had signed a contract, no one would have the right to summon you to the Fortress. You would have closed the remaining rifts, returned to the academy, and in two months everyone would have forgotten that because of you, the Fortress was denied yem. But you refused to cooperate, so Sister Alia had to act with an understanding of the punishment she would face. She took this step consciously, exchanging her life for the chance for you to sit next to me today and watch her endure purification by fire. Everything is the will of the Light."

"She doesn't deserve this!" I refused to give in, ignoring the High Priest's accusations. Everyone and everything was trying to blame me for the girl's impending doom today.

"What does she deserve, in your opinion? To return to the Fortress as if nothing special had happened? As if she did not violate the dogma of the church?"

"She will be my personal servant," I offered after a pause. I did not want to utter these words until I had to, but the desire to somehow help Alia superseded my complexes. "I am ready to sign a contract with her if it will save her life."

"Good suggestion, but too late," the High Priest smiled bitterly. "The decision of the Council of Heads of Regions cannot be changed. Not for me, not for you, not for anyone. Except for the Light itself. Enough, Max. What has come to pass cannot be changed. I hope you won't reject your next personal servant."

The churchmen chained Aliya to a post and descended, removing the ladder. A new figure appeared — a man naked to the waist, wearing a red mask that hid his face. The executioner. In his hands he held a torch. The High Priest stood up, drawing everyone's attention. The hum of the crowd subsided — everyone wanted to hear what Father Urg had to say. The Priest looked at the clock tower — there were only a few seconds left until three. Suddenly, there was a rumble that made the windows rattle — the stormcloud changed directions again, rushing toward the city. The wind picked up, bearing that fresh smell with it, and at that moment the High Priest said:

"May your soul be cleansed, my child. It's time!"

The executioner lowered the torch and circled the pyre, setting the wood aflame. It flared up like dry grass. In just a few moments, a huge flame rose into the sky. For a few seconds nothing happened, but then the square was filled with the heart-rending scream of the girl being burned alive. The flames had reached her feet...

"Don't turn away!" the High Priest ordered sharply as I averted my eyes. Seeing the girl suffer was beyond my strength. "Have the courage to view the last moments of the one who went to the cleansing fire for you. Because..."

The High Priest was unable to finish this thought — the lightning flashed so brightly that I was momentarily blinded. There was a deafening roar and stones rained down on us as lightning hit the top of one of the towers. And then, something out of a fairytale — a downpour fell from the sky. No, not just a downpour — the emperor of all downpours! The dark cloud had finally reached the capital and unleashed all its might. The rain was so heavy that from my seat, I couldn't even see the walls of the Fortress! Alia's scream was cut off — the girl hung helplessly on the chains. The bonfire resisted for a while, trying to fight the sudden elements, but eventually gave up, unable to resist the deluge. The High Priest rose to his feet. Water dripped down his head, his golden robe was soaked through, but the head of the church paid this no mind. He stood and silently looked at the unconscious girl. Soon all the priests joined Father Urg. And behind them, all those who came to the execution. A huge crowd of people stood in the pouring rain, never tearing their eyes from the dwindling fire.

This went on for ten minutes. The wind continued to drive the cloud further along, and soon only the incessant rumble, the blue sky and huge streams of rainwater that the storm drains had been unable to handle were the only reminders. A hum of voices passed through the crowd, but then the High Priest raised his hand, calling everyone to silence.

"The Light has demonstrated its will. The defrocked Alia ascended atop the purifying fire, but the Light showed us that we were mistaken. Everything that Alia did was in strict accordance with the command of the Light! We were blind, but the cleansing fire showed us the truth. No more Sister Alia. She has been cleansed. Taken by eternity. The Light has just given birth to a new woman. Mother Alia. One who has the right to a voice and her own opinion within the church of the Zarak Empire. One that is equal to the priests and obeys naught but the Light itself! If anyone in attendance does not agree with my interpretation of what happened, let him speak now, or remain silent until the end of his days!"

The Fortress was silent. Many people were even afraid to breathe, so as not to accidentally provoke the wrath of the Light. After all, what had happened...could be nothing other than a manifestation of the Light's will!

"Let it be so!" the High Priest proclaimed, and suddenly turned in my direction. "You have expressed a desire to take Alia on as your personal servant. Do you stand by your words or deny them?"

Everyone's attention shifted to me. I became uncomfortable. However, this didn't deter me:

"I am ready to negotiate a contract with her

and sign it."

"Contracts only apply to ordinary servants of the Light, not with the one who has just become Mother Alia. There will be no contract between you. The Light has just proved that Mother Alia is more than just a servant. Your cooperation will be based on pure trust. Just as Sister Alia originally wanted, but I didn't hear her. I was deaf and blind, not realizing that the Light itself was behind her. I await your response, Doomed Max!"

"I accept," I said, backed into a corner. I was taught never to deny my own words.

"Let it be so! By the powers vested in me by the Light and the advice of the Priests of the Zarak Empire, I remove Max's designation of 'doomed soldier.' The as-yet-unnamed man formerly known as Max has escaped the jurisdiction of the Fortress. From now on, the fate of this man will depend on Mother Alia, his personal servant. She and she alone is responsible for the life and actions of her ward. Neither the church, nor the empire, nor the academy have any more power over him. If anyone in attendance does not agree with my interpretation of what happened, let him speak now, or remain silent until the end of his days!"

Father Urg was again met with silence.

"Let it be so! Father Dvar, please release Mother Alia and provide her with a healer. The cleansing by fire has been completed. Everyone may be released."

(Thirty years prior, office of the Priest of the Southwestern Region)

"Father Urg, you must see this! We've never seen anything like it!"

"A magic stone?" The priest glanced at the pebble held out to him. "What is so remarkable about it that Father Gron decided to leave his workshop?"

The owner of the dark robe was embarrassed, but quickly pulled himself together.

"It isn't just a magic stone! It's a solution to all our drought problems! I've conducted a little experiment — we can use this stone to summon rain! I'm amazed we even found anything about it in the archives!"

"Rain?" frowned the Priest. "You came to me for rain?"

"Not just rain!" the researcher scowled. "This stone can summon both a small sprinkle that our crops so desperately need, and a torrential downpour, capable of sweeping away everything in its path. No restrictions — it's all a question of how much mana you spend!"

Rain... Priest Urg thought for a moment — here, in the southwest corner of the empire, they had always had problems with this natural force. Too far from the sea, too high were the surrounding mountains which held back the clouds. In fact, most of the territory was a desert, incapable of producing enough food. If he had the ability to make rain, the food problem would be solved. However, if the High Priest or the chancellor of the academy ever found out about this stone, they would demand it for themselves. No, this cannot be permitted to happen.

"Yes, it is a precious stone. It must not be allowed to fall into the wrong hands. Father Gron, we need to make sure that no one knows about the existence of this stone. It is our key into the Fortress. All we need to do now is test it..."

(The Fortress, two days before the execution)

"Do you think they will decide to destroy it?" Father Gron, head of the Fortress research department, looked up from his examination of the stones brought back from the rift.

"I'm 100% certain. The dark one's life will be spared, but the priests will demand a sacrifice. To make the others uncomfortable. Tomorrow, Sister Alia will be sent to the stake. I'll have to agree with the council's decision. The cleansing will be scheduled for three o'clock, the day after tomorrow."

"Do you think this is a unique case? There will be no second chances," Father Gron warned. "Your decision could spare her life. Send her to the doomed legion, in the end."

"I don't need another doomed soldier. I need an independent force that the Fortress will have to reckon with and negotiate with. Father Dvar confirms that one of the priests is working with the dark ones. Precisely who is unknown. One, two, maybe even all of them. If I manage to get Alia and Max out from under the Fortress' influence, that someone will have to act. They cannot allow the church to gain power again."

"Are you putting them under attack?"

"I remove them from the guaranteed threat of the guillotine and give them full freedom of action. In addition, I want to test Father Nor's loyalty. The old man has grown soft — lately he has become too sentimental. Lost his former rigidity. He needs to be shaken. And the girl herself needs to be tested as well. Will this break her or not? Is she capable of bearing the burden of responsibility, or is it too early? She has been preparing for this for fifteen years, but who knows how she will behave when the bidding is essential. Before we act, we must thoroughly verify everything."

"They brought me a ton of things from the rift to research. It would be a shame to lose all this.""Everything will stay the same, only the flow of finances will change. The money will go to the regions. The priests will have to act, show their true nature, so as not to lose influence. And then we will know for sure who walks in the Light and who has sold out to Skron."

"Well then…three o'clock? I need to prepare. As I understand it, we must start from afar, so as to not arouse suspicion?"

"That's right. At exactly three I will give the order. You must not be late…"

(The Fortress, execution day)

"Sister Alia," the High Priest greeted the detained woman, paying a personal visit to her cell.

"Just Alia," the girl smiled. "I've been defrocked."

"You lose the privilege at the moment of your cleansing," Father Urg corrected. "Until then, you remain a sister in the Light. The dark one has been granted life."

"Glad to hear it," Alia said sincerely. "I hope he can find common ground with his future personal servant. I did not succeed in this. He saw me as a girl, but not a representative of the Fortress."

"It was my mistake," Father Urg sighed. "You shouldn't have been sent on this mission. Not because you couldn't do it. Due to Max's age and the fact that the Fortress made too many mistakes before realizing what a valuable resource he is. I'm sorry you had to pay for our mistake."

"What matters is who he became, not how he got there," Alia said. "But you didn't come here to tell me about the dark one, did you?"

"No, not exclusively," agreed the High Priest. "I have come to you with a request. An old man's final request. Here, take it."

"What is this?" Alia accepted a small jar of ointment and a vial of blue liquid.

"The liquid is an anesthetic. The ointment — a means for quick ignition. It's up to you to decide, but I would very much like you to drink the liquid and completely cover yourself with this ointment. Purification by fire is a painful procedure and, due to the nature of the human body, rather slow. The ointment will speed up the process, the elixir will make it a little easier. This is only a request, not an order. For everything you've done for the Fortress, for Max, for me. For your father. He will also be present — the priests have summoned him. If you are sure that you can be strong until the very last, do not take it. If there is even a shred of doubt, I beg you — use this gift. Light be my witness, this does not violate any of the existing dogmas. It will simply ease your suffering and make your meeting with the Light more peaceful. Think about it, Sister Alia. Think about the words of the tired old man who brought you up almost from the cradle. Now let me hug you. For the last time. May the Light be kind to you."

(The Fortress, a few minutes prior to the execution)

"Everything is ready, Father Urg. You may go out."

"Alia?"

"We checked her cell. The bottle and jar of ointment are empty. She took your advice. Sister Alia will meet the Light without pain."

The High Priest allowed himself a fleeting smile. Ointment for ignition. As if! Anyone covered in this ointment could safely endure the flames for an entire minute without suffering physical harm.

Yes, it would be hot, it may be unbearably hot, but there will be no irreparable damage. The only thing left to do was to properly process the doomed soldier. As long as Father Gron was on time…

(Turb, secret residence, morning of the execution)

"Duke Odoevsky, you've been waiting." The holder of the office measured Count Fardi with a hard look.

"The acolyte was slow, master," the duke bowed his head. "I dropped everything as soon as I learned you wished to see me and rushed here."

"The acolyte should be punished — tomorrow I expect his head in a separate package. You have an important mission ahead of you, Duke. It concerns Maximilian Valevsky."

"The doomed soldier?" Fardi was surprised. "Did he harm my daughter in any way?"

"Karina is fine. The boy has become too important a figure to leave him at the Fortress. He single-handedly closed the eight-level rift and extracted resources that many did not even suspect existed. You must remove him from the church."

"This is impossible. The Fortress will not relinquish a doomed soldier."

"Nobody will ask permission. You will turn to the emperor and announce that you have conducted an additional investigation into the Valevsky case. You, as a true champion of the law, found the court's decision unorthodox. As a result of this additional investigation, you discovered that the judge, the prosecutor and the investigators were bribed by...whoever you can think of. Pick your bad guys. The case must be reviewed and the life of the doomed soldier will be returned to him."

"This will deal a blow to my family's reputation," Duke Odoevsky frowned, not expecting such an order.

"Reputation is nothing compared to what we will gain by bringing the boy back to the big, bad world. He will become a simple baron and will be completely in your power. An eight-level rift, Duke. We have the opportunity to send him to the eight-level rift and take everything he finds there! You have a week to organize your request for the emperor. Maximilian Valevsky must return to the world of the living. That's an order."

"Yes, sir, it will be done," Count Fardi bowed, trying to quell his anger. The order was horrendous, but the duke was used to trusting his master. After all, it was with his help that the simple Count Fardi was appointed Duke of Odoevsky twenty years ago, transferring the western region to his control. One of the nine regions of the Zarak Empire.

"When you complete this task, you will be exalted. You will gain power that you never even dreamed of. I, as the future ruler of the Zarak Empire, guarantee it."

(Capital dark coven, morning of the execution)

"Sir, everything is prepared! We have delivered twenty-one people to the location! Nobody suspected anything! Those who guard the academy are blind fools!"

"Good news." A bloodthirsty grin cracked across Magister Elor's face. "Today at three o'clock, all the heads of the academy will be at the Fortress. This is the perfect moment to enact Skron's will. Tell my man that the summoning ritual may begin. The time has come for the Wave to take the magical academy and the entire capital. The Riftmaster must produce a metamorph, by any means necessary!

End of Book Two

Want to be the first to know about our latest LitRPG, sci fi and fantasy titles from your favorite authors?

Subscribe to our **New Releases** newsletter:
http://eepurl.com/b7niIL

Thank you for reading *Condemned!*
If you like what you've read, check out other sci-fi, fantasy and A LitRPG series published by Magic Dome Books:

Reality Benders
a LitRPG series by Michael Atamanov

The Dark Herbalist
a LitRPG series by Michael Atamanov

Perimeter Defense
a LitRPG series by Michael Atamanov

League of Losers
a LitRPG series by Michael Atamanov

Chaos' Game
a LitRPG series by Alexey Svadkovsky

The Hunter's Code
a LitRPG series by Yuri Vinokuroff & Oleg Sapphire

War Eternal
a LitRPG series by Yuri Vinokuroff

The Way of the Shaman
a LitRPG series by Vasily Mahanenko

The Alchemist
a LitRPG series by Vasily Mahanenko

Dark Paladin
a LitRPG series by Vasily Mahanenko

Galactogon
a LitRPG series by Vasily Mahanenko

Invasion
a LitRPG series by Vasily Mahanenko

World of the Changed
a LitRPG series by Vasily Mahanenko

The Bear Clan
a LitRPG series by Vasily Mahanenko

Starting Point
a LitRPG series by Vasily Mahanenko

The Bard from Barliona
a LitRPG series
by Eugenia Dmitrieva and Vasily Mahanenko

Condemned
(Lord Valevsky: Last of The Line)
a Progression Fantasy series
by Vasily Mahanenko

Loner
a LitRPG series by Alex Kosh

A Buccaneer's Due
a LitRPG series by Igor Knox

A Student Wants to Live
a LitRPG series by Boris Romanovsky

Level Up
a LitRPG series by Dan Sugralinov

Level Up: The Knockout
a LitRPG series by Dan Sugralinov and Max Lagno

Adam Online
a LitRPG Series by Max Lagno

World 99
a LitRPG series by Dan Sugralinov

Disgardium
a LitRPG series by Dan Sugralinov

Nullform
a RealRPG Series by Dem Mikhailov

Clan Dominance: The Sleepless Ones
a LitRPG series by Dem Mikhailov

Heroes of the Final Frontier
a LitRPG series by Dem Mikhailov

The Crow Cycle
a LitRPG series by Dem Mikhailov

Interworld Network
a LitRPG series by Dmitry Bilik

Rogue Merchant
a LitRPG series by Roman Prokofiev

Project Stellar
a LitRPG series by Roman Prokofiev

In the System
a LitRPG series by Petr Zhgulyov

The Crow Cycle
a LitRPG series by Dem Mikhailov

Unfrozen
a LitRPG series by Anton Tekshin

The Neuro
a LitRPG series by Andrei Livadny

Phantom Server
a LitRPG series by Andrei Livadny

Respawn Trials
a LitRPG series by Andrei Livadny

The Expansion (The History of the Galaxy)
a Space Exploration Saga by A. Livadny

The Range
a LitRPG series by Yuri Ulengov

Point Apocalypse
a near-future action thriller by Alex Bobl

Moskau
a dystopian thriller by G. Zotov

El Diablo
a supernatural thriller by G.Zotov

Mirror World
a LitRPG series by Alexey Osadchuk

Underdog
a LitRPG series by Alexey Osadchuk

Last Life
a Progression Fantasy series by Alexey Osadchuk

Alpha Rome
a LitRPG series by Ros Per

An NPC's Path
a LitRPG series by Pavel Kornev

Fantasia
a LitRPG series by Simon Vale

The Sublime Electricity
a steampunk series by Pavel Kornev

Small Unit Tactics
a LitRPG series by Alexander Romanov

Black Centurion
a LitRPG standalone by Alexander Romanov

Rorkh
A LitRPG Series by Vova Bo

Thunder Rumbles Twice
A Wuxia Series by V. Kriptonov & M. Bachurova

Citadel World
a sci fi series by Kir Lukovkin

You're in Game!
LitRPG Stories from Our Bestselling Authors

You're in Game-2!
More LitRPG stories set in your favorite worlds

The Fairy Code
a Romantic Fantasy series by Kaitlyn Weiss

The Charmed Fjords
a Romantic Fantasy series by Marina Surzhevskaya

More books and series are coming out soon!

In order to have new books of the series translated faster, we need your help and support! Please consider leaving a review or spread the word by recommending *Condemned* to your friends and posting the link on social media. The more people buy the book, the sooner we'll be able to make new translations available.

Thank you!

Till next time!

www.ingramcontent.com/pod-product-compliance
Lightning Source LLC
LaVergne TN
LVHW020724200726

843506LV00009B/613